CRAIG HARRISON was born in Leeds in 1942 and educated at Prince Henry's Grammar School, Otley. His rocket experiments in 1958 drew press and police attention, and an invitation to address the British Interplanetary Society.

Harrison attended Leeds University, where he received a BA and an MA. He organised the Liberal Party campaign in Ripon Division, Yorkshire, for the 1964 general election.

He arrived in New Zealand in 1966 after being appointed a lecturer in the English Department at Massey University. There he devised a course in art history, which he taught from 1968 until his retirement in 2000.

His award-winning satirical play *Tomorrow Will Be a Lovely Day* (1974) was performed for a quarter of a century, including in the Soviet Union. The novel that was its genesis, *Broken October*, was published in 1976. He is the author of five other plays, including the prize-winning *Ground Level* (1974), which led to a comic novel of the same name (1981) and a television series, *Joe & Koro*.

The Quiet Earth, a speculative novel, appeared in 1981 and in 1985 was adapted by Geoff Murphy into an acclaimed feature film starring Bruno Lawrence, Pete Smith and Alison Routledge.

Craig Harrison's most recent book, the young adult science-fiction comedy *The Dumpster Saga*, was a finalist in the 2008 New Zealand Post Book Awards. He lives in Palmerston North.

BERNARD BECKETT is a high school teacher in Wellington. He has published ten works of fiction, including the metaphysical novels *Genesis* and *August*.

ALSO BY CRAIG HARRISON

Fiction
Broken October: New Zealand, 1985
Ground Level
Days of Starlight
Grievous Bodily
The Dumpster Saga

Non-fiction
How to Be a Pom

The Quiet Earth
Craig Harrison

Text Publishing Melbourne Australia

textclassics.com.au
textpublishing.com.au

The Text Publishing Company
Swann House
22 William Street
Melbourne Victoria 3000
Australia

First published in New Zealand by Hodder & Stoughton Ltd 1981
This edition published by The Text Publishing Company 2013

Cover design by WH Chong
Page design by Text
Typeset by Midland Typesetters

Printed in Australia by Griffin Press, an Accredited ISO AS/NZS 14001:2004 Environmental Management System printer

Primary print ISBN: 9781922147059
Ebook ISBN: 9781922148131
Author: Harrison, Craig, 1942-, author.
Title: The quiet earth / by Craig Harrison ; introduced by Bernard Beckett.
Series: Text classics.
Dewey Number: NZ823.2

This book is printed on paper certified against the Forest Stewardship Council® Standards. Griffin Press holds FSC chain-of-custody certification SGS-COC-005088. FSC promotes environmentally responsible, socially beneficial and economically viable management of the world's forests.

CONTENTS

No Exit
by Bernard Beckett

A CHILD cries out in the night for its parent. The parent responds. Perhaps it is thirsty, or had a nightmare, or is tangled in its bedclothes? No, it just needs a reassuring cuddle. It needs to know it isn't alone.

In Craig Harrison's *The Quiet Earth*—first published in 1981 and loosely adapted into a cult sci-fi film four years later—it is not a child who awakens, but an adult, our narrator. John Hobson is not alone in the dark, but rather comes to with a flash of light at 6.12 a.m. in a motel room in Thames, on New Zealand's North Island. And when he calls out into the world, nobody answers. Every home, every car, every shop and street is deserted. The concept cuts so cleanly to the heart of our most basic fears that the most surprising thing, as you enter this novel, is the realisation that you haven't read the story before.

Perhaps the reason it is not a narrative staple is that the challenges inherent in telling it are so daunting. At some stage, in a novel like this, the reader must be offered an explanation. Yes, it would be a terrifying, searching experience to wake up as the last person left on Earth, but under what fictional circumstances can that scenario be made credible? In narrative terms, Harrison's opening gambit is like a crime writer opening with an exotic set of clues to a hideous case. It is a wager: stay with my story and I will bring this home. The reader, by picking up such a tale, enters into a contract—one that creates a special tension. We are at once fascinated and wary, hoping the author can pull it off.

The other challenge is the extremely limited palette the writer gives himself. With nobody for the protagonist to talk to, nobody to generate external conflict, the novel must develop through a single character and his response to the nightmare scenario. A short story has permission to observe, to linger inside impressions and fears, but a novel of this type avoids storytelling at its peril. Harrison, who acknowledges his echoing of a 'childhood favourite', *Robinson Crusoe*, instead embraces it.

The artfulness with which both these challenges are met sets this book apart. It is a high-concept novel, and within the New Zealand literary tradition that already places it comfortably in the minority. The greater appeal, though, is not the freshness of the concept but its execution.

Initially, the story moves through the actions and emotions we might expect of the protagonist. Hobson does as we would do: he searches, pieces together tantalising clues (all the clocks have stopped at 6.12, yet surely some should have been running fast or slow), listens in to the radio static, and battles his rising sense of terror. Fear not just that he is alone, but that he is not psychologically equipped to be alone. That he will disappear within the existential chasm.

> *What's happened?* Any, *any* explanation would dam the panic...I struggled to be objective... An enormous isolation and loneliness, a sensation not of being observed but of being ignored, totally abandoned, was all I could separate from the confusion and fear. And this seemed all the more insidious because even now it was recognisable, I could feel my mind shoving blindly against its shape, a distended growth out of feelings I'd always had.

This everyman quality, the camaraderie of the extreme, allows the first of the narrative tricks to be pulled. It is so easy to feel for Hobson's plight that we like him without this likeability having to be established through act or word. And that leaves it open for the author to establish a conflict between our instinctive loyalty toward the sufferer and the kind of man Hobson may actually be. With a certain stealth, the driving question moves from 'What would I do?' to 'What might Hobson do—and have done in the past?' It's a dark and disorienting twist. As the character moves through his broken world, we come to realise that he might be implicated in the breaking of it.

The more Hobson's failure and fragility is revealed, the more we come to doubt his reliability. In clumsy hands, the unreliable narrator is a cheap trick, designed more to frustrate than to manipulate. Here, it is carefully employed. The genetics laboratory in which Hobson worked, the body in the chair, the vision on a dark road, the memories of an autistic son, Hobson's tentative attempts to piece together an explanation: none of this is incidental.

Just as we are beginning to come to terms with the frame of reference allowed us, everything is switched again—and this requires my making one last plot revelation. Hobson is not alone. Another man has survived: Apirana Maketu, or The Maori, as our narrator uncomfortably insists upon calling him (but then, so many things about this narrator are uncomfortable). Here we are, a touch under halfway through the novel, and finally the potential for external conflict presents itself. Harrison gives it free rein. Two men, a Maori and a Pakeha, a soldier and a scientist, each with no one else in the world to turn to. But that doesn't mean they have to get along.

There is more than a little Sartre in this scenario. The worst thing we could ever imagine is being alone, until we imagine being with somebody else. No exit, indeed. And now the range of possible explanations for what Hobson calls The Effect is compressed. Whatever the reason one man was spared must now extend to two, and yet at first glance they have nothing in common. This is a fairly archetypal working of intrigue: beginning with open possibilities, challenging the reader to design their own structure into which these clues can be fitted, and then hitting them with an impossibility. Not progress, but a promise of progress, the reminder that the writer has not forgotten his contract with you.

The second character brings not just conflict, but an alternative viewpoint. Although there is a natural tendency for us to identify most strongly with the first character we meet in a novel, it is not inevitable. The flaws we have already seen in Hobson magnify under his response to Maketu. And therein lies perhaps the most unsettling of all the novel's clues. For not only does the narrator's treatment of his sole companion speak poorly of him, but the way Hobson tells it The Maori's descriptions of himself contain the same offensive reductions and simplifications. Again we are confronted with the possibility—the only palatable possibility—of the narrator's unreliability.

The tension mounts. Tension between Hobson and Maketu, between fact and fiction, between cause and Effect. It is the nature of *The Quiet Earth* that you cannot adequately discuss the ending without saying too much. By the time the inevitable revelation arrives, we understand this story is as much an examination of John Hobson as it is an examination of the circumstances that brought his world to a standstill at 6.12 one sunny morning. We no longer like the man—we now know him to be self-obsessed, paranoid and dangerously violent—yet the intrigue remains. The story, compelling enough as a series of episodes, has one last surprise in store for us. What is it, exactly, that the reader has been witness to?

While some people have claimed there is a deliberate ambiguity to the ending, to my mind this undervalues the author's craft. Craig Harrison, who has been a successful playwright and published five other novels in different genres over the past forty-odd years, knows exactly what he is doing. That there is only one chilling possibility left ensures this book can be rightfully considered a classic.

The Quiet Earth

CHAPTER ONE

The pull of the earth took hold of my spine, my limbs spread over space. There was the breath-beat of falling, spiralling, the air pushing hard for a moment and then letting go. The light split open my eyelids. It was brilliant, drained of colours, painful. An immense silence rushed around me. My throat was trying to make a noise, to beat it back. The light pulsed redness. Then the silence expanded.

I was sitting bolt upright in bed breathing fast and staring at the wall. The daylight was streaming into the motel room through the slats of the blinds. I seemed to have been awake, and asleep, for ages. I lay back and remembered where I was. The silence persisted. My watch at the bedside had stopped at 6.12. Reaching out, I shook it and the second hand began flicking round again. How long had it been stopped? I got up and went to the window which looked out onto the main road; my arm moved up towards the cord of the blind.

What?

I paused. What was happening? The casual movement, everyday, ordinary, towards opening the blind, had been interrupted by something, by an impulse to stop, which had no sensible origin at all. It was so curious and *extra*ordinary that I was pausing not because of the impulse itself but in a conscious effort to find a reason for it. But I had forgotten. My mind seemed to resist. The silence pressed in thickly. It was exactly like forgetting the name of a place you've visited dozens of times; it's just on the tip of your mind but you can't find it. You stop and think, and when there's no answer you go on. Perhaps, later, you will know.

Then I reached up and opened the blind to the enormous light.

CHAPTER TWO

It was still early; possibly, to judge by the sun, about 8.30 am. I looked out at the grass and the road beyond. The air was clear and bright with the promise of another fine summer day. All was quiet. The scene was cut into strips by the slats of the venetian blinds, and I pulled the cord to alter the angle of the slats, looking up, ahead, and down. Perhaps it really was only 6.15; nobody had woken up yet. Saturday morning in a small town like Thames was obviously not hectic. Good. That was why I had come to Coromandel, after all; for peace and quiet.

I showered and dressed. The water pressure seemed weak. Only when I tried to use my electric razor did I realise that the power was off. I tried the lights, the radio, the electric hotplates on the cooker. All dead. Probably a fuse. I went out of the door at the back of the motel unit and looked around from the balcony. There was nobody below in the car park, and no sign of activity. Descending to the office I wandered around pressing buzzers, knocking on doors, shouting hello, but the whole place appeared to be deserted. Curtains and blinds were still drawn and the car park was full.

Curiouser and curiouser: I realised that in all the time since I had been awake, not a single vehicle had gone along the road, nor had there been any kind of noise. Even a sudden breeze rustling the leaves of a tree in the garden of one of the houses behind the car park startled me, and I went and looked over into the garden. Nobody was there. There's a clock in my car, I thought, I'll check the time.

I unlocked the car door. The hands of the dashboard clock stood fixed at 6.12. For a moment the breath went dry in my lungs. I slid into the car, slammed the door shut defensively, put the key in the ignition, drew out the choke, turned the key, revved the engine, reversed, then into first, accelerator down. The Marina skidded on loose stones and swept along the drive away from the motel. The clock had started again. I slowed at the end of the drive but there was no traffic and in a few seconds I was on the main road towards the centre of town.

All this happened very quickly. Because of the sight of the clock. It was impossible. What am I doing? Why am I driving into Thames at about 6.30 am, or whenever, because of a clock? And a power cut?

The first wave of panic subsided, then thickened hard as the total emptiness of the town slid past, stared back, blank. In the middle of the main street there was a car stalled at an intersection. I slowed down, drew over to the kerb and stopped fifty metres away. When I cut the engine off, the silence fell around the car like a solid thing, shutting against me. I tapped the dashboard to make a sound. My ears seemed suffocated. Reaching out I shoved the plastic indicator stick on the steering column to sound the horn, but with the panic still trembling inside me I pushed the wrong one and the windscreen washers spurted two jets of water across the glass. Cursing, I jabbed the other control and the horn bayed into the deserted street so loudly that I let go immediately and it stopped. The water dribbled and sagged down the windscreen, chopping the view of the shops, pavement, shadows, sun, car, car's shadow, into distorted slivers, glistening even clearer. It was all very real and present.

I got out of the car, letting the door swing back and slam shut with a metallic clang which followed the noise the horn had made, spreading away along the street in both directions and being echoed and absorbed as it went.

The sun was now quite hot. I stood on the tarmac looking at the car in the middle of the road, not wanting to go any closer. It was a red Datsun. If it had been left suddenly, wouldn't the doors be open? What the hell. I walked up to it and stared in cautiously, shading my eyes. There was nobody there. I opened the driver's door. Ignition still switched on; petrol run dry; batteries weak. The gear was in neutral; he'd stopped at the intersection. The handbrake wasn't on. It was very hot inside the car and I lifted myself off the edge of the seat and stood up to test the door, to see if it would close by itself if left. It stayed open. As I leaned on the door I looked down at the driver's seat and saw the seatbelt, *still fastened*, stretching loosely across the seat. I slammed the door and stepped back several paces. My first instinct was to run for the Marina and get away. But I stopped the impulse. Many people never use their seatbelts. They leave them strewn all over and never notice. *Fastened*? Yes, why not? People are strange. Do odd things. There are always explanations. What, then? For all this? A set for a film? An experiment? It's a Civil Defence exercise, and nobody told me. I'm a stranger; they forgot. The real thing? A disaster, everyone gone, evacuated, they forgot me. Lots of explanations.

Back at my car I revved the engine loudly and then set off to drive round the town. No signs or clues at the police station or post office. No people anywhere, not even in the residential streets. The houses were all closed and shuttered. Empty cars stood in odd places across some roads. I checked two or three, then drove past the others. The sound of my horn in the streets brought no response. I accelerated back to the main street and parked where I had stopped before. I would have to find a transistor radio. There was an electrical goods shop nearby.

The door was locked. In the window a digital clock showed 06.12. My eyes flicked away quickly from it. I went back, got a tyre lever from the car and smashed the glass door. The noise was a shattering attack on the emptiness. It roused nothing. I waited, listening. There were not even any bird or animal sounds. My feet crunched on broken glass as I stepped into the shop. And I shivered, suddenly, in the coolness.

There was a telephone. I picked it up and listened for a dial tone but it was totally extinct. Selecting a handy portable radio I checked to see it had batteries and then switched it on and ran the dial round all the way on medium wave from 530 to 1600 kHz. There was nothing but static. With the volume up so high that the crackling and hissing sounded like the abrasions of barbed wire across heavy sandpaper, still nothing. After rechecking connections and trying again, I switched off.

A larger portable was next. The moment I pressed the first top button it howled music and my hand jerked back. The sound of Handel's *Messiah* rolled against the walls and surged into the street, alive, thunderous with voices. My skin went warm; there was a slackening of all the tensed muscles inside me. A broadcast, a radio station transmitting!

The relief made me suddenly pathetic and grateful. I wanted to apologise, to make amends for the hollowness of my life and its frightening silences left empty of whatever was needed from me, as though the fear of the last half hour had been made for me, to shake and change me. However late. I wanted to say, I will try to understand what went wrong.

I knew this only for one moment. Then I looked down. The cogs of a cassette tape were churning away behind a plastic panel. It wasn't a radio broadcast. Just a tape. The printing showed: *Selections: London Philharmonic: Thy Rebuke Has Broken His Heart. He Was Cut Off From The Land Of The Living. But Thou Didst Not Leave His Soul In Hell. Hallelujah. I Know That My Redeemer Liveth.*

My fist banged down on the switches. The music cut off, then the radio frequencies glowed in a pale green. The static surged from the speaker. I pressed shortwave and ran the red line up and down at full volume. Nothing, again, except a long-distance surge of falling and rising and fading static, like surf breaking over the planet in huge spaces. Long wave, medium; no other sound. Beneath my breath all the time I was saying, *please, anything, please*, with a bile of anger keeping back the panic. Useless. My fingers wobbled over the dials and buttons, trembling to switch off and stop the hissing.

Silence, then. A vacuum as strong as the light outside, and it seemed to force its way in and flex its strength as though it fed on any hint of noise. To stop the fear in me I crossed my arms over my chest and pressed my hands under my armpits. My heart and lungs were pounding. I felt I had to hold them in, harder, to hold myself together.

What's happened? Any, *any* explanation would dam the panic. Is there really a force that can make everything vanish, that could hear or sense me now, track me down, attack me? I struggled to be objective. After a few minutes I stepped out of the broken door and stood on the pavement. No, I had no feeling of being watched. Perhaps I could have defended myself against that more easily. An enormous isolation and loneliness, a sensation not of being observed but of being ignored, totally abandoned, was all I could separate from the confusion and fear. And this seemed all the more insidious because even now it was recognisable, I could feel my mind shoving blindly against its shape, a distended growth out of feelings I'd always had.

But my brain still works. This is not a dream. I am alive. This is happening. What can I do?

The sun had moved onto my car. I opened the windows.

The inside was like a furnace. I sat down on the edge of the pavement in the shade. A peculiar apathy began to come over me. I felt very thirsty. I would have to break into a shop and get a drink.

Standing, I turned and re-entered the radio shop, now feeling guilty about the damage. A part of me insisted that people would soon be back and that I had better make amends. Conventional sensations reappeared. I felt in my pockets for money to recompense for the mess, but all I had was my chequebook. I took it out, got a biro and wrote a cheque for fifty dollars, cash. I even put my address on the back. Thinking, maybe fifty dollars is too much, I then took a torch from a display and put it in my car.

Ten minutes later I was sitting in the office of a filling station at the end of the street, tipping warm lemonade into my mouth. The heat and light compressed a pain inside my skull into a tight headache. I leaned back and stared up. My watch ticked uselessly away, the only sound.

After thirty years, what did I have or know that could help? No point in wondering, could I cope? No choice. I have to. *I have to go and look in those houses.* Break in, go from room to room, and see what's there. In spite of the fear sticking in my spine like ice.

The dead have no power. They can't harm. Can anyone be more than dead? My head came down and I looked through my image reflected on the glass of the window. No power? I know better than that.

Beyond the window, my car wavered in the heat, marks of evaporated water down the dust of its windscreen, like teardrops squeezed from a machine.

CHAPTER THREE

I walked towards the door of the first house I had selected; an ordinary suburban weatherboard with a neat garden. The occupants of all these houses had obviously not gone anywhere. Their milk was uncollected, festering in hot letterboxes; their doors were closed and locked. It could only follow, therefore, that the inhabitants were still inside, in an abnormal condition.

I stopped. What if it was a disease, a plague? No; I must be immune. I won't be harmed. Go in. Not knowing is worse.

I banged on the door. Only small windows were open and all the blinds were closed. The door was a nineteen-fiftyish ground glass panel etched with a scene of a kingfisher and some mallards. I had brought a large hammer from the garage; I stood back and hurled it at the glass. The mallards shattered. I hung back, waiting. The conventional instinct made me wonder why I hadn't tried the back door. I looked around. Even under normal circumstances there were strong taboos on entering other people's houses. It was another sign of what I was increasingly coming to fear as a dangerous confusion in my mind, that having smashed somebody's front door I should feel it was improper now to enter. I found myself leaning into the hallway and shouting, 'Hello? Anybody there?'

Silence. I picked up the hammer and stepped in. Speckled brown carpet, flowery wallpaper, a telephone on a small wrought-iron stand, a framed picture of waves breaking with sunlight shining through the front wave. The far end of the hall was darkish and the various doors which led off on each side were closed.

The air had the distinctive fusty smell of a closed house, a compound of old carpet and faded cooking, a jumble sale, second-hand, dust-under-beds staleness.

I wondered whether to knock on any of the doors. The first one was on my right. Perhaps surprise would be best. Holding up the hammer in my left hand, I tensed, then pulled the door handle with my right. A heavy white thing rushed out at me, taller than me, falling onto my chest. I made the kind of noise you only make in nightmares, a whimpering attempt at a cry, and I flailed at the thing with the hammer, falling backwards over the telephone table, sprawling wildly.

Then I heaved myself up, cutting two fingers on a shard of glass. The blood ran down my hand. I dropped the hammer and sucked at the wound. With some nervous cursing I wrapped my handkerchief round the bloodstain.

My heart was pounding like mad. I did not think I had ever been so appallingly frightened in my entire waking life.

I had opened the door of an airing cupboard and a large sheet had fallen on me.

The panic subsided. Thank God nobody could see me. But if I have to go through anything worse, let it happen straight away as long as there is some explanation. Anything. Anything I can understand.

I picked up the hammer and advanced to the next door on the right. It swung open easily as I pushed it, and I peered into a bedroom darkened by closed curtains. The sheets and coverings on the double bed were crumpled, but even in the gloomy light I could discern no shapes beneath them, no heads on the pillows. After a moment I walked into the room and drew the curtains open. The bedclothes had not been flung back; they lay irregularly drawn up to the pillows, and each pillow had an indentation as if recently rested upon by somebody. Had the bedclothes been thrown aside, it would merely have looked like an ordinary unmade bed. I balked at throwing them back, but the light gave me enough confidence. There was nothing beneath them. On one side of the bed, a man's clothes were draped over a chair; socks and shoes by the edge of the red tufted bedside carpet. A woman's clothes lay rather more neatly on a bamboo chair on the other side of the bed. I turned away, feeling even more like an intruder than before. My eyes rested on the alarm clock beneath the bedside lamp: 6.12. Yes, of course. But my mind, having almost swallowed this consistent idiocy, finally choked on it. I stood in the bedroom looking at all the normal disorder, and beyond the contradictory impulses of relief and fear at not finding any people, I detected the first tiny anomaly in the pattern of events. It was a triumphant revelation; for a moment it cancelled every other aspect of the puzzle and I had to restrain myself from shouting out loud like a child who suddenly sees through a mystery all at once. Of course! Why hadn't I thought of it before! It was simply this: *The clocks have not merely stopped; some have been altered and then stopped.*

At any given moment, normally, it would be almost impossible to find half a dozen clocks and watches all showing the same time. The clock in my car was always a few minutes fast each day, and I would adjust it when the difference became noticeable. If this had been my alarm clock, here, I would have expected it to be ten minutes fast as I always set it ahead a bit. But so far today I had not seen a single timepiece which had stopped at anything other than precisely 6.12. Surely a few might have shown, well, 6.09 or 6.15, according to whether they were slow or fast? Whatever force had stopped them had also had the power to enforce a unified time on them. This suggested something more than a mere paralysis of moving parts.

I strode out of the bedroom back into the hall and explored the other rooms. There was a teenager's bedroom with posters all over the walls and jeans and T-shirts on a chair, and a children's room with two bunk beds, and clothes festooned amongst toys. The beds were all in the same state, as though the occupants had vanished instantly whilst asleep and with no disturbance. In the kitchen I found another clock at 6.12, propped on top of an old refrigerator. The fridge had defrosted and when I drew the venetian blinds the daylight gleamed on the pool of water on the patterned lino flooring. Some shelves in the living room held badly framed photographs of the family: a formal black-and-white studio picture of a couple in late-nineteen-fifties styles on their wedding day, and several garish coloured photos of children squinting towards the camera on bright sunny days in back gardens and on beaches, the sky turquoise Kodak. I looked at the photos with a heavy feeling, a sensation of having been excluded from all the processes which had operated these people, of being as separate as a creature from another planet, unable to divide the ordinary from the extraordinary. I feared that although these people might not be dead, might not have ceased to live in any ordinary sense, nevertheless they would almost certainly not be coming back here. The arrangement of objects in the bedrooms seemed to be hard evidence of something irrevocable, of an event which was irreversible as well as mysterious, just as all photographs show an unreachable past.

The images of people from my own life who might have vanished held me fixed there for a while. I wondered if they now only existed in my mind. I was unnerved, briefly, by not being able to feel any very powerful emotion about that, and by a deeper disturbance in my memory relating to Auckland and the past which had no apparent cause. I turned away from the photographs. Was everything irrevocable? A force which can stop clocks is one thing; a force which fixes all timepieces to one setting is quite something else. It has a purpose, surely?

There was a dull, heavy thudding and rustling noise from the kitchen. I tensed and crouched behind an armchair, estimating the distance to the door which led to the hallway. No, to get out that way I would have to turn my back towards the kitchen, and I had left the kitchen door open. I waited, holding my breath, holding the hammer even tighter. Nothing happened. Slowly I stood up and advanced. There was no sign of anything in the kitchen. After a long pause I kicked the door wide open. The same thud and then a slithering came from inside the fridge. I walked across and opened the fridge door. A mass of melting ice fell out onto the lino. A large block, shaped with the ridges like a mould of the cooling unit, sagged onto the plastic tray on the top shelf. Water dripped down. A faintly unpleasant odour hung in the air, a cheesy, meaty staleness which would be the beginning of the decomposition. I closed the door hard against the slush. Microbes? The decay of meat was a process involving living cells. People had vanished leaving no trace, but meat remained and was decaying normally.

I unlocked the back door and walked out into the strong, hot sunlight. There were some scraggy rose bushes in the back garden, red oleanders, the inevitable marigolds, and the white buds of a magnolia opening like poultices. Screwing my eyes up against the powerful light I wandered around examining the flowers. There were no aphids or insects on them; none, at any rate, that I could see. A spade was leaning against the corrugated iron fence; I put my hammer down and got the spade and began to heave aside lumps of the dry rock-hard earth. It wasn't easy. The earth I uncovered seemed as dead as sand. There were stabs of pain from my cut fingers. Sweating, I blundered back into the kitchen and turned on the taps over the sink; the water pressure was low but the dribblings soon filled a small basin I picked up from the draining board. I took the water outside and splashed it on the soil. After two or three trips the soil had darkened and become softer. The spade sank in more easily. When about twenty centimetres of soil had been levered out I fetched more water and poured it into the hole. It formed a slurry with the loose earth. I stirred and prodded at the sides of the hole as the water sank away.

Suddenly, into the mud, there was a movement, a writhing. I laughed out loud. Carefully lowering the tip of the spade into the hole I edged it into the mud and lifted up part of the dark mass like a goldminer peering for a glint of something precious. And there it was! Wriggling, bluish-pink, coiling, enormously alive: an earthworm.

I released the earth gently and knelt in the heat of the early afternoon watching the only other living creature I had found or detected in six hours of searching. A common or garden worm. I laughed again. The worm burrowed out of sight. I said, 'Hey!' out loud, putting my hand down to part the earth. My companion crawled off in another direction. I watched it go. Don't start talking to worms, I thought.

I sat there for perhaps five or ten minutes, the strain ebbing away, a sick weariness mixing with the elation, until the sun on the back of my neck drove me to the shade of the carport.

So: I was not alone. The effect, or whatever, had not eradicated the microbes which made meat decay, and it had not removed life beneath the surface of the soil. I felt sure now that there was a detectable pattern to the Effect (I consciously christened it there and then) and that I would be able to make deductions, as a scientist, and that sooner or later some sense, if not some cause or explanation, would emerge. There *must* be a pattern; there always was, to any process. Perhaps normality would return, reassert itself, by degrees. Normal processes would continue; entropy still applied, growth and decay seemed unaffected. I lifted my roughly bandaged hand to wipe the itch of sweat from my face, and then stopped the movement because my fingers were caked with the earth I had unburied. I dashed it off on my trousers, convulsively, walking back into the kitchen and turning on the taps to wash my hand, to clean the cuts and run water over my fingers and wash and wipe them until they emerged from the rubbing of dishcloth and towel quite clean, scrubbed blue and pink.

CHAPTER FOUR

I drove at random around the streets in the afternoon, occasionally stopping to enter a house and walk quickly through its rooms. It became easier to do. The clocks all showed 6.12. The houses were all void of human beings or animals. All pets had vanished. Milk in saucers lay curdling on kitchen floors into blue and yellow liquid.

In one house I was startled to find the bedclothes thrown back as though the occupant had got up; in the kitchen there was evidence of a breakfast in progress, and, most chillingly of all, a loaf of bread on the formica bench with a breadknife halfway down a slice. I thought, for the first time, of the *Mary Celeste*, the abandoned ship with its half-eaten meals on the table. No doubt there were more grotesque sights in store for me. I removed the knife. The bread had begun to dry and curl. If the people returned, would they reappear at the same points in space? Was I interfering with the conditions for their precise reappearance? An academic question. Whatever I did would alter some aspect of this frozen six-twelve moment.

Less academic was the worry about my cut hand. There didn't seem to be any slivers of glass or traces of earth in the wound. What would happen if I became ill?

What if I got tetanus? In one house I found a first-aid kit in the bathroom. I bathed antiseptic onto my fingers and sealed the cuts with band-aid. Each closed house held its own distinctive staleness. I held my breath against the smell of beer and ashtrays, remnants of exhausted Friday nights; bedrooms heavy with dead sweat and cheap scent, the curtains drawn to preserve the secretions; children's rooms full of the breath of highly flavoured sweets, toothpaste, chewing gum, and stale urine. There were bathroom scents, soapy, antiseptic; chemical lavender disinfectant and the sharpness of chlorine scouring powder in obsessively neat houses where none of the surfaces had traces of human beings on them. One older house was filled with a feral air of animals and damp newspaper; another, unbearable, like the inside of a diseased lung, sweet, tubercular, breathed to the death of all its oxygen several times over, every door and window shut tight. I had to stop. A revulsion I had always felt about the physical secrecy of other people, the solid, hidden strangeness of their lives, formed into a nausea with these smells, the almost tangible presence of people who had sweated what they had eaten all their lives: dead mutton, sour milk.

Should I go to Auckland? Now? I didn't want to decide. I wandered around gardens checking for insects. Even the woodlice, the slaters normally crawling frantically under old lumps of wood or large stones, had gone. No aphids, greenfly, codling moths, slugs, snails, wasps, mosquitoes, mice or rats: a dream for gardeners.

But also no butterflies or honeybees, no spiders, no background hiss of cicadas. The silence was still absolute and terrible, the gardens like cemeteries for the deaf. I wondered if nature could survive for long without insects as pollinators or without the complicated interlock of predators and victims. Surely it couldn't? They would *have* to restore themselves. It was too vast a disturbance.

I discovered that my mind had begun to adapt its functions to the new conditions automatically, as though an unknown set of evolutionary switches had tripped, closing some circuits as temporarily useless, sending others into overload and short circuit, and activating new areas. It was reassuring to realise this. Whenever my progress from one house and garden to another was stalled by these vague and at times dangerous speculations which threatened to branch out into unpleasant conclusions and fear about the enormity of what was going on, then my mind would close down those circuits and redirect me to the sheer physical effort of going on, of not stopping still. The resilience of this mind amazed me; it was almost a separate phenomenon, a part of myself which had instinctively sought to protect itself from breakdown and to prepare defences to ensure its own survival as an organism. The question of whether I was really seeing what I seemed to be seeing kept recurring. I might be mad. This was met with a dodging agility. Madness is a deviation from what is normal, I thought; it is abnormal for people to disappear; I have not disappeared; I *am* now normality. *I think, therefore I am.*

Me: and the worms? No, madness didn't need witnesses any more than heroics needed onlookers. If a tree falls in a forest where there are no ears to hear it, then you can argue whether it makes a noise, but whether it makes a noise or not, it still falls.

What will you do tonight?—a demand from my mind, overriding the contradictory impulses with an insistence on practical action. Was there any danger that if I fell asleep I might be scooped up by the Effect? What would happen when 6.12 came round again? Should I go back to the motel room or get out into the countryside?

I drove the car aimlessly along the main street again and then on impulse decided to go up to the lookout on the hill overlooking the town. The road curved up past closed, silent houses and emerged on a small car park at the top of the hill next to a large tower-like structure. I got out of the car and looked across the town in the late afternoon sun. The houses, churches, gardens, garages and streets lay below; there were greyish mudflats beyond, then the glittering spread of water, and on the far side the distant hills, blue, insubstantial. Beyond the hills would be Auckland. Empty?

For more than half an hour I sat on the steps leading up to the tower and gazed at the immense lifelessness of the scene. It did not even seem to have acknowledged the change which had come over it; there were no visible clues as to what had happened, and no sense of any further imminent changes. The stunned clarity of the landscape seemed almost insulting; but even this was only like an extension of the indifference it had always radiated. I had felt it often when driving through remote hills in the past, on deserted roads. The clear light which scrubbed the hills into such precise definition, which polished seas and rinsed distance from time as well as space, had not changed. The nothingness stretching over huge sections of land infinitely had extended itself everywhere; it had penetrated towns, cars, houses, rooms, an irresistible, magnified vacuum. I had once driven through enormities of emptiness towards the south-east coast of the North Island, to Cape Turnagain. All the way the loneliness had dilated and rebounded from the vacant ranges of hills setting up a frightening reverberation. The beach was being sandblasted by a ferocious north Antarctic wind pressing back the curling tops of the breakers as if trying to cancel and dissipate their energy. There were no human beings in sight. The atmosphere seemed hostile to any kind of vitality that was not destructive; the wind and clear light beating down forced raw, instant, hard reactions, did not allow rest or thinking, denied something that was essential to your humanity. The landscape held no possibilities other than those of that moment. You felt you had seen it all forever. It had no psychic resonance, no memories, no past; nothing human had ever happened there. That was not unusual for parts of New Zealand. But that place also had no potential, no projections from ahead; its future gaped into nothingness too. It was inconceivable that humans should ever settle there and endow it with traces of their lives. I had been chilled, appalled, at the boldness and ferocity with which it revealed its nature.

Even then I had wondered as I drove away from it what would happen if that emptiness set up an echo, or found reverberations inside the people who nominally laid claim to the land; what would happen if you were insidiously affected by it, and weakened, losing the power of resisting it, until you might find yourself trapped in the same kind of abhuman present, transparent, unending?

I returned to the motel, stopping en route to recheck the radio wavebands. I had once read that the ionosphere undergoes alterations in the evening. But there was only static again. The motel was as I had left it. The door to my unit was still open. As I walked in, I felt a thickening sadness and depression. It was as if everything there belonged to another life, penetrated by the act of opening the blind that morning, fractured finally and beyond help by the most casual exit from the door I had just re-entered. I had intended to investigate the room to try to see if it contained any clues as to my escape from the Effect, and perhaps to lie down and reconstruct my movements from the moment I had awoken, like the re-enactment of a crime, to unearth, possibly, a missing link, a detail forgotten. Instead I slumped on the unmade bed, choking on feelings for that finished life all around, its closeness pressing against its remoteness. The ceiling was covered with a roughcast stipple of some sprayed, congealed composition, and the softer late sunlight revealed glints of gold and silver specks mixed in with the stipple.

Then the light slid into new shapes and the surface liquefied and trembled. Reflections flicked about on the upper surface of the liquid becoming quick and brilliant. I was floating beneath the surface with a hissing in my ears, the kind of hollow sea sound which comes from the pale bone of a shell held close to the coil of your ear, covering all other sounds. I pushed my hands down to try to rise but it had no effect. The terror was beginning. Slowly, as if going through space, I felt myself being turned. The hissing stopped and there was silence, dead, total. A face came drifting into view, the face of a person dead under water. The eyes were open, the nostrils flared, the mouth gaping fishlike, the long tendrils of hair slowly moving like saliva in a tide of greenish water round a pale drowned face. I could not move. The sound came back in echoes of human voices, very distant. But I couldn't reach them or speak for help.

I woke up, staring at the ceiling. It was not yet dark but the sun had set. Perhaps I had only been asleep a short while. The voices in the distance had woken me but they were not real, only part of the dream. I went to the window and stared out. The sky was turquoise and gold towards the sunset and a deep indigo overhead, into which the stars were beginning to glint. The universe was still there. The same.

Having had nothing to eat all day I now felt hungry. The sick feelings of panic and depression had gone, leaving a hollow. I decided not to venture back into town. I would stay here for the night. It wouldn't be possible to cook anything but I had some fruit with me and the motel milk was still drinkable. Before the evening became completely dark I went down and looted the motel office and rooms, getting some packets of salted nuts and potato chips, a lump of cheese, two cans of orange juice, a tin of pineapple cubes and a transistor radio. Then, with the car safely locked, I took all this and the torch I had obtained from the shop earlier, and went up and locked myself in the motel room. I decided to barricade the door, and heaved the spare twin bed against it. With all the curtains and blinds closed I felt reasonably secure. It was now deathly dark and the silence was pressing in, but this was easier to deal with at night since it was usually quiet at night.

Yes. Usually quiet.

I ate by the torchlight, stopping every few minutes to freeze and listen intently for the faintest suspicion of a sound. Nothing, not even a breeze to rustle the trees at the back; in fact with the door and windows closed the humid evening was doubly oppressive. Should I drive up to the lookout and see if there are any lights in the distance? No, better not. I would not like to go out there.

It will not, I thought, be easy to sleep. The dreams are bad and I am afraid to go to sleep.

Perhaps even the dreams would have been better than what followed. I switched off the torch; the darkness was as complete as the silence. It was all very well to think that it was usually quiet at night but in my desire to stay awake for as long as I could, I found myself sitting listening to the silence, holding my breath, hearing even my own heart-beats, in the effort to hear something. I felt sure that I had heard some kind of noise from the direction of the car park below at the back of the motel. It was something moving, and when I listened intently it stopped as if conscious of being detected. For what seemed ages I strained to hear, but when there was nothing further I decided I had imagined it and relaxed, wiping the sweat off my face with a towel in the bathroom. Whilst I was doing this the noise briefly penetrated the room again, furtively. I stood petrified. The hairs on the back of my neck crawled like insects. There was something outside. There, again. This time it was a movement on the loose gravel of the parking area.

I cursed that I hadn't picked up a gun or any weapons from the sporting goods shops in town. Creeping quietly back into the kitchen, slowly in the dark, feeling my way along the edges of objects, I gently withdrew the cutlery drawer and fumbled around until I touched the large breadknife. With this in one hand I stood by the back kitchen window steeling my nerves to the action of carefully, slowly, lifting the end of the blind away from the window by no more than a centimetre. From this angle I could see along the balcony by the dim starlight (there was no moon) but it was not possible to see down into the car park or to see the steps which led up to the first-floor units on my left, out of my angle of vision. The steps would be visible from the other end of the window but to lift the blind slightly there and look out through that narrow gap, I would have to climb on top of the electric cooker, and this would be precarious and might make too much noise.

Nothing happened, and I seemed to stand there for ages, aching in one position. The sweat made its way endlessly down my face. Whatever was outside must know I was here. And it must be evil. There was a furtive slyness about the sounds. I was sure that was not imagination. I could sense it.

The steps up to the balcony vibrated, as if someone, or something, had advanced onto the first step and paused. The vibration was detectable because the steel framework of the stairway was attached to the wall of the motel and the iron handrail acted like a tuning fork. But again, after the agony of waiting, nothing else happened, and I could feel numbness in my hands and feet as cramp began to set round the tensed muscles and veins. I realised that I had been exerting every cell in my brain towards the thought, directed at the steps, that no object of any kind should come one centimetre closer to me. The totality of this effort to repel and prevent seemed to have drained away all the resources which usually fed oxygen to nerve centres and muscles, so the slightest relaxation meant a lapse into instant weariness. At one point I must have been asleep, or unconscious, or hypnotised into a staring dream condition, for how long I couldn't tell, perhaps only for microseconds, maybe for several minutes, until another slight sound brought me back to the full intensity of listening and concentrating again. And then I was not sure if there had been another sound or whether I had created the sound in the reflex of returning suddenly to total wakefulness in an instant. I had never before in my life passed through such a condition of terror, and to find this peculiar hyper-sleep or super-consciousness on the far side of fear was unbelievable.

After another huge void of starlight and dark and waiting, I moved very slowly from the window and slid down to sit on the kitchen floor with my back against the sink unit. The lino was cool. I held the knife in my left hand.

The silence seemed to have taken on its former solidity, and instead of being threatening it now felt protective. But I wanted to avoid thinking that the noises outside had gone away or been defeated; I was afraid that any relaxation of that kind would somehow provoke a response from whatever was out there.

Sure enough, there was another sound: the crunch and rustle of loose stones again. The stairs had been abandoned, then, and it was back in the car park. I could hardly move, but I dragged myself up and gently lifted one slat of the venetian blind. It was not possible to see anything. After only a few minutes, the same sound of gravel, but further away and to the right, beyond my angle of vision. Was it going away, or trying another route? I strained to see, then carefully let the blind go and stood in the silence for a while. It could have been entirely my imagination, but I believed I could actually sense a lessening in the feeling of evil which had earlier been so oppressive it was almost touchable.

Groping my way across the room I sat down in an armchair by the door to the bathroom. A slight trembling and shivering came over me. The room had cooled. Against the fatigue which pushed me deeper into the chair, I tried to think about what had happened. The idea of an evil as some kind of personalised thing had not occurred to me during the day. I'd been scared in the first house I'd entered, but those were merely momentary shocks, irrelevant to the bigger puzzle, easily solved. The disappearance of every living object, the fixing of all time mechanisms at 6.12, the absence of radio transmissions from all wavebands surely couldn't be connected to an Effect which manifested itself as a specific thing corporeal enough to creep around and squat for hours on staircases? Perhaps there was nothing outside except a stray dog or cat or opossum, any odd animal which might have escaped the Effect like me?

The fact that I could consider this was, I realised, a sure sign that the menace outside had gone. No animal could have radiated malignancy like that. If I'd survived the Effect because of some freak or accidental immunity, then I might have a special resistance which something was trying to break down. There might be no logic to these phases, just a sequence of threats or attacks. I shall find out more, I thought. The dark lightened, my bravado increased. I know it's evil, it comes at night, and I *think* I can keep it at bay with my mind under control. If I hold that control I can survive.

When I woke up the sun was streaming in from the bright silence.

CHAPTER FIVE

For a few seconds of course I wanted to believe that everything would now be normal again. The absence of sounds defeated this idea even before I moved to peer through the blinds. The moment I moved, a succession of powerful muscular pains wrenched at my spine and shoulders, then at my legs. I remembered what had been happening and that it was acutely real. My bad dreams had never involved physical pain; they had been memorable for terror, the vertigo of falling or slipping down slopes towards chasms, or the impulse to run from some horror but not being able to, or the feeling of slow suffocation under deepening water; there had even been dreams in which I had to wander through strange buildings, opening doors of rooms which contained unrevealed horrors. But never physical pain.

I walked around the motel unit, wincing, looking out. Was it safe to go outside? All seemed clear. The word 'normal' would not do. I packed up my belongings and the food so that I could load the car quickly. The sooner I got away from here, the better. The Effect was so closely tied in my mind to this place that I thought its force might weaken the further away I went. The place to go, obviously, was Auckland. There were sure to be people there out of half a million. Surely.

Having moved the barricade from the door, I checked again and then unlocked the door, opened it, and stepped out onto the balcony. Nothing had changed. I went down the stairs and glanced at my car, turning round slowly as I moved, my eyes checking the other cars, the back fence, the motel doors, the exit road, the cars again. When I felt reasonably safe I unlocked the boot of the car and went back up to the room to get my things.

Five minutes later, sweating, slightly out of breath, I had packed and loaded everything I thought I might need, including some blankets, sheets and pillows from the motel beds, plus some pots and pans, cups, cutlery and plates. There was no question of leaving a cheque; yesterday's confusions seemed ages ago. Yet when I was ready to go, I found I was pausing, standing at the foot of the steps in the shade, trying to recollect something, reluctant to leave. I sat down on the steps and wiped my face with a handkerchief. As I pushed the handkerchief back into my pocket my arm banged against the iron railing of the stairs, and the whole rail vibrated. The sound came back from the darkness in the night. I realised I must be sitting exactly where the object had been; right there, the menace, the thing, the embodiment.

Once more, with an awareness now of following a repeated series of actions, I was leaping into my car, slamming the door and driving away from the motel onto the main road, a spit of loose stones under the wheels. And again I was heading into town, to the right, instead of away towards Auckland to the left. I was badly shaken. The tremor of the staircase had set up a resonance inside me which was acutely unnerving because it wasn't wholly accountable merely as the memory of last night, allied to the fear of the thing outside. It was more, but it was inexplicable. My mind had marked a threshold; I knew that. And the full reason for this attack of nerves lay well on the far side of that threshold, locked away.

The town was unchanged, silent, full of hot light, narrow shadows, stopped objects. The locked houses were as dead as yesterday, their shut blinds like white eyelids across empty sockets.

I located a sports shop. The door resisted my attempts to break in; I had to smash the window and clamber in through the display of fishing rods, aqualungs, and golf clubs. Finally I found the gun cabinet, the rifles padlocked to a rack. It took an hour to pillage every cupboard and cabinet and drawer, forcing them open with a crowbar from the garage down the street, sorting out cartridges, bullets, and bolts, hacksawing the locks on the rack, cursing and sweating all the time, before I finally had a serviceable Remington hunting rifle and a large, wicked-looking pump-action shotgun, a 12-gauge which took six cartridges. I loaded the car with the guns and some boxes of ammunition, putting the Remington handy on the passenger seat.

The shotgun made me nervous. I placed it on the back seat on pillows and rugs. I also took a gas-operated cooking unit with spare cylinders, a sleeping bag and some containers to hold water or petrol.

The car had filled up considerably by the time I drove to the garage again. Robinson Crusoe, I thought. Self-sufficient, ready for anything. I was feeling more confident. I filled the petrol tank, hand-cranking the pump; checked batteries, oil and water, then filled a couple of the plastic containers with petrol and stacked them safely in the boot. Safe? If I had a crash, the detonation of all this would wake the dead.

The phrase disturbed me as it went through my mind, and I stopped, closing the boot, leaning on the sun-hot metal.

But the rush of practical concerns over-ran the pause. A few minutes later I was driving out of town, the doors locked from the inside, the windows half open, fresh air drying the sweat on my face, the loaded guns at the ready.

In the whole landscape nothing else was moving or alive. I sped faster and breathed deeper with a sudden exhilaration. Everything was shining in an empty clarity stretching away in all directions. There were no problems except the Effect. It had drained the world of every other puzzle and mystery. Except me.

CHAPTER SIX

I drove west through empty settlements and towns, abandoning more and more of the road code, cornering recklessly, not expecting to meet any other vehicles. Then, suddenly, I came round a bend and there was a milk tanker across the road and I was skidding sideways and braking, ramming the grass verge on the right. The car bounced violently, all the loose objects, guns, cans, were knocked off seats, clattering around, whilst I wrenched at the wheel. I missed the tanker by centimetres and came to a stop on the verge, the air shaken out of my lungs. The smell of burned tyres drifted in with the taste of dust. After a few deep breaths I opened the door to get out, but it jammed against earth and grass. I had to reverse onto the road.

There did not seem to be any damage. I opened the doors, rearranged the jumble of equipment. The sun was beating down from a shiny featureless sky the colour of blue enamel. There was a faint stench from the tanker. I climbed up and peered into the driver's cab. It was empty. The keys were in the ignition. The engine had not been switched off, so the fuel had run out and the batteries were dead. After the disappearance of the driver the tanker had just coasted to a halt, slewing slightly to the right across the road. He would have been pulling the wheel over as he came round the corner, I thought. For the first time I wondered what exactly happened at the precise moment of the Effect. Was it painless and instantaneous?

Above the fuel gauge with its needle resting at E, there was a dashboard clip stuffed with papers and documents, and a photograph facing the driver's seat. It showed a smiling Maori woman with several children who were grinning, frowning, or staring vacantly at the camera lens, the camera presumably being held by the father. Now, faced by bright light, the faces were staring into the empty cab of the tanker on the deserted road. The heat on the tarmac in the distance waved evaporated, detached images of road surface way beyond the cab windows. I climbed down and went back to my car. The long scar in the earth of the verge made me think how close I had been to an accident which could have killed me. I could have been trapped in a mess of metal under the tanker and spent days dying. Any injury would be fatal.

I drove away slowly. The steel glare of the tanker drew away and shrank into my rear-view mirror. After a while I calmed down and even began to feel tired. Somehow the milk smell, blended with hot stainless steel, reminded me of school, memories surfacing through twenty-five years;

the fights with other kids, the hollow noises echoing down corridors, the massive silence of mid-afternoon playgrounds when you were sent outside because you felt sick and time seemed to have gone somewhere else and dried hard like a stain.

Now the danger was that I might fall asleep. The drone of the road in the heat was hypnotic. I had to force myself to concentrate.

Soon I reached State Highway 1 and turned north. I would be in Auckland in half an hour. I had reset my watch and the car clock to an approximation of correct time; it would be about midday. There must be somebody there. The expectation set some adrenalin flowing, and I began to tense and stare ahead. My sunglasses toned down the glistening of the road to sullen purple and indigo and projected a pattern of bluish marks from the windscreen's toughened glass like faint bruises across the landscape.

A certain uneasiness, prompted by the photograph in the tanker cabin, made me wonder about driving off the motorway across to Pakuranga to Joanne's address. I decided against it. There were many reasons why we had separated; she had made it clear that she held me responsible for the death of our son; that was enough. What would I be able to say, even if she might be there? Could I say, this world, at least this world of people he never seemed to see, and we could never quite cope with, has disappeared; can we now speak plainly and deal with what was left unsaid? Bathos. It would make no difference anyhow. What's done is done. I have no photograph staring at me. No commitments. The child was dead. She, the mother, had wanted to abandon him to an institution because of his strangeness. She had not been able to cope with it. Or with the reactions of society to him, to herself. When he had died she blamed me. Any psychiatrist would have diagnosed a case of transferred guilt. I read a book about it. It is apparently relatively common. I was to blame. So she had gone away. There was nothing very much to leave, she said; I ought to be left alone with my conscience. Then she had gone to live in a flat in Pakuranga to be alone with hers.

I think she had believed that she was doing me a tremendous favour by not running off to some other man. I had to admit that she had been faithful. But by her own definition she had been faithful to 'nothing very much', to a form of words, a contractual obligation only indulged in for the sake of convention; so the effort could hardly have been very great. For better or for worse; what did that mean? Anyhow, at least she hadn't returned to her parents, her precious family in Remuera, that clan of self-righteous hypocrites. It had never occurred to them that whatever genetic aberration lolled inside the brain of my child just might have been inherited from some dormant idiocy of their own chromosomes. I imagined them seized by yesterday's 6.12 disappearance. It would have been irresistible, the Effect would not have spared Remuera, it would have flicked across the tight lawns, high fences, alarms, through clinker-brick walls and thick upholstery, velvet and fur and deep-pile Axminster; relentless, sudden. *The owners disappear*, every last executive belly, sauna-soft torso, sagging chin and lifted face, every piece of sclerotic organ and half-digested pâté of bowel pulp, all gone like magic, along with all their slavering animals, leaving untouched everything they really valued and guarded and thought they owned: real estate. Loot.

I sped onto the motorway just before noon, guns at the ready, driving fast by the few deserted cars and trucks, heading straight into and over this immense spread of houses. Corrugated metal rooftops flashed far off; blinded windows glinted. The air was clear and silent. The city blocks in the distance stood against the sky like headstones, empty boxes in a vast garbage dump, ratless and Sunday. Shadows were pulled tight everywhere, drawn in. The motorway rolled across, glaring, a dead concrete runway fixed at the centre of all this, littered with pieces of exhausted technology. I was elated, overcome by the enormity of what I was seeing and surprised by the power of the feelings of vengeance and triumph. Driving alive over all the deadness I realised how much I had always hated.

CHAPTER SEVEN

I had hoped for a clue. Why I had hoped to find it in Auckland I could not have said, even if there had been somebody to ask, and there was not. I had become more unique than I had believed; half a million people had vanished from here without a single survivor. Was I really the only living human being *anywhere*? That would change everything. It would mean I had been exempted by a process beyond mere random chance.

Driving up and down these central city streets which had nothing more than a few pieces of paper drifting around them, it was easy to believe that the larger the anomaly of my survival, the greater the likelihood that there must be a particular reason for it. In half an hour the scale, the hugeness of the abnormality, pressed in on my mind and was met by the same stubborn resilience. This was all so great it must have a meaning, and that meaning would soon reveal itself to me, otherwise it would all be pointless, and I should have vanished yesterday too. I even smiled. Two days earlier my existence had been more or less pointless. Now it seemed that it might be the point of the universe. Could it be as great as that? What power did I have? Would it be revealed or would I have to find it out?

I climbed laboriously up a concrete stairwell to the top of one of the large hotel blocks and found my way onto a lookout balcony. Here I could see great distances. I was out of breath. I sat in the shade and looked south.

The sun blazed. It was hard to hate the city like this. It seemed helpless. I looked down. Beware of high places. Temptations. I sat down again.

Once I had seen a collection of early photographs of mid-Victorian city streets, taken when the exposure time of the light-sensitive plate was more than five minutes. Moving objects—people, animals, carriages—did not register on the photograph, so that the streets appeared empty, except for faint malingering smudges here and there. People were in those streets, but the machine's perception process was too slow to record them. They had been rendered irrelevant. I had wondered: were there other objects at the other end of the time spectrum which *we* could not see or sense in everyday life, because our perceptions were too slow? This was not a speculation I felt like extending now. My mind dismissed it. The resemblance of this scene to the photographs, in any case, was only superficial. I could see pieces of paper moving in the streets. There was a slight breeze coming in from the sea. Getting up, I walked around the other side of the balcony and stared at the glittering water and the low curve of Rangitoto Island. The sparkle of the water was a reassuring movement.

I put my sunglasses on. The light calmed. I scanned the bridge. There were only a few specks and dots of stopped cars on it. Then, north, in the distance—something? A smudge on the skyline. It was very faint but it looked like smoke. I strained my eyes into the haze. Yes, it *was* smoke.

My heart shivered. I took the sunglasses off and rubbed them on my sleeve. My eyes narrowed against the strong light. After a moment I looked again. The smoke was definitely there. I walked up and down the balcony, peering intently. No, it wasn't a mirage.

Down and down and down the flights of stairs and back into the car. How would I get to the bridge from here? I drove along the wrong street, reversed, turned left, got lost. At one point I found myself dutifully obeying a one-way-street sign and looking for an alternative way. Eventually I reached the motorway and zoomed down to the bridge. There were two articulated trucks on the motorway, one of which had trundled down and jack-knifed across three lanes. I dodged them and sped up and across the bridge, crossing to the southbound lane to avoid the toll barriers. Coming down into Northcote I could no longer see the smoke; I slowed down, then decided to stay with the main road north. Yes, there it was again, a blue-grey haze towards Glenfield. I turned off to the left past the golf course and went down Archers Road. Now the smell of burning, pungent, penetrated the car. I was getting lost in a maze of suburban streets, going down a no-exit road and seeing the car reflected in the blank panes of ranch slider doors from vacant houses. I stopped, checked my loaded guns, reversed, U-turned across dry lawns; then halfway down the next street, jammed on the brakes, hard.

It looked as if a mass of rubbish had been strewn across the road, over the gardens and trees, and even on the roofs of the houses.

I took the rifle and cautiously got out of the car, locking the door. The burning smell was very strong. From behind the houses there came a crackling noise, suddenly, into the quiet. I walked along the side of the road. A pale-orange object which was lodged mysteriously in a broken tree proved to be a battered suitcase.

The rubbish everywhere was a compound of torn clothing, papers, odd shoes and shredded material; plastic bags and cups, personal effects. I stared at it. There were more suitcases. Going into the smoky gloom I found my way down a drive and emerged into what had been back gardens. An enormous burned scar ran across the ground. The houses in the next street were in ruins, just smouldering remnants, collapsed and buckled roofing iron and mangled carports, masses of brick here and there; black stumps of trees still glowing with hot charcoal. White ashes lifted in the slight breeze. Heaps of incinerated houses, huts and garages had been hurled all over the place. Skeletal cars, everything burned from them, were lying haphazardly around, some overturned.

I clambered cautiously over hot acrid remains of objects which had become indecipherable. Melted tarseal stuck to my shoes. The stench in places was particularly stinging, and my eyes were soon streaming with tears. Coughing and sweating, I stumbled as quickly as I could over more ashes, broken concrete and drainpipes, until I emerged on the other side of the smoke. It hung in a cloud across several streets. Further down, a fire was still burning, slowly, making loud snapping noises. Even out of the range of the burned and wrecked area, houses had been partly demolished and domestic wreckage flung across lawns. One house had been sliced in half and stood open in cross-section to the dull sunlight; a living room with pictures on the wall, a television set, a brass lamp with a turquoise shade, imitation-leather lounge suite; and purple curtains waving in the slight movement of air. I walked past. A tartan slipper and the door of a refrigerator were lying across some ripped cushions on the grass verge, the innards of the cushions spilling out amongst shards of broken glass and the decaying remnants of food, eggshells, oranges. At the end of a long scar across the lawn there was a metal object embedded inside the caved-in wooden wall of the next house. I went down the drive and crunched over the broken glass of the windows and doors. The house had been partly knocked off its foundations, and the front door was leaning to the left, its glass panels shattered. I climbed in. There was a smell of plaster, dust, fibreglass pink insulation disembowelled from the ceiling, and a rubbery, oily machine odour. Wedged into the centre of the ruined house, blocking the hallway and kitchen, were the huge black tyres and hydraulic mechanisms of an aircraft's landing gear. One set of wheels, at any rate. The metal struts were buckled in places, otherwise scarcely damaged. They had thrust into the house at speed, locked in a senseless rigidity. The pink fibreglass hung down from the ceiling in tendrils with ripped corrugated iron and long, dead, cobweb filth. I looked in the nearest bedroom, just to check, but of course there were no people. My shoe crunched a small object: a glass ornament, one of several knocked from the dressing table. It had been a swan, the glass streaky white like petrified milk, translucent; I had broken its neck.

I went back outside. The smoke across the street parted and I could see the great tail fin of the crashed plane looming out of the debris, unburned, the Maori logo of Air New Zealand on the side like a brand on a shark fin. Everything else was charred, an empty carcase in pieces. I only walked far enough down what had been the street to discern part of a starboard wing and a massive engine, crushed and mottled with dark patterns of fire, still hot, wobbling the air with heat; then I turned and made my way up the street and across and back to my car. My eyes were acid from the reek of burned plastic, vinyl and styrofoam. The sharpness scalded my sinuses and throat. I put the rifle in the car and stood wiping my eyes. All the time I was thinking of this plane, yesterday, coming down at dawn from thirty thousand feet, from—where? Los Angeles? Tahiti? Singapore?—suddenly empty, spiralling down, metal and petrol, across the spread of deserted streets and houses.

And I'd thought I was driving towards some part of the answer, that I might begin to understand, to detect a pattern.

I could scarcely see the wreckage as I stood there, the heat blotting illusions into the air, my eyes watering. God, this couldn't have any meaning, it was too insane.

I suddenly felt irrelevant and weak. The sun behind the smoke was dull orange, and it made the light very strange with a faded muddy pallor. I stared at the sky. The physiological mechanisms of weeping were operating on my face. I had not given way to the real reaction for a long time. Hardly ever, in fact.

CHAPTER EIGHT

The research centre, where I normally worked, was closed as usual for the weekend. I locked the car and walked to the main doors of the windowless concrete block, my rifle in one hand, the keys in the other. I had no specific reason for coming here, except that the centre was near Albany, a short drive north from Glenfield. And I felt uneasy about going back into the city or to my flat at Takapuna. Perhaps this building would be a secure place for the night. I felt defensive at the prospect of nightfall.

Once inside the doors I relocked them by slipping the catches back and went across the reception area to the door labelled RESEARCH 2. The air was cool and scented faintly of floor polish. The clock stood at 6.12. I took my identity card from my wallet and slotted it in the decoding unit. The power, of course, was off, so I flicked the battery switch. A green light came on and the door opened with a buzzing noise. Retrieving my card I entered, switching on all the emergency power. The door closed behind me and dim lights flickered on along the corridor. Hidden air conditioners began to hum. I went down the passage, turned right and descended to the door labelled SECURE UNIT. My card opened this door too. Antiseptic white light flooded down from panels in the ceiling. I felt stale and grubby as I walked along the inner corridor to my room, the polished lino sucking at the flecks of tar under my shoes.

Everything was as I had left it two days earlier when I went on leave. My desk, chair, books were all in their usual places. The air here was cold and I switched off the circulator. Partly from habit, partly to keep warm, I put on a white coat over my shirtsleeves and went to the research lab.

All the security devices had been no protection against the Effect. Every biological specimen and experimental animal had disappeared, even Atkinson's collection of insects, the *Drosophila melanogaster* on which all his research had been based. The dead ones, of course, were still in their transparent plastic cases. The dead had survived. I wrinkled my nose at the laboratory-formaldehyde smell and sat down in front of Perrin's half-completed three-dimensional genetic model. To the left there was the great double helix of the Watson–Crick DNA structure, spotlit by a special lamp like an icon in the sanctuary of a temple dedicated to mysterious rituals. Which, in a sense, it was. I had felt sure that Perrin worshipped it. He had claimed to be working towards a new understanding of the relationship between the ribonucleic acid molecule and the chromosome evolutionary model which he was constructing. He spoke of this in almost religious terms, a mystery revealed only to one who had been prepared to sacrifice. 'Nobody finds out anything without sacrifice,' he once said, pompously, just after I had begun to work here. It was one of his catchphrases. He was not a very sympathetic character. Perhaps none of us were. We didn't have to be. I suppose we all had our eccentricities. As a research assistant I was very involved in what we called Section 2 Special Project, of which Perrin's work was a part.

It would not have been easy to explain to an outsider what we were trying to do, even if the project had been taken off the secret list. Joanne thought I was treating her badly because I was so involved in the work and yet unable to tell her anything about it. But I was sure we were on the verge of a breakthrough in one of the basic problems of biomolecular genetic research and we were going into areas which strictly speaking were marginally beyond what we were supposed to be doing and for me that was very exciting and challenging and all-absorbing. I was the youngest member of the team, in my late twenties, and it was a chance I might not get again.

Perrin was investigating dormant genes. It had been discovered that within all species of living creatures there were some individual members—very rare, about one in a million for human beings—whose genes contained an inactive, apparently useless 'pair', chromosomes without any discernible function. Scientists had been trying to activate these. Atkinson had been using fruit flies, Drosophila, because of their simple genetic structure and rapid rate of reproduction. Perrin had extended the experiments to include mice, rats, dogs and rhesus monkeys. We were using radioactivity plus low-frequency sound waves. The problem was to energise the dormant genes without destroying the others at the same time or producing lethal factors which would cause the organism to self-destruct. Nature had been very careful here. A whole complex of natural prohibitions existed which ensured that mutants and abnormalities failed to reproduce at a basic cellular level, or aborted, or were suicidal, or fell mysteriously into recessive or lethal phases, or, if they survived at all, turned out to be sterile. And usually the radiation would produce abnormalities or sterility.

Perrin wanted to use the sound waves to induce a 'resonating effect' on the ribonucleic chains which would confuse the 'alarm systems' and at the same time protect the basic proteins from the bad effects of the radioactivity being used to activate the dormant genes.

All this research had originally sprung from simple experiments in stockbreeding, always well funded in New Zealand. Officially we were hoping to make farm animals genetically more efficient and productive. We had been given rather more remote and secret facilities when we started using radioactive isotopes. The government didn't want us pestered by some unholy alliance of anti-nuclear protestors and animal lovers. At least that was the official, or rather, unofficial, reason for all the security. But of course secrecy had bred secrecy, and it had become difficult for a research assistant such as myself to find out, to know exactly, the full range of activities even in our own department. We were investigating the dormant genes 'because they were there'. It was pure research. Nobody knew why dormant genes existed. We were going to shake them awake from the thousand million years in which they'd mysteriously coasted through evolution as an unworking elite. It would be an achievement beyond Rutherford's dissection of the structure of the atom, which had been started in an even more rudimentary way in a cellar in Christchurch.

Naturally we did not trumpet our project, not even to our funding agencies. There was a general feeling that they would stop us. As Atkinson had remarked with his usual dryness, we would be poor scientists if we could confuse the incredibly subtle and complex alarm systems inside proteins, yet not be able to do the same for the alarm systems of a few thick-headed politicians and bureaucrats.

I sat in the empty laboratory staring at the DNA spiral. It was a tangled helter-skelter of different coloured plastic marbles curving round in chains of partners, held in midair by steel rods on a frame; a frozen dance, infinitely elegant. I remembered Perrin standing by it one day, when I'd said, 'What do you think will happen?'—meaning, when we resonate the cells at the correct frequency to wake the dormant genes. He had peered at me, resettling his steel-rimmed spectacles on his nose with his forefinger.

'Evolution,' he said; 'the next phase. A quantum leap. We have some idea. The timing can't be accidental.'

'Timing?'

'If there's intelligent life out there'—gesturing not at Auckland but up at the universe—'it probably follows the same pattern as ours. Nuclear physicists develop the ability to destroy the planet. We risk being destroyed because our moral and ethical development has lagged behind too far. We're moral cretins playing with hydrogen bombs. But the odds are, that every civilisation which can unravel the atomic nucleus will also unravel the protein chains of evolution *at the same time.*' He paused, and put his hand on the DNA model. 'Nuclear fallout leads to radioactive mutations. The clue for waking up the dormant genes. It's a coding system. They're there to save us. From ourselves.'

He knocked the DNA structure with his knuckles, gently, making it vibrate.

'But we can't be sure,' I said. I could hardly grasp the full implications of what he'd been saying. Perhaps he was trying out an elaborate patronising joke on me, I thought. They sometimes did. No, he was serious. I had seen him reach out his hand and knock on the next billion years; the chains of protoplasm trembled. I had been thinking of unravelling a secret from the past, as Watson and Crick had done with DNA. Ideas about the future had not occupied much space in my mind. A quantum leap. He was supremely assured. He looked at me, his glasses reflecting the gleam of the spotlight.

'What else could it be?' he said.

At that time I was sufficiently surprised by the fact that he had floated these speculations to me, to be able to ignore the feeling that he was still concealing the greater part of his 'mystery'; and to disregard any doubts I might have had about his sanity. Objective standards of sanity didn't exist. Even if they did, it would have been pointless to judge the people who worked at the unit by them.

Then later, I began to see the flaws in his argument. And I started to worry.

The quantum leap would be a leap in the dark unless it could be controlled. If the genetic developments could be controlled absolutely then they would be absolutely corruptible *and* corruptive. Secondly, Nature might have prepared not a mechanism for saving us, like a fire alarm behind thick glass, but a final defence mechanism for preserving the rest of creation against us. Perrin might have seen all the right clues but constructed the wrong conclusion from them. The evolutionary charts showed our ape-brained predecessors loping down the dead ends of genetic failure into extinction, and Man striding serenely along the broad path of development *ad infinitum*. We might have been mistaken. Worse, we might have fallen deliberately over a tripwire set a billion years ago to catch us if we became too clever for the good of the universe. Finally, it was useless to pretend that we were a vastly superior group of people in this unit, immune to the general retardation or to human frailties. *That* was the crunch.

It had been another of Perrin's mottoes that 'you never see the obvious'. I stood and switched off the spotlight on the DNA model. There was no sense in wasting power. The image of his hand reaching out to the structure remained in my mind. What he had failed to see had been very obvious and yet I hadn't worked my way round to it easily because it involved the kind of admission which broke down secure barriers inside oneself; it had been one of the factors which had led to the eventual nervous crisis, or whatever it was, culminating in my having to take extended leave from the unit.

It consisted of the simple realisation that if moral cretins were playing with hydrogen bombs, then moral cretins might also be playing with DNA molecules.

In order to dismiss such a thought I would have had to find an area inside myself which could resist it with unquestioning assurance. It was useless to speculate about other people. I had to answer from within my own resources and with scientific objectivity because it was a serious problem demanding a high degree of careful assessment.

In the end my resources had proved inadequate and I had been unable to resist the most adverse conclusion.

The irony was that I should have reached this crisis as a result of a cold scientific problem, after all the years of apparently much greater turmoil stemming from the disaster of my own life. But the two fitted together inextricably, like the paired molecules chained inside the DNA spirals. It seemed strange that at this precise moment, I could not remember exactly how. The links seemed numb, nerves paralysed at the root by some local anaesthetic.

Well. It was all irrelevant now. I wondered if, at the moment of being obliterated or transmuted by the Effect, Perrin had been vouchsafed any sudden revelation to compensate for the waste of his life. His world had always been so orderly. Did he have a final instant of surprise?

The door leading to the corridor on the other side of the lab was unlocked. That was odd. I walked along the corridor under the dim emergency lighting. There was a thin glow of brighter light from beneath one of the research supervisor's rooms. It was Perrin's room. I paused, then pushed open the door. The lights were switched on but of course the room was deserted. Perrin must have stayed behind late on Friday to put through an extra programme; yes, there were computer printout sheets on his desk. He often worked late, sometimes until the early hours of the morning; it was easy to lose track of time inside the unit when there were no windows to remind you of day or night. And my absence would have meant extra work for the senior staff. A glance at the programme heading surprised me; he'd been trying my suggestion for B12 on a high frequency waveband. That was very much a shot in the dark. What was he doing? He had seemed very noncommittal when I'd proposed trying high frequencies only a few weeks ago. Yet curiously I felt I knew about this. The surprise was not as strong as it should have been. Perhaps I'd suspected him without really admitting it to myself.

A sudden thump inside me bounced my heart against my ribs like a physical blow. What if—

I threw down the computer sheets and ran out of the room, down the corridor, along to the left, then down more steps and round another corner past the DANGER: RADIATION signs, and there was the steel security door leading to the radiation unit with the spokes of the radioactivity warning light above the door shining a dull red. That meant a danger level of radiation in the plutonium storage area and in the experimental chamber; not a high level, but enough to cause mild radiation sickness after exposures of longer than a few hours. I stared at the warning light, then ran to the door and looked through the small pane of thick armoured glass inset into the solid steel. I could see into the experimental chamber. All the emergency lighting was on and Perrin was sitting at the panel of the remote control handling device, his arms extended so that his hands were buried inside the thick gloves of the device.

He was peering at the screen in front of him. *Perrin was there!*

I shouted. Not his name, or any recognisable noise; just a yell of sheer relief and excitement bursting the suffocation out of my lungs and throat.

Then I did a stupid thing. Without thinking, operating the manual control, I swung open the door into the radiation unit. Bells clanged the alarm. A series of dull slamming noises reverberated throughout the whole wing of the research centre. The air conditioning stopped. The whole of Research 2 Secure Unit was now automatically sealed off from the outside world to prevent any radiation leak.

I scarcely noticed; it didn't register. Striding through the doorway I called to Perrin, and stopped. Then I walked slowly towards him. He was quite dead.

The Geiger counters above the control panel were stuttering erratically. Whatever animal or specimen he had been handling inside the glass box with the spastic armatures and clamps of the metal extensions to the gloves had vanished. The transformers and circuit breakers on the sound modulator had gone into overload and tripped, as though a surge of energy had been pushed back into the main power supply, and there was still a faint smell of burned insulation material in the air, along with hints of a more hideous disintegration.

I did not touch the body. The eyes were open. A reflection in the screen gazed out with the same vacancy, grey fixed on bone-white. He must have died before the Effect had struck, or he would not be here. Electrocution? No sign of that. The radioactivity wasn't strong enough to kill. Natural causes, then; a heart attack? No expression on the face. No clue. What happened? For God's sake, *what*?

For minutes I stared round the room, in a daze. A bile lump of frustration and rage churned inside my stomach. Damn, damn, *damn*. I kicked the remote control device. And again, and again. Then I retched on the solid bitterness coming up my gullet to meet the smell in the room. Out. I went to the door, wrenched it open, blundered back into the corridor, slammed the door and vomited, leaning on the wall and hearing the spatter on the concrete floor. Sour tendrils of saliva swung from my mouth. My eyes streamed again. I destroyed Perrin in my mind ten times over for being arrogant and devious, for being so clever and stupid all at once, for shunting me off on leave so he could try my idea out, for being here, for being dead when he should have been alive, and finally for stinking in his deathness like any putrescent piece of rotting offal.

I staggered back along the corridor and sat down on the steps leading to the laboratory, wiping my face on the sleeve of my white coat.

It was about ten minutes before I realised that I was dead, too.

CHAPTER NINE

The whole research unit was designed so that any radiation would be confined to the section I had just entered. If the door between that section and the rest of the unit was opened by manual override whilst the danger level sign was at red, the exterior doors from the unit would seal themselves shut. The air conditioning would stop and metal panels and grilles would close over the ducts. I was now trapped inside the unit with about thirty-six hours' supply of air and no hope of getting out.

My identity card was useless for operating the doors. The two heavy steel doors by which I had entered could now only be opened from the outside by the security controller. They would have extended their core of titanium steel reinforcing rods out into the thick ferroconcrete wall in a complex locking system. All the walls were impenetrable. Even the waste pipes from the sinks and toilets ran laterally through the walls for a metre before they too encountered metal seals which blocked their exit to the outside main drain in an emergency. There were no windows and the ceilings and floors were ferroconcrete layers.

In an emergency there were several ways of getting out. You could wait for clearance, when the security controller would override the emergency locks from the outside. There was telephonic contact. There was even a hand-cranked device for setting off bells and sirens on the outside of the building, in case of total power failure. That was the worst-option situation. Everything had been thought of. The system was infallible.

I walked slowly back to the laboratory and sat down in a swivel chair. What could I do? I had my rifle and clip of bullets, but shooting the locks off the doors, or even emptying the bullets and stuffing the locks with cordite, was wishful thinking. There were no conventional locks.

I swivelled slowly in the chair, gazing at all the scientific equipment. The absurdity of what had happened was unbelievable. I had come a long way on a hot sunny afternoon, as the sole survivor of God knows what, to trap myself in this fail-safe technological tomb surrounded by the products of centuries of intellectual research. And now I would die here like any Stone Age cretin mouldering away amongst a heap of toys and trinkets. Idiotic. But fitting. Perrin's metabolism has already started down the journey. We go together, even our stench sealed off from the world. Will anyone ever force a way in and wonder what happened? Or is everything extinct now?

What the hell. No point in waiting. Get it over with quickly. There are poisons in the chemical store.

I stood up and went out into the corridor at the far end of the lab. The third door down led to a small room lined with shelves of medical chemicals in hundreds of different coloured bottles and containers. My knowledge of these things was vague. Even during the worst crises, I had never resorted to tranquillisers. Joanne had been fond of magic potions and tablets. And the doctors had prescribed every latest corrective-behavioural pill and injection for Peter. Child, what we did to you.

There are no means for me to make amends. No life after death. For you, not much before death either. I only did what I believed to be right and it was not easy.

My eyes ran along the shelves and fixed on a squat bottle. The memory of long-ago chemistry lessons returned, not very clearly, only a dim recollection of a warning and the curiosity aroused by the warning. An idea. My mind seized on it, coming back to life.

I raced out into the corridor and along to the wash-room. There, neat and clean, were the three metal sinks whose outlet pipes ran down into the concrete wall. The far ends of those pipes would now be firmly sealed with metal caps where they joined the main drain. The concrete wall was about twenty-five centimetres thick here, and the outlet pipes ran along the inside of the wall for a metre.

I began to run back to the lab, but slowed to a quick walk. Must conserve oxygen. I have plenty of time if I *think* and keep calm.

There was an adjustable spanner in a bag of tools which we used for fixing models and repairing clamp stands. I got it, went back to the washroom and grovelled under the end sink until I had unfastened the S-bend from the wall pipe. Water and slime slopped out. Then I dried the mouth of the pipe which projected from the wall.

Yes. It might just work. Well, I'd die trying. I had nothing to lose.

Ten minutes later I had found half a dozen Pyrex beakers ranging in size from 500 ml to a litre capacity, tipped their contents into a bucket (not down the sinks, their pipes had to stay empty) and carefully cleaned and dried them. Then I paused to think. I was going to have to mix guesswork with memory. And be very careful, and very lucky.

I heaved acid containers out of the chemical store and fetched some acid-proof gloves from the lab. With great delicacy I poured out measures of acid into a jug which was marked in cc. units on the side: I transferred these measures into each Pyrex beaker in turn. The fumes hovered above the liquid, bitter and sharp, mixing with the vomit bile in my mouth and throat. I coughed away from the bench, knowing that any drop of moisture could explode the acids in the beakers.

It took two hours to make the mixture. But finally I had, at a rough reckoning, about a litre of highly explosive, extremely dangerous nitroglycerine. I slumped into a chair and tried to work out the next move.

How could I detonate it? My plan was to pour the nitroglycerine into the waste pipe which led to the wall from the sink unit. Normally the liquid would simply flow out into the drain. Now, because of the emergency blocks, it would fill the pipe inside the wall and I would have—I hoped—a ready-made bomb powerful enough to blow a hole in the concrete. But it needed a detonator.

Of course: the bullets in my rifle! I emptied the clip and moved to the other end of the lab. Then I patiently rigged up a contraption that, when the gun was fired, would explode and detonate the nitroglycerine. With luck.

Another two hours had passed. I was feeling light-headed; was the oxygen running out already? Perhaps it was just fatigue and hunger.

I picked up the first jug of nitroglycerine and carefully, slowly, walked out and down the corridor and into the washroom. Kneeling beneath the sink unit I placed the lip of the pourer to the edge of the pipe leading to the wall and trickled the yellow liquid into the pipe. It went in soundlessly. When I had poured it all, I put the jug down and lay back on the floor, taking several deep, slow breaths, aching with tension. Then I crawled up and walked back to the laboratory to get the second jug.

As I was carrying it out, I put my foot on one of the fallen plastic molecules from the DNA model, and I almost fell. The jug lurched, the nitroglycerine slopped, and I felt death. Luckily I was moving so lethargically that I regained control and froze. '*Hard luck*,' I said out loud, kicking the molecule away.

When I had poured the second lot of explosive into the pipe I brought the rifle into the washroom and used three heavy clamp stands from the lab to hold it so that it pointed down into the pipe with the metal detonator tube right inside the pipe and hopefully dipping into the nitroglycerine. To make sure the rifle would not drag back when the trigger was pulled I jammed a metal chair between the stock of the gun and the sink, and bound them with tape.

The final problem was pulling the trigger. In theory it seemed easy, but it was hard to arrange properly. I had to be as far away as possible. I decided to descend into the concrete bunker of the radiation unit. The air pressure of the blast might damage my eardrums. It took ages to fix a long reel of twine from behind the steel door of the unit, up the stairs, along the corridor and into the washroom. I had to make sure that the tension of the string would be strong enough. There was no way of testing it. There would only be one chance.

At long last, I slipped the loop of string over the trigger and retreated to the radiation unit. Perrin's corpse sat in front of the screen still staring at whatever had gone beyond the clutch of the mechanical arms in the glass box.

'Here goes,' I said, evenly, to myself. I left the steel door ajar about six inches and crouched down with my hands raised and palms covering my ears, holding the string up in my right hand. Then I pulled. Nothing happened. I tugged. Still nothing. Maddened, I took my hand away from my ear and heaved hard on the string.

There was an enormous, thunderous explosion. It banged down the corridors in a push and suck of blast, whacking the door against my knees, thumping vibrations inside my lungs and ears. The door drew back. Gulping air, I got up and hauled it open. At the top of the stairs I met a cloud of dust. Down near the washroom part of a chair had been blown out across the corridor, and the air tasted of cement and plaster. The lights in the washroom had gone out and one or two had failed in the corridor, so it was hard to see anything. I scarcely dared look. There was the spattering sound of water from a broken pipe or tap. Pieces of concrete and twisted metal on the floor made me stumble. The air was stirring. A draught!

A black mark extended along the pale concrete wall beneath where the sinks had been. I kicked the rubble away and knelt down, my hands groping in the half-light.

There was a hole in the wall, about a metre long and slightly less than a third of a metre high at its widest point. I put my head down and craned my neck sideways. I could see part of the car park, and a tree against the indigo of the evening sky. The sun had set. The air on my face was warm and thick, like scented blood.

I was going to go on living.

CHAPTER TEN

It took another two hours to get out. The iron reinforcing rods which had been set inside the concrete had been bent and broken and were sticking out at odd angles, but I had to twist them aside even further and use a hacksaw from the lab toolkit to amputate several of them before there was a space big enough for me to slide through. Even then it was a squeeze.

Before leaving, I went to Perrin's office and checked his papers. I was so exhausted that I hardly had the energy to search very closely, and the emergency lights were growing dimmer by the minute, closing the whole place in what would be the final all-time darkness. However, I found the small metal box in which he kept his personal papers and confidential notes. It might contain some answers. I carried it through the shadow-growing laboratory feeling uneasy and increasingly uncertain about the nature of some of the shapes in far corners. I realised I'd been talking to myself too much, not merely swearing in irritation, but reassurances spoken for my own sake, with taunts directed towards an incoherent feeling of malice which the building seemed to generate. This malice appeared to have grown and to be present in the air like static electricity. Perhaps it was all a result of my weakening concentration. I hurried to the shattered washroom and pushed the metal box out. It fell with a thud onto the grass below.

When I squeezed out, feet first, slowly, trying not to get cut on prongs of steel or serrated concrete, it must have looked as if the building, squatting there in the twilight, was extruding a live object created inside itself by unimaginable processes. I finally dropped onto the grass, smeared with blood and peculiarly humiliated; peculiar, since there was nobody to observe all the squirming and slithering. I stood up from the grass, inhaled the warm air scented with earth and plants, and it was like being re-created. By myself. No witnesses. Only the stars.

The southern sky with its vast spread of starlight was pulsing and flickering with intense energy over the dead city in the distance and the empty countryside. I arched my neck back and stared up, overcome with the magnificence of the display. It was incredibly beautiful. It seemed that at any moment the stars would make some kind of sound. I felt that I would *hear* them. The ringing echoes of the explosion were still inside my ears and I could sense the resonance of that sound wave expanding outwards, my own message of existence. I had blasted my way out of a tomb. There ought to be some response to a pulsation like that, a recognition of my evolutionary skill. My uniqueness demanded an answer. There *would* be one, somewhere.

I was swaying with fatigue beneath this mute, deaf brilliance, nearly fainting. With a great effort I groped on the ground for the metal box, found it, and stumbled to the car park.

There was a secluded block of private motel units across the road, used by scientists attending research conferences. I drove there, broke in, found an unused room, and after carrying in the shotgun and a few essentials from the car and locking the doors, I slumped onto the bed and straight away fell asleep and unconscious.

CHAPTER ELEVEN

There were no dreams. I woke feeling hungry. It must have been about midday, hot and bright again. There was enough cold water for a shower. I dressed in fresh clothes. Yesterday's were torn and stained, and I had acquired a set of bruises and scratches. My cut fingers were healing, though. After eating a large quantity of the food I had brought from Thames, I took the gun and walked around exploring the motel and the area nearby. I soon felt tired, so I went back to the room, moved everything of importance in from the car, parked it beneath some trees, then locked myself in the motel and lay down to sleep again. My brain seemed to want to run low and repair circuits. I didn't know what to do.

There was nothing on any radio wavebands. I tried several times. In the middle of the night I woke up, tried the radio, ate more food, drifted back into sleep. It was more like a coma than sleep. My first thought the next day was about time. I had to calculate that it must be Tuesday. It was important to keep a check.

I examined Perrin's box but it was securely locked and impossible to break into. It would have to wait. The food was nearly all gone, so I drove back to the nearest shops and stocked up. The smell of decaying food in the melted freezers was becoming very powerful, a putrid compound of meat, ice-cream, fish fingers and blue-vein cheese. Luckily there were still no signs of a resurgence of rats. I was dreading encounters with rats or rabid dogs. When I'd looted all the provisions I wanted, I returned to the fastness of my motel unit. The absence of noise and people seemed less unnerving out in the countryside, and it was good when a fresh breeze sprang up and made reassuring sounds as it rushed through the trees.

I went out in the early evening and looked at the stars again, still intrigued by the memory of their effect on me. I pondered the thought that they were beautiful, and scanned the panorama now, head back, eyes wide. Planets, clusters of radio stars, the hydrogen of broken galaxies and remote blurs of mist which were themselves huge spiral nebulae: all this had always yawned up there above my indifference to it. I'd never believed there could be any purpose in those atoms churning in a vacuum, blurting and speckling across nothing. But nor had I ever previously felt that the sight was beautiful. Normally I tried to avoid using such words. It had been part of my scientific training to avoid them; or rather, part of my own discipline of mind. Did it now matter that I should experience such a feeling, admit it, and transmit that response outward? I lowered my head from the vertigo which came from the draining of blood from a brain not prone to any form of mystical confusion. For a moment, the impression of *falling upwards* had nearly floated me onto my back on the grass. The air rushed around. I steadied myself.

Answers? Not in the stars. There was still the enigma here, the planet gone dead. It stretched out to expose its deadness to the lights pointing down from the dark.

Perhaps all this had happened countless times out there; it could be part of the nature of all processes. Even most of those star-images were points at the end of nothing. The light entering my retina was ages old, a message from objects which had ceased to exist an unimaginably long time ago; millions of messages from death, extinction, space now empty. The glittering diamond display up there was an illusion, covering the most colossal irony with its apparent hardness, eternity and brilliance. It represented the past. Yet at the moment its radiation passed into my eyes it was the only reality I could know of those objects. What reliance could you place on all those lights with the annihilation of their origins racing at the speed of dark behind the end of each beam? Could that be beautiful?

Somebody had once written, the universe is not only stranger than we know it is stranger than we *can* know. I remembered feeling sorry for physicists when I read that. They saw everything as a model of their own confusion. A hundred years ago Michelson and Morley had demolished classical physics; the Fitzgerald Contraction had proved there was no possibility of measurable objective single truth in the universe, all was relative, subjective, multiplex. Einstein had theorised about curved space. His equations had been questioned and then the radio astronomers had found massive problems with the whole new structure of ideas. The physicists had developed a death wish. They had no clear notion of what would happen when they exploded the first atomic bomb. Some of them believed it might set off a chain reaction with the hydrogen in atmospheric water vapour which would destroy the whole planet. But they went ahead anyway. Now they spent their time arguing about black holes, and about particles which went backwards in time. All suicidal, nihilistic ideas. A subjective and relativistic universe moulded by neuroses.

I went back into the motel, locked the door, and lay down to think. What did the curvature of space mean? That nothing really ended? That the stars which faded from one place reappeared somewhere else, and events curved back on themselves? If that happened, time would crumble, causes and effects would cease to be linear and sequential, and the laws of thermodynamics and entropy would contract from general principles to purely local phenomena.

Taking a strip of cardboard from one of the packets of food, I folded it into a loop. Inside surface, outer surface; top edge, bottom edge. Now, what was the trick? You disconnected the ends, twisted the strip once, and reconnected the ends. That was it. A Moebius loop. The inside and outside surfaces become continuous; and there is only one edge. Neither have any ending, they have become infinite. And the object only two dimensions. Yet it still exists in the three-dimensional world. Shadows are two-dimensional.

You cannot pick them up. So this loop, this spiral, must be a trick of some kind. Or an anomaly in this universe. An ordinary shape with one simple kink in it becomes an impossibility with no beginning or end. Yet it exists.

What would I do tomorrow, and tomorrow?

CHAPTER TWELVE

Great questions; small answers. I would drive south to Wellington. Perhaps I might meet somebody or come across at least some form of clue or revelation. So far I was not able to piece together even the beginnings of a coherent idea. I did not consider returning to the research centre. I could not have forced myself to go back in there. The smell of death had gone too far down my throat. My escape, when I thought it over in the light of day, had been the result of a controlled scientific deduction, the application of logic to a problem. There were chemical equations to account for even the decomposition of the corpse which had been Perrin. I was aware that beneath the surface of all that logic were atavistic impulses and private terrors; they had always been there. As long as they did not link themselves to the phenomenal world created by the Effect, I would be safe. And yet every day seemed to set a greater space between my optimism of a solution and the likelihood that there would be one. It was like being on the platform of a deserted railway station wondering if you are too early or too late. You pace around, and wait, and look hard at ordinary objects; you stay, and wait, and nothing happens. There is no announcement. The waiting in one place becomes intolerable. Something terrible has occurred along the line. The explanation is somewhere else.

On Wednesday I loaded the car with my gear and drove to my flat in Takapuna. I approached it carefully, with a vague fear that it might contain a vengeance from forces cheated by my absence, a vacuum wanting my presence, impatient at waiting. Absurdly I checked the letterbox, as if expecting a summons. Shotgun cradled in my arm, I then unlocked the door, paused, and went in quickly. Of course the place was as I had left it. The normality was unnerving. I looked around, feeling intensely sorry for the person who had left here on Friday to go to Thames, gone so unsuspecting into such an enormity. This was the old world, like a museum now, full of objects that no longer worked or had any meaning.

I stayed only long enough to pick up some clothes and a few odds and ends, then drove away, back onto the motorway and across the bridge into downtown Auckland. The weather had changed. Grey clouds hung over the city. But it stayed hot and the clouds pressed the humidity closer. At first it was good to be rid of the bright of the sun beating down from empty sky, making day after day seem the same and searchlighting every millimetre of space. I was glad of the change. Then the clouds packed together overhead and stopped moving, and the density of the air buried even the sounds I made, and lay thick over the inner-city blocks.

I broke into a shop and took some clothes. There were stacks of cardboard boxes in the back of the shop. Heaping them in the middle of Queen Street I made a bonfire, ensuring plenty of smoke with the spare tyres of nearby abandoned cars before retreating to the vantage point at the top of the hotel building to scan all the streets for any signs of action or response. An hour went by. There was nothing. I toyed with the idea of setting fire to one of the insurance companies' office blocks to make a real blaze. I could spread petrol over the ground floor; it would go up like a torch. Part of my mind was disturbed by the thoughts of destruction and the forward thrill I derived from this. The desire for violence, for an act of great power and senselessness that would be all mine and my gesture at the universe as well as at this city which had consumed my life, all this was immensely compelling. I went down the stairs to my car and drove away fast, dodging stalled trucks and fareless taxis to the motorway, south, the sweat flattening my shirt to my back. It had never been the buildings I had hated, only the people, and they were beyond retribution. Burning a tower would be pure spite, no catharsis, just kicking a hollow coffin.

Driving south I kept looking left. *Had* there been anything in Thames outside my room that night? When I thought about the sequence of events I realised there had been a close connection between my mind and what happened. What I had feared had seemed to happen. Then when I set my thoughts to resist the consequences, I had beaten them back. Was this a world in which the mind could promote events which then proceeded outside the mind, objectively, yet still capable of being influenced by thoughts? The boundaries between subjective and objective seemed to have blurred. The shift from one to the other was like looking through a window at an object and then finding yourself staring at your own reflection in the glass; a medium had changed its nature for no apparent reason. No; the medium stays the same, the mind makes the change.

Perhaps I had been in shock. But I couldn't stop glancing left, down each road that led east. The nervous impulse persisted.

Hamilton was desolation. It was easy to see that nobody had survived, because nothing had been changed in any way. I dutifully checked the main streets, post office, police station and hospital. And there, outside the casualty entrance, an ambulance stood abandoned, its rear doors open. I got out of my car, the sudden tension liquefying my insides as usual, and walked past the vehicle into the hospital. A short way down the corridor there was a trolley topped with red blankets. Inside a nearby room there were beds. The first one I saw was as empty as the rest, but there were bloodstains patching the indented pillow dark brown, and a big spilled stain on the shiny lino floor by the bed. It had come from the inverted transfusion bottle hooked above the bed; the tube hung down loosely into space above the dry iridescent blot. The antiseptic scent in the room was mixed with a suffocating stench, a mucous of stale excretions. I turned and half-ran out, fixing my teeth and lips tight against the reflex of retching, holding my breath until the car was accelerating down the road and I could inhale fresh air.

Then, south of the city, I found the smashed cars which must have been the source of the casualties. Two impacted wrecks locked together were hemmed in at the side of the road by black and white traffic patrol cars, a fire engine and an ambulance, dead warning lights, then a line of stopped cars and trucks. The tarmac was scattered with crystals of windscreen glass, a woman's shoe, a paperback book, a tartan blanket, a handbag, stretchers and tools. Black sump oil and dried rust-water stains ran away across the camber of the road like bleed marks spilled from the death of machinery, with broken flecks of rust and mud which had been bashed loose and flung all over.

I did not want to stop. The car on the far right was half crushed and I could see indistinctly the head of a corpse tilted sideways in the wreck behind the gap where the windscreen had been. I would not normally have stopped. The obscenities of public accidents, of somebody struck down and suddenly an object at the centre of the stares of strangers going by and looking but not wanting to see, that was all indecent enough; but now all the witnesses crowded around had vanished, and it was as if the horror had been arranged just for me, spread across the road like a display, waiting. Here is another human being, it seemed to say; go on, look closely, you know how rare they are, now, you can't pass by. But I did go by; I only slowed to avoid bits of stuff on the road, then I pressed my foot on the pedal and the Marina gathered speed.

Soon the accident was miles behind. A weak sun came out. The air freshened.

The leaves of the old trees lining the streets of Cambridge were hissing in the air, the town empty but filled with this noise and the shadows breaking and flickering over the moving car. I did not feel any particular uneasiness, yet when the sun went back into the bank of cloud behind me as I drove on, the day became much darker and the clouds ahead drained the light away from the eastern sky and made the hills into which I was going seem dull and threatening. The road squirmed towards them. I tried not to anticipate anything. My mind went back, pushed by the scent memory of the hospital, and I thought of Joanne and of Peter. There were times, like now, when I could think of certain parts of my life quite easily and without feeling that compulsion to close my mind in the way I'd closed my teeth against retching.

We hadn't known, or really admitted, that there was anything seriously wrong with Peter until he was nearly three years old. Then the strangeness of his behaviour had become more acute and unavoidable. We were forced to face the prospect that it would not go away or get better or that he would grow out of it. Quite the opposite; it seemed he would get worse, and grow into it. The medical, neurological and psychological analyses finally delivered the word 'autistic' as the term which was supposed to describe his condition, and then, having presented us with this word, the experts had relaxed into noncommittal inaction. The word was their achievement. There was nothing else they could do. Little research had been done, they said. Their expressions of helplessness, masked behind the urbane professional courtesies, had stared pensively across polished desktops or out of air-conditioned windows towards clinical parklands. Their voices, hands, and doors, opened and closed softly; I seemed always to be watching soft fingers toying slowly with gold and black pens resting on white blotters of infinite resilience. The sounds I made, the words with which I had tried to wrench some sense out of these people, had been absorbed into thick carpets and upholstery, or reflected back from sterile surfaces. Would he be like this all his life? Well, it was possible...highly likely...no appreciable change foreseeable...

The child was otherwise healthy and normal in appearance. He merely disregarded most of the world in which we lived. His eyes were always averted, darting away; he would never look directly at anybody. He would spend much time looking at nothing in particular, fixing his gaze towards a part of the room which had no visible object there, or at least nothing capable of exciting such intentness. If you moved into the area towards which he was staring, he would turn away. The presence of people and buildings seemed to cause him merely momentary and minor irritation. He was aware of them, but they came very low on his priorities, and his fleeting expressions of annoyance suggested he would rather not be bothered with them. I once saw him sitting on the carpet in our front room making an endlessly repeated but highly complex series of movements with his arms and head, as if operating an intricate machine. Suddenly he stopped (the doctors asked us to note the 'cessation of hyperactive function') and turned to stare quietly at the blank wall to his left. This was so odd that Timmy, our cat, who was lolling in front of the fire, turned to follow his eyes. Peter looking at nothing, frowned and tightened his lips for a few minutes, and then smiled. The cat, still fixing its eyes on that spot, rose, stared, and then crouched into its tense predatory position, bristling, as if a rat had appeared. After a pause, the two of them transfixed, Peter turned back abruptly and the cat fled. I felt a curious chill, quite different from the unfathomable wondering of what, if anything, was going on inside the brain of my son. And as his eyes had swept round the room darting at random across surfaces which included my face, I thought I detected a remote flicker of sadness passing from their indifference, little more than the quick beam of a light moving across shapes in a dark room.

The cat abandoned us a few days later and never returned. I had always believed them to be very intelligent animals.

One of my earliest memories, which had formulated itself into a set of images characteristic of a dream, and which may in fact have been a dream or a fantasy dramatised from a real incident, was of being alone in a large hall of enormous height, the walls stretching away on each side in a blaze of white light; and this hall was filled with great echoing sounds, footsteps, whispers, talking, rattling, slamming and scraping noises; all seethed and boomed in emptiness. There was a bench, and doors. I had to sit and wait for my parents because they were to come and meet me there. It was a railway station. Or a hospital. A waiting room. The sounds of people who must have been outside or passing by resounded on every side of me and I jumped and turned when a door slammed loudly or papery whispers seemed to hiss in midair nearby, but when I looked there would be nobody there. At some time or in a way connected with the waiting in this hall I became aware that my parents were never going to return because they were dead in an accident and my being alone foretold that or was the result of that discovery. It was my earliest traceable sensation. Twenty years later it still had the power to panic me into one of those nightmare awakenings which had so alarmed Joanne. The psychological experts tried to probe these memories seeking clues in the past for Peter's disorder. The neurologists thought they were wasting their time, that autism had purely physiological origins, perhaps a chemical imbalance, oxygen deficiency, specific brain damage, an endocrinal or pituitary conspiracy. I agreed; I didn't believe in the psychological theories either. It seemed to be typical of that pseudo-science to avoid looking directly at any real problem, and to writhe off into irrelevant areas. They hadn't a clue about Peter, and since part of his condition consisted of an absolute refusal to speak to psychiatrists, or to anybody, they were reduced to interrogating us. I had wondered later if this demonstrated a state of hyper-wisdom on Peter's part and imbecility on ours. Peter communicated by a repertoire of noises conveying states of mood by changes in tone; so did the psychiatrists, with the modulations of their jargon. During those years I listened to many theories, and nobody anywhere seemed to be willing to ponder for a moment the possibility that a human being who refused to participate, who refused to speak or listen, who failed to 'interact with his peer group', might not be all that crazy, and might even have arrived at an understandable response to the world in which we lived.

I was fooling myself, of course. I did want him to respond. I would have given anything for it. I even began to want to seize the child, shake him, *make* him see me; the eyes which regarded me as of no more significance than a chair or a table were becoming insufferable. 'Are you saying he thinks I don't care about him?' I asked one of the psychiatrists.

He swivelled away. 'Oh...no.' After a pause he said, 'I'm sure you do. Both of you.'

This needled me. Joanne was not there at that interview; she had begun to attend some absurd classes in transcendental meditation or whatever the latest cure-all craze was at that time. I had cared about her, too; once. Looking back on my life I thought how enormously strange it was that I should have found myself giving so much affection to two such unresponsive people, like somebody squandering a small hoard of valuables on indifferent recipients.

Small? I admitted that to myself, yes. I had never been one for self-deception. After my parents had failed to return, my father's older brother had gloomily taken me in. He and his wife had no children of their own. He was a bureaucrat in an insurance company. The house was a chilling, neat, carefully painted and polished place in Herne Bay. Time went by. I withdrew into books. I had few friends; I did well at school, especially in science. I read science fiction a lot and made my own worlds in my mind. My surrogate parents seemed pleased at my school reports. They only ever surprised me once; and that was over their reaction to a Maori family which had moved into an old house in the next street. One day I was mowing our front lawn, the strip bordering the footpath, when the mower began to fall apart. A Maori boy of about my own age appeared out of nowhere and offered to help. He asked if I had some kind of spanner; we went into the garage to look. I saw my aunt in the front room cracking apart the venetian blinds to try to see who I was talking to. In the garage the Maori saw a few drawings I had been doing on white card; they were mathematical circles and spirals formed by moving a biro round several discs of transparent plastic. This was about as artistically creative as I had ever been, and even this had been consigned to the garage workbench. I showed the Maori how it worked; he tried a drawing himself but with odd results; he was left-handed and moved the discs anti-clockwise, producing odd patterns and reverse spirals. In the middle of this my aunt put her head out of the back door and shouted for me to come in for a minute if I had finished the mowing. The Maori boy moved away. I said something like 'Come in,' but he looked away, shook his head and mumbled, 'Nah, better go, eh,' and walked off.

I was surprised, not merely at the warnings my aunt and uncle gave me about the undesirability of associating with Polynesian children, since I already had a vague idea that they disliked Maoris, and remarks about contagious scabies and head lice were familiar in the form of general warnings against people one should not mix with; no, what amazed me was the extent of my own naïveté, revealed by the fact that the Maori boy knew more about my surrogate parents than I did. In the shake of his head he had expressed a whole world of intuitive knowledge of which I was quite ignorant, knowledge gleaned in ways which I couldn't even begin to guess at. The hand forcing apart the slats of the blind, the tone of my aunt's voice, had been noted and evaluated and acted upon. There was no bitterness in his gesture. In any case I was concerned with my feelings, not his. I thought I had sensed a form of casual pity towards me and this enraged me. After all, I was, I thought, better off than him in every way. He lived in a squalid house, crammed with drunken relatives who were always in trouble with the police and welfare people; my aunt, in the succeeding months, filled out the details whilst my uncle nodded and worried about Islanders moving in nearby and the decline of property values. I walked past these houses and saw heaps of children playing in the overgrown gardens and heard laughing and music from the wide-open doors and windows, and when my uncle had said solemnly one evening that they were 'lowering the tone of the district' I suddenly found myself saying, 'Well, altering it, anyhow,' which astonished him as much as me, since it surfaced from this rage inside me and the need to strike out randomly at somebody in retaliation for what I still couldn't understand. A whole space of experience had been locked away from me. I felt I would never make up the lost time, that it was already too late.

'You like those people, do you?' my uncle asked, after a pause.

I considered. 'No,' I said. It was true. I realised I hated them. Hurt pride, I suppose, demanded it. Yet I felt later that this was the moment when I took control over the values which had up till then been imposed on me by others; I made them my own, and this denial, made for my reasons, not to please anybody else, was my assertion of control.

The sky had darkened even more by the time I reached the junction of the roads at Tirau. I stopped at a filling station to refuel and eat some canned pineapple and a few biscuits. A metal sign overhead was squeaking and banging in the uneasy gusts of air; the sky behind me, to the west, had curdled into grey banks of cumulus occasionally shot through with insipid yellow. It looked as though there would be rain soon; the mass of hills and dark forest towards Tokoroa was an unnerving prospect. I consulted a map. The sign above me swung and screeched. I decided to turn onto State Highway 5 and make Rotorua before the light failed. Map folded, windows shut tight, I set off.

The saturated green of the trees and grass seemed to intensify against the thundery sky. I had still not seen one living animal. There were empty cars and lorries on the roads and I had had to drive carefully. Now I switched on the headlights full beam. Soon there were gloomy stacks of forest on each side. The headlights made a space in the dark for a hundred metres ahead and the car hurried onto this light and pushed it forward, the white centre-markings on the road flashing up out of the night like tracer bullets.

Joanne had insisted we spend our honeymoon in Rotorua. She said she had been told that the place didn't really stink all that badly and you soon got used to it. Of course this was not true, and even I was taken aback by the unbelievable putrescence of the hydrogen sulphide from the thermal decay fuming underneath everywhere. The ground wobbled. It could have been an omen, as it turned out. At the time it seemed funny. The hotel was shaken by a small earthquake one night; not, unfortunately, at an appropriate climactic moment. Joanne was already pregnant, anyhow.

We had met at university. I had left the house in Herne Bay and taken a flat just off Parnell Road. The university work was easy and I felt free. That was the best time of my life. I imitated the way of life of the other students and did a lot of pretending but generally I was really happy. Perhaps the confusion began during those years; maybe I came to deceive myself into thinking my sociable, amenable behaviour represented a complete deep change; and I fell for that, at least for a while. I met Joanne at a third-year party. She was intense and intelligent, but with a nice sense of humour; and she was attractive. Her parents disapproved of me. She defied them, and occasionally stayed weekends and overnight at my flat. I think it was her first fling at independence. After I began doing postgraduate work I took a flat in Northcote to be nearer the research unit at Albany because the university had leased research facilities there. Joanne moved into my new flat with me, in spite of her family's de facto objections. We decided we both valued our independence too much to make firm commitments. I did well at the unit and gained a full-time job there after two years.

We had already begun to test the effects of radioactivity on chromosomes and although it was early days I knew it was going to be important work. When Joanne became pregnant we married for the sake of the child, and it looked for a while as if the breach with her parents would heal, and we would get a house and settle down and have kids and that would be life. Yet looking back I wouldn't say either of us really wanted that, we just seemed to...

Christ! *There was something ahead*, on the road, *running* into the car lights! I jerked the wheel hard across, braked, swerved, nearly lost control. There was a wild screeching. The car tipped right, skidding, and I flinched, expecting it to roll. It didn't. The wheels lifted, then fell back. The car stopped, sideways across the camber, headlights whitening trees. What in the name of God had I just seen?

It had appeared out of nowhere, loping diagonally along the road from right to left, glaring hideously in the lights, an unrecognisable thing. I sat paralysed, then wrenched my eyes to the left to look back, but outside the patch of car light there was only the black of the road and forest below dull sky. First move was to grab the shotgun. Then panic. The engine shuddered and died. Sudden, heavy silence packed the car, pressed in. I writhed around, left hand frantic for the ignition, found it, turned the key, the engine dead, stalled—come on, again, again, for God's sake—it started. I rammed down the accelerator. Not in gear. First, first, where the hell was it—*there*. The gears crunch-connected, my foot came off the clutch and with a muscular spasm hauling the wheel round I was off. Wildly. The car lurched all over the road. My arms had no strength, I couldn't steer. The terror had done something to my spine and the nerves of my shoulders; my right foot went numb thrust down on the speed pedal. Space rushed past. The black came quick at the patch of light. Faster.

I had glimpsed, briefly, a bone-white beast the size of a big dog or a calf, hairless, wet and pallid like an abortion. Its head was deformed, a mutant of dog and goat, yet fat and imbecile, wide mouth snarling to the roots of its teeth, and glistening with spit; the car lights had glared back from red points of eyes rimmed pink. I had never seen such a monstrosity, not even amongst Perrin's worst experimental aberrations, and *they* were all mercifully dead. The double shock here was that this nightmare was alive, the only other living thing—

The car ran round bends squealing and roaring. How did I miss hitting the thing? It had gone straight at my left headlight but there'd been no sound or impact. I kept staring in the rear-view mirror half expecting the abomination to be coming after me; no, nothing but dark. That sounded biblical: *abomination*, it surfaced like some diseased vision from Revelations. The way the creature *moved*! The slow lope totally alien to the run of a dog or calf, a kind of upright slithering...

Overwhelming fear had been dreadful enough inside the motel. Now it struck at me here, in half-dark on a remote road cut through hills and forest in the back of nowhere. I struggled to stop the panic. Calm down. It's gone. You're safe in the car. You have the gun. You're safe. It wasn't real. You were asleep for a second, it was a hallucination. Don't think about it. Just a stray dog, or something, distorted in the light. *Control it.*

I drove on to Rotorua, the whole place standing dark, powerless, empty. The stench was the same as ever, like shit in hell. Clouds of white steam lurched in the distance and spurts of vapour were dissolving in midair over the road. There seemed to be movements everywhere. When I turned to look, they vanished.

I went fast down the main street, saw a hotel block on the left, turned off, drew up next to the main doors, switched off, and got out with the shotgun ready.

The only sound was a background hissing and rumbling, becoming more violent nearby in the bushes beyond the car park. Boiling water spattered up in a roar for a moment and then subsided. The bushes were coated with sulphurous powder. Some were dead. They stood out very pale against the edge of the darkness, trees from another planet, fuming suddenly. The air was thick, evil with heat.

I grabbed what I needed from the car and locked it. The hotel doors were open. I entered and latched them behind me. Shining a torch around I got a room key from reception and found the stairs. I went up six floors, let myself into the room, then locked and barricaded the door.

I stayed awake. My mind raced.

I know what I saw back there. If it was real then there were now things living on earth which should be dead, which defied every law of nature I ever knew. And there must be a reason for that. Something I could not live with, in any sense. It demanded my death.

And if what I saw had slid into my retina from inside my mind, then God help me.

CHAPTER THIRTEEN

I put the muzzle of the shotgun in my mouth and reached down to the trigger. My fingers touched the trigger guard. The gun barrel was hard steel. It tasted of metal and machine oil, a sour, hard taste. And I could do nothing. I took the gun away and laid it down.

When I was small there was a story about a boy in a forest walking along a path as night draws on. The trees make strange shapes. Shadows move and rustle. He is afraid to look back. He walks faster and the path strays until he is lost. The forest has a power to transform itself and to sense fear, and a power to change people. They never return. If they try to turn and go back they meet a terror.

It was so dark in this room. The night was starless, it seemed to go on forever. A long time in the past I would keep my eyes closed if I woke from a bad sleep and would think of words to plead for help, for the night to stop; but

I never spoke them. When scared, I always thought, Oh God, or said to myself words like 'God help me', but they were just words and meant less than nothing. I had never been able to believe in God. Teachers had ransacked the Bible to cram morals into our minds like metal fillings drilled into teeth. There was small forgiveness in those stories. Animals were slaughtered, vengeance extracted, cities desolated, eyes and tongues rooted out, spikes hammered into wrists; the pain demanded belief to make sense. The more pain, the madder the belief. I remembered a man holding a Bible, his face tense, and the way the vein on his forehead writhed as if there was a worm beneath his skin straining to get out. *God is not mocked. God is just.* Close your eyes, pray, and you will be heard. I had not believed it.

At some time a rainstorm rattled across the space outside, running against the glass of the high windows. It went on quick to the west. I closed the curtains.

The beam of light from the torch revealed the things in the room one by one: chair, bed, gun, lamp, mirror, picture, chair. I moved to look at my image in the mirror and there was a pale skull there, shadowed black, the bone only millimetres beneath the stretch of skin. I propped the torch on a chair. My fingers went towards the glass and touched the tips of the fingers of the image. I put my hands up to my face. The reflection obeyed. It looked sad. And frightened. The eyes were hard to see, the shadows deep over lids and sockets. There was a frown.

I remembered being here with Joanne years ago. She would now be dead. Like everyone else. That was what the remnants of the crashed plane had meant. The passengers and crew could never return. Where would they return *to*? The plane had crashed because everyone had vanished. The crash had not killed them. They could not reappear dead in the wreckage; they had never been part of that event. It had been caused only by their absence. They could not reappear alive unless time ran backwards and the plane somehow reassembled itself and flew back together again as it had been at 6.11 am five miles high. Both options were equally impossible. Time has no way to run back. Events are sealed.

Everyone has gone forever. Face it.

The image in the mirror moved its mouth. It was forming the beginning of syllables, fractions of words. The words had never made their way so far before; even now they carried scarcely any weight of meaning. They were worn down. The restraint normally held by the brain over the larynx and tongue and lips loosened now that acknowledgement had been made that there was absolutely no one to hear. The words were about love; a declaration, an admission, that once there had been somebody who had been loved. It was not extraordinary. For most, a fact as conventional as the word. But to the reflected figure now mouthing syllables of affection to shadows in a concrete cell on an empty planet to someone seeming dead so many times over, it had all been unbelievably strange and unexpected. How could expressions of love have been used? What emotions did they refer to? There had been no standard of comparison for those feelings. A life had functioned without them. How could they be known?

As a child I had waited in the dream room, deaf to sentences of consolation or attempts to distract me from the realisation that my parents had left me alone. I deflected it all, I let it pass by. I knew the truth. Once was enough. I wouldn't risk so much again to the chance of betrayal.

Then Joanne, smiling across the isolation, weakening me, vulnerable herself, had unfolded with hardly a move of my hand. She stayed with me. At first nothing involved us with each other beyond the skin-deep, the pleasure of sensations. Or that was what I wanted to believe, then; because I was still unsure about the distance between independence and loneliness. One sounded so brave and decisive, the other so pathetic and helpless, that I'd always imagined they must be separated by an immense space and time. When we started to depend on each other in small ways, hardly noticing it, I began to realise the closeness of the two. They could be only minutes or inches apart. One morning as we were lying in bed in the Parnell flat, I had woken early and stretched out my hand to draw aside a strand of hair which had fallen across her face in sleep. An expression like a smile had formed on her features for a moment, half-conscious. And I had moved the tips of my fingers down her face very gently and traced them down her throat and over her shoulder, and at that moment, with the waves of early light breaking through the curtains onto the walls of the room, I realised with a distinct and separate surprise that there were reserves of emotions somewhere inside me which I hadn't suspected. There was no reason for their existence. If evolution and adaptation counted for anything in individuals, then expressions of tenderness, if that was what this gesture involved, should have been extinct.

If she'd gone away, after those first few weeks, I could still have coped with that and made my own sense of it and not been changed. Of course I would not have found it easy; but it would have fitted into the view of the world, the ideas about people, which I already held.

But she stayed. In secret I was amazed. Even more, when we invaded each other deeper, discovering more needs than a few millimetres of skin; that marked the start of waking to a new set of chances for my life. If I concealed from her how much I needed that chance, it was only because I was afraid of trusting so much to someone whose judgement I suspected, someone I didn't fully understand. Our dependence on each other even made me think, suddenly, that perhaps she might be very like me. I pushed the idea aside. It was absurd; frightening. Anyhow, it could not survive in a time when I was happy. I held very close to that happiness and gave most of myself to what was not understandable.

So without my conscious awareness of how it was happening, the bitterness in me had retreated and faded. Yet my mind would run ahead at times in half-panic like a recluse in a remote home might rush to empty rooms, make them look used, open the blinds, check on what the light might show, then turn a casual face to the unexpected. The danger was alive.

Finally in spite of myself, I did trust too much, I ran risks, I got kicked for it. Self-pity? Why not? Who the hell else is there?

The image in the mirror dissolved to a blur as the eyes blinked liquid. Useless; a spill of saltwater down a face. But not selfish. The point of deception was gone now.

Steel oil from the gun barrel soured the inside of my mouth. Lifting the torch I walked slowly to the bathroom. The light picked out the dull cool of chrome and porcelain. Another mirror gave back the face with the silver trails on its paleness. I turned a tap and ran some water into a glass. The pressure was weak. The taste, in a quick rinse and spit, was musty. I threw water on my face and pushed a towel across it. Behind me in the mirror I could see the outline of the white bath.

In the nightmares I see it like that. There is the wet hand of a child holding the edge of the bath, tightly, then weakening. The hand lets go and the arm and hand slip back into the water and sink beneath the reflections of the fluorescent light. Beneath the clear water the eyes are still open. They collect images the brain never receives.

I shoved the towel over my face and pressed it against me, groped for the torch and stumbled out of the bathroom, closing the door securely.

'He wanted to drown,' Joanne had said; 'I know he did.' And she had looked straight at me. 'It frightened me.' When I shrugged as if I didn't really believe her, she flared up; 'Yes, I know what you think.'

'Go on. What?'

'I'm inventing it.'

She was right. I thought she was finding reasons for having Peter committed to an institution. She couldn't cope. Of course she presented it as a humane answer. They would look after him properly there. He would be in the care of specialists.

'Don't be silly,' I said.

'Tomorrow night, you give him his bath.'

Peter was eight. A special nurse came several times a week to supervise him. This was to take some of the burden from Joanne. There had been no suggestion that Peter might be a danger to himself or to anyone else. I had noticed, though, a slight change. His invisible world seemed to be failing him in some way. He had begun to push it away, turning from whatever images were there for him in the empty parts of rooms, literally pushing back the air with an odd tightness set on his face, frowning and thin-lipped. I had only seen this once or twice. And once or twice, also, I'd seen him shake his head at nothing as if making a decisive denial, an absolute no to some unimaginable problem or object.

I gave him his bath, talking to him sensibly as if he could understand what I was saying, a technique one of the psychiatrists had suggested. I had hoped that sooner or later at least some of my words or even the tone of my voice might awaken just the slightest response in him. That evening he'd gone from hyperactive to passive and withdrawn. The bathing went without incident. Joanne was watching television.

Earlier he had refused to eat. I thought he might now be hungry. When I had got him into his pyjamas and dressing gown I led him into the kitchen and hauled him up onto a chair by the table. He sat with one arm rigidly extended across the table and the other loosely by his side, his head turned sideways and eyes staring at the blank wall.

I opened a can of mandarin orange slices and spooned some into his plastic dish. It would have been wildly optimistic to have said that my son liked mandarin orange slices; all I knew after eight years was that often it was easier to feed him these than most other things. So I placed the dish in front of him and held the spoon up with two slices of orange on it, and spoke his name, tugging gently at his extended arm. Sometimes he would take the spoon; sometimes he had to be fed.

Now a terrible, horrifying thing happened. He turned his head and looked down at his arm. I took my hand away. His eyes flickered over the orange slices and back to his arm. The arm, still rigid, lifted, stopped, banged down on the table, lifted, banged down again, and again. He looked at it with a detached curiosity. Then he frowned, and a determined fierceness went across his face for a moment. His arm stopped banging and rested tense on the tabletop. He seemed to concentrate on it. My hand, holding the spoon, trembled. His arm relaxed and lay soft on the table, fingers uncurling. Then it moved towards the dish and stopped. It went no further. The determined look faded from his face. In a sudden movement he jerked his head back and stared straight at me. It was a gaze focused for the first time directly on my eyes, totally conscious and aware, only achieved with enormous effort. The message was unmistakeable, of immense pathos; it sprang from some trapped and defeated source of will inside him which said in effect, I don't know why my arm behaves like that, I don't know why I am like this, there's nothing I can do about it, I hate it. And his eyes brimmed and there was a sudden run of tears down the sides of his cheeks before his head wrenched itself in another direction and ignored the world again as though nothing had happened.

I was devastated. My throat had gone dry and when I tried to say his name I couldn't speak. I put the spoon down. After a few moments I pronounced his name and placed my hand on his arm. There was no response. In a way, it was not 'his' arm at all. It was not under the control of the intelligence which had just unblinked itself at me; there was nothing else he could do. I took my handkerchief and dabbed away the tearstains from a face as blank and indifferent to my presence as an abstract sculpture. In my own daze I fed him the orange slices, lifting them to his lips one by one on the spoon, knowing that he wanted to eat them. His mouth functioned. His throat swallowed them. When I had fed him I manoeuvred him to his bedroom and into his bed. His head lolled to one side and he made strange convulsive movements with his shoulders and hands as I took off his dressing gown and I gave way to the selfish weakness of embracing him for a minute, but was repaid with the usual inertia. I sat in the dim room and watched until he fell asleep. Joanne came and looked in and said, 'Well?' and when I didn't reply she watched him for a few moments and then went away.

I sat there thinking: how much does he know? Does he understand what we say? There had never been any very certain way of knowing. But now I was sure that some part of him knew that he was locked fatally, for always, in an uncontrollable physical shell in a world where every conscious instant could produce neural nightmares, the realities of his own cerebral cortex which he could never escape and which—I assumed—were getting worse, becoming more repellent to him.

And perhaps knowing this, some inner force was trying to find a way to end the whole organism, to self-destruct. Whatever happened, I knew there was one certainty: I would never abandon or fail him. It was possible that the look I had just seen in his eyes was purely the expression of a frightened animal and that no part of him knew any emotion as complex as love or had any awareness of other people's feelings or of the passage of time and what it would mean to be sat down at a table day after day for seventy years in an institution with a plastic spoon pressing congealed baby food into a mouth which would never speak. But I would never abandon him because I knew myself what it meant to be deserted and if there was only a one-tenth of one percent chance that some tiny fragment of the child's mind would feel what I had felt, I could never risk that. He had, after all, looked at *me*.

'What happened?' Joanne asked, when I returned to the front room.

'Nothing.'

'Something happened. I can tell.'

I sat down and stared at the television screen. Newsreel pictures of a soldier firing a heavy-calibre machine gun from a helicopter into thick jungle; then bodies being dragged into a clearing. She got up and switched it off.

'I don't know why you are so secretive.'

'What? Why should I be?'

'You are. You never told them the truth about the research centre.'

'I told them as much as I could. Anyhow it was irrelevant.'

'You could have let *them* decide what's relevant. Unless you were afraid of what they might find.'

We had battled through all this years earlier. Now it resurfaced. I ignored it.

'Don't you think we tell each other the truth, then?' I said.

'Did we ever?'

There was a long pause. We avoided looking at each other. Then I said, 'I never had any illusions.'

And she had said, 'You get worse.'

A few nights later I was supervising Peter's bath when he suddenly slid beneath the water. I tugged on his arm. He resisted. His face, pallid and neutral, drifted under the surface of the clear liquid. There was a weird determination about the way he pushed me back. I had to haul him up with both my hands hooked under his arms. He exhaled, spluttering. Perhaps he was testing me. But the silent plunge and struggle had been frightening.

If he wanted to kill himself, what could we do? I knew what the official answer would be; he would have to be placed under close watch in a mental hospital. If necessary, under restraint. So he would be forced to survive. Because this hypocritical society insisted at this level that life was sacred. At every other level it encouraged people to smash themselves to bits, to inhale cancer, to drink themselves to death, all for fat taxes on the profits.

But officially, life was sacred. To want to escape it to stop pain was listed a crime.

When I thought, I don't want him to die, that was only a natural reaction. Yet considered more carefully and objectively perhaps it was little more than my selfishness operating again.

Now I stood in the dark hotel room and shone the torch down on the gun. Death seems difficult for so long but then it must become easy. How very hard to find the easy part. The brain seems demented for survival. It has a core of power to protect its functions from termination, to drag its host organism back from actions which spell body death. Pathetic arrogance and panic even invent the idea of an essence within the self which is immune to extinction. For some reason this is supposed to be consoling. I had never understood why I would be afraid of a universe which arranged immortality for people so incapable of coping with something as small as life. It would be a sick joke, an obscenity. I never had any illusions about *that*. What prevented me from killing myself now was ice-cold cowardice. No. More than that. Worming inside the absurdities of what should have been the final reduction there was still something of mortal importance to discover. It had no firm shape. But it would impel me to go on. No matter what I saw.

Peter began to utter screams. There would be no word in the dictionary adequate to describe the actual noises which came from him; 'screams' would fall far short. He didn't seem in any physical pain. His expression hardly altered, there were no warnings beforehand or traces of any trauma afterwards; it was as if the screams were being irregularly transmitted through the child's throat and mouth from a distant source. They suggested dreadful terror and agony. The doctors and psychiatrists did tests, summoned us, and spread out encephalograms on their desks showing the jagged electrical pulses inside the child's brain like edges of broken ice. Then they said: Well, we really don't know. They spoke of electro-convulsive therapy. At any rate they proposed that we consider placing the subject in a special clinic. Whilst we talked, the subject sat in another room waiting, ignoring the nurse who was there; it was a soundproofed room, and we could see him through a one-way mirror. At one point he turned and seemed to stare towards us and his mouth opened in what may have been a scream; only later did I remember that he was not looking at us but towards his own reflection.

We took him home, and argued as usual. I felt my opposition weakening. The screams, sporadic, shocking, were unbearable. I had seen history-book pictures by medieval painters, where faces were spread out in terror and split open soundlessly, the noise left to your mind. Peter's cries were like that, as if a door had opened and slammed shut on hell.

What followed, a few weeks later, was still not easy for me to remember because my mind had insisted on being evasive, and this was part of the nightmare, the thing I wanted to elude. Now it presented itself in the form of disconnected images as a waking memory, held in me like a shout without sound.

I am sitting on the edge of the bath. Peter's eyes are devious, they glance in all directions and then again with a wrench of his head they fix on my face. I know what will happen. Holding the sides of the bath, he sinks back, slowly. His face goes from the air by inches, mouth closed, the edge of the water sliding up his face in a silver glint of surface tension, the trapped bubbles of air bright like chromium beads, his eyes open beneath the water. His hair floats and drifts, rising from his forehead, combed in slow motion by the lift of the silver line. Now I have to decide. Ten seconds. Wet skin glitters. The eyes widen. I stand, trembling, the reflections slipping over the brilliance. Goodbye Peter. He will only see my lips move. Then the lights.

I go down the hallway and into the kitchen. I go back into the hall. My child is dying. I go into the front room. Joanne is out. He knows that. I go to the kitchen. How long? I shall tell the inquest I went for a towel to the airing cupboard. Some things fell out when I opened the door. Then the phone rang. Wrong number. Then it was too late. I go into the front room. Dear God. I wrap my arms around myself. I am shivering. The sky dark blue. There is no noise.

CHAPTER FOURTEEN

The grey haze lightened and paled from clouds of rain mixing steam and mist. Buildings, dark macrocarpa trees, wet streets emerged and receded. The day uncovered the landscape cautiously, but the clouds still waited round the lake and hills, and I waited and looked out from the drawn curtains of the sixth floor of the hotel. The volcanic areas heaved with steam. Some craters seemed dead, scabs of white-yellow sulphur amongst pools of acid, as though the moon had pressed an infection onto the surface of the earth. The rest boiled and spat, expelling the smell of decaying innards into the thickness of the atmosphere. When the clouds moved there were glimpses of wounds gone septic, erupting from beneath pieces of loose cotton wool.

I did not believe that I could go on much longer without having a complete breakdown. There was no option but to keep going until I lost control, but the end was inevitable.

It shrank closer all the time. What day was it today? Friday? No; Thursday. I might not even last a week.

The city cleared itself into a more intense daylight. The structures of motel signs, motels, car parks, filling stations, shops, take-away food bars and used-car lots solidified from the dawn and set their colours against each other to catch nonexistent eyes. How familiar. It would all go. The corrosion would eat into it. The fraying edge would make its way across like gangrene. It would all go. The makers and users had ceased to exist. Now the bits of city appeared to be nothing but lost luggage which nobody would ever claim, a dump of non-returnable objects.

When I used to look down from high buildings I always wondered about the hidden lives of the people who were hurrying around, coming and going, all fixed on errands and purposes I could never begin to guess at. How did they live? Were they content with their lives? The Maoris in the next street in Auckland, twenty years ago: why did they seem happy? Did they really have good lives? Inside all the faces you saw in the streets and on buses or behind blinds, all the minds in those miles and miles of houses, under every corrugated iron roof, in the dark, awake at night: what were they thinking? Were there bound to be so many mysteries? And secrets? I wondered how much was concealed from the world or how much was concealed from *me*; my life had been a very narrow channel, and I'd edged along it knowing almost nothing. The life everybody else was leading had seemed vital and purposeful, as if meanings had been found; it went on apart from me, and I picked up faint images from it, echoes, muted sounds, filtering down my narrow channel. I watched people from a distance, I read books, I glimpsed hints from films and television advertisements. But my detachment, my amazement at the way life went on without me, stayed the same. I would feel bitter, and bury that feeling, and direct rage outwards to easy targets. I was doing it even now, when everybody had vanished into an even greater mystery, a communal secret hidden completely from any ignorant speculations *I* might make; *me* of all people. It had been left to *me* to break into their locked houses, look at the evidence, and make sense of it.

The light gathered in the room like a damp powder. Everywhere it would be filling millions of closed places uselessly. I got ready to leave. Holding the shotgun and torch I unlocked the door, went out into the corridor and down the stairs. Near the lift there was a trolley laden with early morning breakfasts intercepted at 6.12 last Saturday; amongst white cups and plates stood a jug of rancid milk and wads of green fur which had been bread. The silence was stronger than ever. The carpet absorbed the sounds of my movements. In the lobby of the hotel the large window walls were slanting great rectangular plots of light across the floor. The sun had come out. Enormous pleasure and sadness mixed together and welled up within a rush of new sensations. My shadow moved over the carpet, across the furniture. It was as if the world had been re-created. The dreadful night and the image of the abomination of the dark road seemed to fall back into the distance with the other bad memories. My arm brushed against the branch of an indoor plant fading to brown for lack of water, and a few dry leaves detached from the stem and rustled to the floor. Soon it would all be dead.

I unfastened the main doors and walked outside into the damp warmth. The car was covered with condensation. I wiped the windows. Cancerous waves of stench from the pools. I drove round and back onto the main street, turning left out of town. The air soon freshened on the way south. My mind began to clear. But I was achingly tired and increasingly hungry. The road went through desolate and strange-looking country with ragged hills here and there, and then carved its way through vast forests. It was a wide new highway with a cleared space on each side reaching to the blocks of trees. Even though the sun was bright there was a thick darkness in the packed forest and nothing else was growing except a few feeble ferns at the edge of the gloom. The columns of pines went back on all sides into the distance.

I did not think I should stop. After a while I saw a police car which had trundled to a halt off the road; and for the first time I thought about the emptiness of the jails. Had that happened everywhere, too? Even in the worst places? No one in the world being tortured or murdered; all the armies and secret police vanished... The world wiped clean. And then: what if there were survivors in jails? Why should I think that might not have happened? Because criminals wouldn't have *qualified* for survival? That the Effect had moral scruples, an ethical mechanism? It couldn't have, or I wouldn't exist. I might have been in jail myself. Less than a year ago I had lied my way through an inquest on a very strange death, afraid to be worried too much by my skill at deception and the confidence of the face that answered every question. It should have been harder to do.

I glanced in the rear-view mirror, briefly, for reassurance. The road receded behind my face. Rotorua had been absorbed behind my image, a patch of weakness on the earth's surface, a singularity, a local aberration. Was the world so much better now, all cleaned and redeemed? My face – I looked again – was pale, and the skin seemed stuck to the bone by the pressure of the light. No assurance at all. What kind of unstained world would forget or release *that*?

The trees stood back on each side of the road like armies of dead soldiers standing to attention.

CHAPTER FIFTEEN

The river was clear and deep, shading to a dark green by the far banks. It swirled past in a heavy silence. Every few minutes the suck and slap of ripples breaking the surface from deep uncoilings gave the only hint of movement around the island. Beneath the water by the bridge the riverbed was visible, with small stones rolling along under the mass of transparent liquid.

Taupo was dazzling in its emptiness, the sun hot on tarmac and car metal, the shop windows blinded, doors locked. The light beat back from the lake fading all the colours and fading the hills even further away. Chip shops and burger bars stood unattended along the street smelling of grease and dead meat, and ranks of motels faced the lake with NO VACANCY signs raised for last weekend. I didn't want to invade a room, but I was tired of driving and decided not to go further. A street map at the public relations office revealed the ideal place: a small island in the river to the north which had been developed as a tourist attraction. There were a few souvenir shops and a restaurant next to a bird sanctuary. The island was connected to the riverbank by a narrow footbridge. I stood on the bridge and thought about the old superstition that evil spirits were supposed to be unable to cross flowing water. Then, as I looked down, I saw a swarm of fish glint in the river, all moving against the sunlight for a moment and then darting away. They were only a few centimetres long, quite small, but brilliantly *alive*. They had survived! The Effect had not gone below the surface of water!

I hung onto the railing of the bridge and gazed into the water trying to see them. Yes! Again! The points of light flashed up all at once. How could I have racked my brain, driven all over the place, looked for everywhere, considered every aspect of the mystery, and not once wondered about the sea or the rivers?

It was a long time before I could walk onto the island. The sudden excitement drove the tiredness away. Then it came back, heavier. I couldn't make any more sense of the Effect with the new information. Perhaps, if there was some significance, I would see it later. At least it was reassuring, to see living creatures and realise that lots of life still existed and went on existing as if nothing had ever happened. There was something defiant about the quickness of the fish, the way they caught the light in the clear water and flicked round all together in a crowd.

I broke into the small restaurant building on the island, went upstairs, and spread my sleeping bag on cushions on the floor after carrying in some of the equipment from the car. There was a handy kitchen in which I set up the gas-operated cooking unit and warmed up a few tins of food. After eating, before going to sleep, I cut the mould from a loaf of bread I discovered in the kitchen, and went back to the bridge. The loaf was dry and hard, but I pulled it apart and dropped the pieces into the river. The fish lunged at them. My hands were trembling.

I had a completely unconscious sleep, dreamless. It was early evening when I woke and the sun was saturating the air with a powerful golden radiation. I took the gun and crossed the river, drove back up to the town, and parked by the lakefront. The hills were slate-grey and purple, the sky an intense green towards the horizon. The sun went down with its light on the landscape like a nuclear forge throwing out a spectrum of all the elements: strontium reds, barium and copper greens, sodium yellow, silver chromates, blue cobalt, quicklime whites of calcium and magnesium, and brown ferrous oxides. And from the west the shadows spread out like heaps of carbon black tipped beneath the hills. My senses had extended and become more acute in the isolation of the last week, and visual images had taken on an energy of their own as well as the power to break into heightened perceptions from other senses. The force of the chemistry of these colours gave me the taste, scent, and touch of each separate element. The whites were hot and crumbling, the greens sharp, pungent, acid, the carbon soft and slippery like powdered pencil lead with its smell of sweat. Only my hearing had retreated from lack of work. The soundlessness of the beast that had slithered across the forest road had been as frightening as the sight. It might almost have been formed out of the solid silence which was squatting everywhere.

I turned to get back in the car to return to the island for the night, when I thought I heard something. From a long way off, seeming to come from as far away as the mountains at the southern end of the lake, there was a long booming noise, vibrating and changing pitch. It was impossible to tell what it was. The bellowing of a machine; an indecipherable compound of tones. Then it sounded again, or perhaps echoed, either from the hills or inside the drums and canals of my ears; I was straining hard to listen. It was mournful and weird. When it died away, the silence stood even thicker until a slight breeze began to ruffle the lake and hiss in the leaves of the taller trees by the shore. Perhaps it had been the movement of air, setting up a resonance, seeming further away than it was. Or even a volcanic, or a thermal noise; this was all an unstable area. Or maybe I had imagined it. I listened for several minutes, then, as the sun fell and the darkness began to grow, I got in the car and drove back to the sanctuary of the island. The river was like cold metal, the liquid of dead hills.

I had never considered what it would be like to become insane. The worst thing would be knowing it, being aware that it was happening. It would be gradual. The little rituals of sanity, the small items, would slip away. Lucid patches would contract and the light go thin until there would be huge areas of uncertainty. It seemed to me to be extremely sad and at the same time in the whole mystery of the world amazingly trivial that I should be insane.

In the night I woke and listened helplessly to the trees and the river. I wept for about five minutes. When I woke again it was a clear day.

CHAPTER SIXTEEN

I loaded the car and stood on the bridge looking at the water rolling beneath. There were broken clouds in the sky and the sun was being cut and dulled. Then the clouds would go and the heat press down on my neck. My reflection was on the surface of the water and my shadow lay on the riverbed below.

I put my sunglasses on and drove up the hill through Taupo, and left on the lakeside road south. The road swept up and then crawled down awkwardly between hills in sharp bends. Round one bend I nearly collided with an empty sheep truck and trailer jack-knifed across the road. I stopped, got out, and looked. The way was blocked. On the left, a wall of cliff and bush. On the right, a patch of soggy earth and ferns, then dense bush. I couldn't move the truck. The batteries were dead and it had run dry of petrol. I consulted a map; either go back and round the lake on the other side, or go down State Highway 5 to Napier. It would take ages, and those roads would be narrow and might be blocked as well.

After testing the muddy patch and pulling aside some plants and tree branches I thought I could make it past the truck on the right. No sooner had I driven off the road than the back wheels sank and churned up the mud and in ten seconds the car was stuck. I got out and unloaded the boot and back seat to lighten the weight.

Then I wrenched some planks from the sheep truck and shoved them under the back wheels of the car. I found some rocks, rammed them into the ground, jacked up the right rear wheel and pushed rocks and a piece of plank under it. At the first attempt the wheels kicked out the wood and sank again. Covered in sweat and mud, I tried again. On the third attempt it worked and the car lifted out, found traction, and lurched forward over the firmer ground, scraping bushes on the right and bouncing back onto the road. Then I had to carry all the stuff round and reload.

The immediate problem had taken my mind off everything else and I felt better. I drove on along the winding road by the lake and past empty motels, caravans and campsites. Half an hour later I stopped on the bridge at Turangi and opened tins of corned beef and pineapple for a snack. The sun was coming and going. Turangi seemed less altered by depopulation than anywhere else I had seen. I couldn't imagine anyone would live there by choice. The makers of the place must have been struck by the same puzzle, and had thrown the houses down and run away. The road, as I drove past, was like an escape route made for a massive burglary; but what had been stolen from this desolation was a mystery. The hills ahead on the right were dark against the sun, barren and sullen, as if vengeance had been involved and was not ended yet.

I speeded up for a couple of kilometres, then slowed down, cursing. There was another sheep truck and trailer across the road. This time there was no way round, just clumps of tussock and embankments of red earth. To the left, about thirty metres back, there appeared to be a way through the knots of gorse and small mounds of scrub and bracken-covered land. It might even have been a well-used track at some time. The ground looked quite firm, but in the distance there were blots of steam which suggested thermal pools. Maybe the track once led to a thermal area and there was no way back onto the main road. But it was worth trying.

I walked back, got into the car and reversed, then cautiously turned left and nosed the vehicle slowly into the wilderness. The hills were about three to five metres high and obscured the view on both sides and in front; the way curved slightly right, then left again, and the fronds of vegetation brushed against the car in places. Sulphurous smells confirmed that this was a volcanic area, or at least an area of geological weakness. I peered out intently at the track, watching for danger signs or patches of treacherous mud. The way led towards the steam. Ahead on the left I could see a pool half-overhung with dead ferns, steam drifting from the water across the track. The windscreen hazed over and the humidity increased. I stopped. This was too risky. I had only come this far because there was no room to turn around, no way to go back. Reversing would be awkward.

I opened the door and carefully got out. There were bubbling, demonic noises from the pool on the left, and similar and other sounds nearby from behind the hills. I trod along the track into the steam, but it seemed to thicken and become more clammy and hot, and I couldn't see any further. The tangle of plants rising up on both sides seethed with vapours, a dead dark green and brown; the sun had vanished, and the atmosphere and odd sounds closed in on me. I stopped. The noises were secretive, unnatural. A pressurised hissing broke through undertones of heavy exhaling and mixed with the bubbling water to sound like a series of sighs trying to force their way up from beneath the surface and being drowned, falling back, trying again, the bubblings expelling furious energy out of suffocation.

I suddenly felt the onset of terror, a bad, hard fear coming at me from all this, the place, the noises, and something else watching me, consciously, very close.

There was a rustling in the ferns on the small hill to my left. I hadn't got my shotgun. I turned to run back to the car, not wanting to see whatever was behind the mist. But the haze cleared for an instant and I couldn't move a muscle. For a fraction of a second I might even have been unconscious with shock. Then stupefied.

It was a human figure. A man.

Pointing a gun at me.

CHAPTER SEVENTEEN

'Stay there. Don't move.' Keeping the gun trained on me, he sidled down and stood about five metres away on the track. 'You alone?'

I nodded. I couldn't speak. The steam moved between us; his hands were raised with the rifle and his face obscured. He seemed to be wearing army gear, khaki trousers tucked into his boots, an anorak stippled with dark camouflage green, and a black woollen hat. He kept the gun levelled at me.

'Put that bloody thing down,' I managed to say. I hadn't spoken to anyone for so long, my voice sounded unconnected to me. He stayed as he was.

'Where you from?' he said.

'Auckland.'

'Just you?'

'Yes.'

'How many people up there?'

'None. Nobody.' The realisation that I wasn't alone was beginning to penetrate my mind, pushing aside the fear and danger. My voice caught in my throat. 'I haven't seen anyone since last Friday,' I said. He seemed to hesitate and began to lower the gun. 'Look. For God's sake—'

There was a breeze from the south, and the air cleared as the steam was blown aside. He suddenly came into focus and I could see his face. He was a Maori. We stared at each other, and he relaxed even more, the tension going from his arms and shoulders. He held the rifle down.

'Nobody?' he said. I shook my head. The intentness of his eyes and face drained away and he looked as worn out as I must have looked and felt. 'What the hell's going on?' he asked; 'Where the bloody hell *is* everyone?'

Something crumbled inside me, as it must have inside him, with the revelation that we had each been alone and could tell each other nothing. I shook my head again.

'I don't know.'

Perhaps the disappointment was greater for him than for me, since I might have seemed to him more likely to know an answer. In that moment we appeared to have said everything we would ever say to each other; we had exhausted what was important. We faced each other blankly. He was uncertain what to do, and the gun made me nervous. Cautiously holding out my right hand, I said, 'I'm John Hobson.'

There was a long pause, as though we were both frozen in an event which had slowed down outside normal space and time. Then he advanced towards me, the rifle held down in his left hand, his face still almost drained of expression, his right hand reaching up to clasp mine. The formality of shaking hands in the middle of so much strangeness reminded me of pictures of British explorers meeting after months of forcing their way through remote jungle alone. I didn't know what else to do. We managed to smile at each other.

'Apirana Maketu,' he said.

What was even stranger was the fleeting idea which seemed to link us at the same moment, immediately after the reassurance of physical contact had confirmed for us both that we were real, living, flesh and blood human beings and not illusions or apparitions; and that was the faintest hint of recognition as our eyes stared closer. 'Recognition' would have been too decisive a word. It was rather more like a vague questioning look which people exchange when they mistakenly think they know each other and then realise they don't, or can't possibly, and yet in the act of dismissing the idea they're really putting it to one side for further exploration. There was reassurance, and caution; for this and for all sorts of reasons, we weren't sure about each other.

'You've not seen anybody?' I asked. He shook his head.

'Went down to Napier, Hastings. Nothing. And up to Wairoa, Gisborne, all up the coast. That's where I'm from. Tolaga Bay. Nobody there, back home, it's just...'

The words had come out in a rush and he stopped and swallowed. Then, 'D'you reckon...you reckon they're all...?'

He was obviously thinking of his family. 'I don't think they're dead,' I replied, sensing that I ought to sound decisive and assert something, however little I might know. He very much wanted an assurance to hang onto. 'Dead things didn't disappear.'

He gazed at me, thoughtful, far off, his eyes still fixed on my face.

'No.' He nodded. ''S true.'

I'd avoided saying 'corpses'. He knew that much, then; he must have found corpses. He nodded again, and came out of his thoughts with a tighter smile, lifting his right hand and clasping my left arm in a friendly gesture.

'Gee, it's good to talk to somebody,' he said; 'I was...I begun to think I was...you know? *Porangi.* Crazy. I mean, I couldn't figure out why it was me, just me—'

It was my turn to nod agreement, but I couldn't bring myself to return his gesture. I wasn't in the habit of grasping people in matey embraces and it would have looked awkward and phoney if I'd even tried. Yet without knowing what to do, how to respond, I did feel the same thankfulness and rush of emotion.

'And I thought it was just me,' I said, and we grinned at each other. The puzzle seemed to have changed shape elusively, to have shrunk and expanded in different areas. Yet I felt it could be cornered now, and defeated.

'Why us, then?' he asked; 'we must be special, eh?'

'We must have something in common,' I said, absurdly. He stood back and looked at me, in mock confusion. His face was lightened by very white teeth and the going of the frown, but he was quite dark-skinned and his eyes were very black and quick, scanning me up and down.

'You don't look like Ngati Porou to me,' he said.

As if on cue we both burst out laughing like madmen, reeling around the ridiculous landscape, eyes watering, lungs heaving. The release was more than just the collapse of fear, tension, isolation, and everything else, it was a burst of noise for its own sake, for being alive, for getting our own back, for defiance and mockery at whatever had messed the universe into such clueless stupidity. Five minutes earlier, alone, it would have been a sure mark of mental disintegration.

We leaned on my car, weak. When I got my breath back I looked at him.

'I think we'll get by,' I said.

'I think we will,' he replied.

Euphoria. Brains short of oxygen.

CHAPTER EIGHTEEN

He had blocked the road with the sheep truck and driven along the track from the south in an army jeep to the point where the steam drifted over the way. He'd pitched a tent behind the small hill on the left. It was a carefully calculated ambush. The previous day he'd come up from Waiouru to Turangi to check the power station at Tokaanu. He didn't know much about all that, but he thought there might have been a power surge at 6.12 last Saturday morning, since some equipment at the army camp at Waiouru had gone into overload and all the circuit breakers had been tripped. As far as he could tell this had happened at the power station too. He was a lance corporal in the army, by the way, and I should call him Api. He'd had four years' service. Weapons instructor. Wanted to be a mechanic, really. Anyhow; yesterday he'd been at Tokaanu, about midday, and he thought he'd heard a noise coming across the lake from the north, from Taupo. What kind of noise? Well, hard to say really. Maybe an echo, like a foghorn gone wrong, but a long way off, and sort of distorted.

I said I'd heard a sound in the evening a bit like that, only I was in Taupo and it seemed to come from the southern end of the lake. No, he'd not heard any sounds in the evening. But he thought it might be a car, so he'd set up the road block south of Turangi to catch anything coming along either the east or west sides of the lake.

He was very well prepared and equipped; I was a little surprised to realise that he seemed to have been coping very competently, perhaps even more adequately in some ways than I had, though this might be, I thought, in fact it probably was, only a superficial impression. We always overrate skills in other people we don't have ourselves, and it couldn't take much genius to pitch a tent and cook up a meal or two. Boy Scout stuff.

I sat on a folding chair whilst he uncorked a bottle of wine and produced some cold chicken and potato salad from a polystyrene container off the back of his, or the army's, jeep. We drank several glasses of wine in celebration. It was a good New Zealand riesling, not the flagon of sugary sauterne I expected when he offered me white wine. He talked as he unpacked and readied the meal. I drank enough to become pleasantly relaxed, and sat there watching him with the thought drifting into my mind that maybe I had acquired Man Friday.

He didn't have very much to tell which could decipher the mystery. When he woke up last Saturday he'd found the camp deserted and imagined that some exercise was under way and he'd not been told or forgotten. Like me, he panicked slightly, and like me, he checked all the radio wavebands. There was no power problem because they had auxiliary power supplies; all he had to do was to set the generators going. The clock phenomenon and the total absence of radio signals or transmissions had had the same unnerving effect on him. When he found Waiouru town empty as well, he had to decide what to do on the basis of his training. His instincts were, as he said graphically, to 'run away and shit myself'. It was obvious, when he looked through all the barracks and living quarters, that people had not got up and gone, they had just—and here he spread his hands out and looked at me for a word, helplessly—well, they had just gone. Those that had clothes on had disappeared with their clothes. That was weird. He had remembered a lecture they'd had a couple of years before on the neutron bomb. It was supposed to kill people but not damage buildings; the radiation did it. Maybe some new weapon like that had been used? He concluded that it was his duty to stay in the army camp, so he'd surrounded himself with weaponry and waited.

'If you run away, it's desertion,' he said; 'on active service you'd get court-martialled.' He paused. 'It looked like the real thing to me.'

'What if everyone runs away?' I asked.

'That's a strategic withdrawal,' he said, seriously.

'What they used to call a retreat?'

'Uh.' He shrugged, not detecting any irony. 'If you're the odd one out, you usually cop it.'

'That's what they tell you?'

'That's how it is.' He ate some chicken. 'How it was, then. Hell, I don't know. If we were being attacked, I couldn't see anyone. Except...' He stared pensively, looking away and then back at me in an almost furtive manner, as if dubious about what he might say.

'Except what?' I felt my stomach constrict.

'I got this feeling...there's something around, like something you think you just might see out of the corner of your eye, or like hearing a noise and then you listen and there's nothing, and you can't be sure...And it's not everywhere, only in some places. And worse at night. Don't you feel it?'

I had hardly spoken. For some reason I was wondering how much I ought to tell him about what had happened to me since Saturday.

'Yes,' I said; 'I know what you mean.'

He sighed with relief.

'Jesus. I thought it might be all in my head.'

'Well it's in mine as well, then.'

There was a pause. He drank some more wine. His eyes fixed on me above the glass.

'Did you see anything?'

'I was driving to Rotorua. It got dark, there was a storm coming on. I saw a thing like a...dog or a calf, come running at the car. No sound, and it seemed to vanish. It scared hell out of me.'

'A *dog*?'

'Like nothing on earth. Bits of dog, bits of other animals. Teeth, like a wolf. No hair on it. White all over.' I drained my glass. He uncorked the wine bottle and refilled it, his lips compressed, the frown dark on his face again. 'You haven't seen anything?' I asked. He shook his head.

'You reckon it was really there?'

'I saw it.' I held the glass in both hands. The pale straw-coloured wine reflected the sky and the glass held my distorted, curved image. 'It's evil, whatever it is,' I said; 'it gave off evil like a smell. I could feel it.'

'Yeah. I know that.'

I gave him a questioning look, and he held his hands up, pink palms outward, as though pressing on a sheet of invisible glass in midair.

'At times I can feel it,' he said, 'very close. But I don't know what it is.' He lowered his hands. 'When I was a kid, about nine or ten, I woke up one night and there was my cousin Hemi standing outside the window looking in. It was moonlight, I could see him as clear as day. I said, "Hey Hemi, what you doing out there? Come on in." And he walked off round the side of the house and I waited but everyone was asleep and there was no knocking on the door. I woke my brother up and told him and he said, "You must've had a dream, go back to sleep, Hemi's in Whakatane." So I went back to sleep. But I knew I'd seen him. And next day we got the news, Hemi died suddenly in the night, at Whakatane. Appendix or something. Well...' and here he rubbed his forehead with his knuckles, nervously; 'the next night, I saw him again, outside the window. And I thought, if Hemi's dead then that thing out there shouldn't be walking around looking like Hemi. It must be bad, and why is it after me? Wants me to join it, maybe? I mean, dead is *dead*, all the way. You might have liked somebody a hell of a lot, I liked Hemi, we were good friends, but you don't want anything like that, not all dead, not staying dead, so I yelled, "Hemi, you're dead! Go back, go away, you're dead!" 'Course it woke everyone up and they reckoned I was having a bad dream. But when I shouted, that thing outside the window seemed to know. Like it was him, eh? And he really didn't know he was dead. It just faded away.'

The Maori clenched his fists. I moved the wine glass to my mouth and tipped some of the cold liquid between my lips and teeth. He closed his eyes tight. 'I think that was one of the worst things I ever did: I still dream about it. They thought I was a spooky kind of kid. I had dreams. *But that was real.* It wasn't a dream. I know who he was and what I said. For people who're alive you can go back another day and say, "Look I'm sorry I hurt you." And explain, and get it right in your mind. But this was forever. It was worse than if I'd killed him. The look on his face.'

I wished he would stop. It was not the kind of thing I wanted to hear. I hadn't found the only other person perhaps in the world in order to listen to this kind of thing. He stood up and put the empty wine bottle back in the jeep and then faced me again, holding his hands up.

'That's like the feeling I've had this week,' he said; 'something bad, weird, just trying to get through to me, not far off. And I don't want to know.'

'Neither do I,' I said. He seemed to sense the tone of my dismissal, and lay down on a groundsheet, his head propped up on a rucksack. After a silence he said quietly, 'You missed the point.'

'What do you mean?'

There was another pause, and he toyed with a piece of fern with a sad intentness before replying. 'I mean, what side of the window are we on? What if we're the ones who don't know, and we have to be told?'

I looked away. My stomach was churning.

'For Christ's sake—' I said.

'You must have thought of it.' His words were soft and slow-spoken, with an odd insinuating quality. I resented the way he had somehow placed me on the defensive and pushed these words and ideas so easily through my defences.

'We eat and sleep and breathe,' I said, with as much force as I could, 'and when we get cut, we bleed'—I held up my fingers, sealed with pink sticking plaster—'and the wound heals. And you think we may be dead?'

He avoided looking at me.

'How often you been dead, then?' he said.

'Alright. What do we do? Dig a couple of holes, crawl in, and lie there till we go cold?'

He didn't answer; he threw the fern aside and stared gloomily at the ground. I felt I had to assert myself, as much for my own sake as for his.

'Apirana,' I said. He looked up. 'I don't know what being dead is like, but I do know about being alive, and this is it.'

The statement, packed with ironies as it was, swelling into a massive lie, still had a power to it as though the words could harden in the air and make their own reality in the same way that an exorcism might have strength to push against a manifest threat.

'We are both alive,' I said deliberately; 'don't fool yourself.'

A trace of smiling went into the expression of his lips and he nodded.

'Okay. Sorry.'

'You don't believe New Zealand really is heaven do you?' I asked, anxious to break the mood. His teeth showed. We laughed.

'I reckon not,' he said, then pretended to sniff the air in the direction of the sulphur pools; 'could be the other place, though.'

I was slightly drunk, which made it easier for me to play the part of somebody with a fairly developed sense of humour. I held up the glass.

'No, it couldn't be hell. They wouldn't do a good riesling.' And we laughed some more. He relaxed.

'It's three dollars a bottle,' he declared.

'Did you pay cash?' I asked. His face clouded for a moment and he nodded.

'Habit,' he said, curtly. I hadn't meant to suggest anything. This was treacherous. My experience of talking to Maoris was almost zero. All the time there were sharp points and bad patches, like walking barefoot over a lawn with bits of broken glass hidden ready to draw blood.

'I left cheques,' I said lamely.

'You put your address on the back?' he asked.

'Of course.' A pause. 'I'm a good keen bloke.'

He leaned back and folded his arms, pushing his head against the rucksack so that his black woollen hat tipped down his forehead and shaded his eyes. The teeth appeared again.

'Good,' he said; 'makes me feel safe.' And he laughed

in a very Maori way, his chest heaving and expelling deep throaty noises. It sounded like the kind of laugh that would be shared amongst friends and directed outwards at other people.

'I'm the one's been doing all the talking,' he went on, after a pause, becoming more assertive; 'how about you?'

'What do you mean?'

'Well. Job? Family? All that.'

The chance to strike back was there, and I took it.

'I'm a research scientist. My wife left me last year. We had an eight-year-old boy. He drowned...in an accident. She blamed me. So, no, no family. My parents died when I was a kid. No brothers or sisters. I didn't have anybody to go looking for.'

He lifted his hat and sat up, staring at me.

'Nobody?'

'Nobody.'

'Hell. I'm sorry, man.'

It looked and sounded like genuine sympathy, and I was taken unawares again. He accepted what I told him without question, and seemed to be affected by it as though he'd known me for ages.

I covered my confusion by giving an account of what happened to me since Saturday, describing the crashed plane but not my escape from the research centre or Perrin being dead in there, and only giving the briefest summary of our research in terms which I hoped he wouldn't understand. And whilst I was telling this, I was trying to cope with the way Lance Corporal Apirarna Maketu had pushed his naïve pity onto me like a condescending social worker—

and I'd known a few—looming into a personal crisis for a bit of emotional indulgence, the voyeur at somebody else's accident handing out pity like paper handkerchiefs. Luckily my isolation had spared me most of this during the worst times. Now, after everything I'd been through, I was faced with the casual presumption of this particular perfect stranger doing me the honour of being sorry for me. And in any case, all I had told him was that I had nobody to lose. If he pushed his flat nose into the implications of that, then he might realise it could be strength now, not something to be sorry about. He should consider that.

He interrupted me to ask what kind of research I did. 'You use radioactive stuff?'

'Well, yes. But I'm in biological science. I don't know anything about radioactivity as such; that's another area, that's physical science.'

'No theories about what's happened, then?'

'I don't think it's anything like a neutron bomb—'

'Nah.' He shook his head. 'Not so simple, is it?'

'We have to get all the evidence together. There was a power surge, it knocked out electrical equipment, it stopped clocks, but it didn't reverse the polarities or anything like that—'

'What do you mean?'

'Well, if you restart electrical equipment, generators, batteries, and so on, it still works. Radios still work but don't pick up anything.'

'Because nobody's transmitting.'

'Or because the ionosphere's been mucked up, or the wavebands have been jammed by some force. What else do we know? It didn't affect insects and worms below ground level, or anything beneath water, sea level—'

He sat up again, inspired, suddenly.

'What about blokes down mines? Or in submarines?'

'I doubt it. Rats and mice could have been underground and survived, but I haven't seen any. My guess is that only small things escaped.'

'We don't know for sure, though.'

'Submarines...it's possible.'

My idea of a world magically disarmed by the Effect had been weakened by the survival of the lance corporal and his gun. The thought of fully manned nuclear missile submarines bursting through the level of the sea on panic red alerts was hard to take. But the universe was obviously in the mood for grotesque jokes.

He reached into the rucksack and produced a small compass.

'Still points north,' he said. 'Course, it *would*, eh?'

'Mm?' I was musing on the submarine problem and thinking that people down mines would not have survived merely by being below ground level, because that would have saved people in basements and cellars, and there were quite a few all-night clubs in Auckland basements but no survivors in evidence.

'You were on about reversal of polarities. What if it happened to the whole world? North and south poles, everything? We wouldn't be any wiser, would we? This would still point north because this compass would have reversed its polarity as well. Same with the electrical stuff. How would we know?'

I stared at him. Was he really only a lance corporal? I nodded.

'I think I once read about the earth's magnetic field reversing itself millions of years ago,' I said. 'Maybe it could happen. I don't know. But I doubt if it would affect electrical equipment or small magnets. The compass needle would point north, but only if you faced geographical south.'

He looked down.

'Bang goes the Maketu theory. North's still up there.'

I would have to watch my step; bright people could be dangerous. That much I did know.

Putting the compass away, he stood up and stretched. It was late afternoon now and the sky had cleared to a deep sea-green. The clouds had dissolved.

'We'll sort something out,' he said. 'What worried me was, I thought, what if it depends on me? If there's something I've got to do, to make it all right? To make them come back.' He darted me a forlorn look in which I recognised reassuring signs of self-doubt. 'I'm not used to being on my own. Not much good at it.'

'You seem to be doing alright to me,' I replied, gesturing at his tent and jeep. He shrugged.

'Basic training.'

I stood up. He looked around, then turned towards me and said more or less exactly what I wanted him to say.

'What's the plan, then?'

CHAPTER NINETEEN

'The object is to sink the black,' he said, 'when everything else is down.'

Leaning over the pool table he drove the cue onto the white ball, sending it with a loud crack at the triangle of other balls. They scattered across the green baize. He lifted the cube of chalk and screeched it on the end of the cue.

'You're sure you don't play?'

'Positive.'

'I never met anybody who didn't play pool.'

'We've both led sheltered lives, then.'

He laughed, and began to move round the table lining up shots and cursing when he missed. We were in the games room of a Turangi motel, having taken over a two-room unit for the night. Apirana, for some reason, didn't want to drive down to Waiouru and stay at the army camp. 'It's only crummy barracks,' he said. After the trauma of last

Saturday he had stayed dutifully at Waiouru for two days, then abandoned the camp and driven down to Hawke's Bay and up beyond Gisborne in search of his relatives. And finding nothing, had come back.

The sun was setting and the darkness gathered in the room. I sat by the open ranch slider doors looking north, the sun on my face. I had noticed that Apirana was left-handed.

'You've never been to Auckland?' I asked.

'Nope.' He tapped the cue ball gently and it missed its target. 'Been to Singapore, though.' The ball missed again. '*Whaka*—nui!' This, I gathered, was his swear word. He put the cue down and came and sat in one of the aluminium chairs on the patio, holding a glass of beer. 'Too dark in there.'

After a pause, I took a deep breath and said, 'The reason I asked, was...because when I first saw you today, I could have sworn I'd seen you somewhere before.'

His face was turned towards the sun and the light was being absorbed into his features and reflected from the bone beneath the skin, pale almond under coffee. His eyes were almost closed.

'Lots of Maoris in Auckland,' he said softly.

'Didn't you think we'd met somewhere?'

The face was expressionless.

'They say we all look the same to the pakeha.'

'I don't think so.'

A pause. He drank his beer. It looked gold; it slid into his mouth. Then, placing the glass on the concrete floor, 'How many Maoris did you know?'

'One used to live near us, twenty years ago.'

'What was his name?'

It was my turn to pause.

'I don't remember.'

'Did you ever know?'

'No.'

He didn't move. His face was set like an Easter Island monolith against the sun on a hillside.

'Anybody else?' he asked quietly. My irritation began to increase.

'A bloke at the supermarket. A mechanic at the garage. There weren't many at university.'

'No, I reckon not.'

It was obviously useless trying to get behind the mask he'd assumed. A sullen reticence had come over him, an apathetic weariness rather than defensive hostility. The shadows stretched across the grass towards us as the light faded. When I looked at his face again the dusk had gained such depth in the porch that only the whites of his eyes reflected glitterings of light.

'So we can't have met before,' he said, finally.

'But you did think you recognised me.'

A long sigh came from the gloom.

'Yes.'

The eyes closed and cut out the last points of light, and the place where his face was seemed darker for a moment than the shadows behind and all around.

'I was wondering what it might mean,' he whispered.

I felt very calm; the admission reassured me, it justified my persistence, and even its obscurity blended easily into the mass of darkness. He had delayed, waited for the day to evaporate.

'What do you think?' I said. There was this calmness between us, as if we had settled into an awareness of our fixed situation on a planet that was moving, slowly but perceptibly turning its axis against the sun and taking us through space with some immense purpose.

He stood up, suddenly.

'Don't ask me,' he said; 'you're the *scientist*.' Pause. 'It's too dark. I'm going inside.'

Lying awake in the night I wondered why we should think that we could understand what was happening. We would have to pretend, perhaps, so that we would have something to do, to impose at least a surface of purpose on our actions. But after all, nobody had understood existence as it used to be; and here we were, hoping to unravel an even stranger set of trickery in a few days.

At school there had been an experiment in which a clear, highly saturated solution of a chemical could be made to transform itself suddenly into a dense white solid, a crystalline mass, merely by knocking the side of the jar in which it stood. The sudden disappearance of solid objects such as people and animals might be analogous, in reverse; perhaps the universe reached a point of saturation and then an instantaneous transformation took place to another dimension. It would be what we called, in jargon, a 'major event anomaly' or a 'singularity occurrence'. Many experts no longer believed in the Darwinian theory of evolution; they said that the appearance of *Homo sapiens* was inexplicable, a sudden phenomenon for which science as we knew it could never find a cause. The 'quantum leap' wasn't merely a 'missing link' but a random event, a quirk in the universe. We had discarded religious fables of creation. Sooner or later we would have to discard the evolutionary fables. If these experts were right, then a 'major event (positive)' could very well be annulled by a 'major event (negative)'. A few apes had survived the first; we had survived the second. The lack of completeness was characteristic. No theory could account for a hundred per cent of any phenomenon.

Obviously the world had undergone a psychic jolt; the Maori had confirmed that a change had occurred. The world we were in was almost exactly, but not quite, the same as the old world. A subtle dislocation somehow involving the processes of perception had shaken the normal boundaries out of place. It was hard to detect, like a familiar room in which something is very slightly changed. And it induced the same unease.

I had no concepts or words to apply to this. I had to struggle with the realisation, also, that I wasn't unique, I wasn't the focal point, I hadn't been especially chosen for some revelation or saved for a purpose. The universe was simply careless. Its disorder seemed to me to be a betrayal. The calm I had felt earlier was eaten up within me by a cancerous rage. *The universe was simply careless.* After the silent bang, there remained a few pathetic whimpers. I was one. Asleep in the next room was another, making occasional sounds very like pathetic whimpers.

Perhaps that was how I slept, too.

*

In some dreams I see photographs of my family which were never taken. They show Joanne and myself, and Peter as a normal child, with such clarity that even as the dream is going on I wonder if this is a future which does exist somewhere in the universe. We are on a boat, a ferry, in what seems to be the Bay of Islands, leaning on a white-painted rail, laughing. Another shows Peter reading a magazine on a beach. He is slightly older than he ever was; about twelve or thirteen.

Then, sometimes, there are events from that alternative world, in which these people move and talk. I am taking a piece of meat from a barbecue grill and putting it on a plate held by Peter; he makes a face and complains that the steak is burnt, and Joanne laughs and asks why I insist on cooking outdoors but hardly ever in the kitchen. Peter groans and says, Mum, for heaven's sake, don't encourage him. Then there are other segments of clearly defined events, frighteningly vivid. It worries me that they should have such clarity. None of them are significant, they lack any specific meaning, their ordinariness is equally disturbing. We move through rooms which must exist in the real world somewhere, and from which we could not be subtracted without violating the rules of the universe, without creating an absence and a vacuum as impossible as that which I had felt in the succession of empty houses I had entered all through the afternoon at Thames. And yet now we are not there; the impossible has happened twice. I move through an empty room towards a mirror. When I stand in front of it, and look into it, I cannot see myself. There is nothing.

*

The road wound down and around awkwardly and then came up, turned, and pointed straight across the desert plateau. The day was cloudless, the sky acid-blue behind the snow on the tops and slopes of the mountain volcanoes to the right. They looked ruined, as if the white was quicklime corroding their solidity. A smear of vapour from the height of Ruapehu stretched east on the top of the sky; there was fire inside the snow.

Apirana drove ahead in his land rover. I followed about fifty metres behind in my car. We had agreed on my plan to go to Wellington. The first stop would be Taihape. He said there was no point in stopping at Waiouru; he had double-checked everything.

The air thickened as we drove down from the plateau through great clefts in the hills. The scrub browns gave way to greens, faded on the sheep-eaten hills, dusty by the road. The road slanted down. More vegetation appeared, some undefeated trees and patches of bush. Mostly it was chainsaw land. Every now and then, week-old dead possums lay on the road where trucks had hit them, bits of fur and leather innards, no flies or hawks to worry what was left. The land rover made swerves.

At each small town we halted and Apirana detonated a training grenade, a thunder flash. He showed me how they worked, compared with real hand grenades made out of metal, of which he also had a boxful in the land rover. The thunder flashes blasted violent waves of noise into empty streets and back at us from buildings and hillsides. Then silence. We would wait, then go on.

South of Taihape there were vistas of endless hills, like broken bones hidden under green baize. In places the road sliced through lumps of land leaving cuts exposed in the air. They were being corroded; gangrene had set in. Subsoil had fallen and dried. Yellow dust came up and powdered the windscreen. I wondered how long it would take for the bush to grow back and the hills to get firm roots again. A feeling of violation welded the past to the present, of extinct life forms feeding on extinction for revenge. The same negative presence was seething in the vacancy of human places as in the spaces where the forest had been and where the excavators had amputated whole sections of hills. I remembered driving from Cape Turnagain years before and feeling the threat of the emptiness getting at places inside myself. Even here where there were buildings, roads, and farms, they appeared furtive, as though not properly seen or not meant to be closely looked at for long; made in haste, unrepented. People spoke of the land being settled; in fact it had been unsettled. And now, absolutely.

The windscreen wipers cleared the view, made it hard. Suddenly I was startled by swarms of darting flecks in the air, swirling in the wake of the land rover. Thistledown. Like butterflies. Billions of seeds. For the rest of the way down to the plain there were these clouds of floating white specks. The weeds were on the move, not wasting time; it would be all theirs.

We detoured to Palmerston North. Apirana fired grenades, and we climbed to the top of a tall insurance building to scan the horizon with binoculars. There was a whitish heat haze, and no sound or sign of life. Descending, we ate what would have been lunch under the shade of a tree in the square. A white marble statue of a Maori chief stared from a dead rose garden at reflections in shop windows. Apirana walked around.

'Why would they build a statue to a Maori?' he said. He peered at the inscription. 'Oh, yes. Might've guessed. For his loyalty in the Maori Wars. You know what that means?'

I said nothing. He shook his head.

'Means he fought against the Maori.'

'It was a long time ago,' I said.

'Not so long.' He pointed. 'It says, "I have done my duty. Do you likewise." Well, well. How about that?'

I could tell he was trying to irritate me. We were both a bit on edge from the heat and the weariness of the drive through the vacant towns. Yet something about the words of the inscription seemed to goad him.

'Who decides all this?' he asked, tapping the letters with his knuckles. 'They do. The ones who win. The ones who get the land in the end. He just backed a winner, that's all.'

He came back and flung himself down in the shade. I wasn't going to fight the Maori Wars with him. I could never understand this obsession with the importance of the ownership of land. Your people might have scratched around for a few generations on the top ten centimetres of a land two hundred million years old which had another four hundred million to go. In what impertinent sense of the word could you claim you 'owned' that piece of geology? By burial rights? Surely that would reverse the titles of claim and claimant? Nor had I ever sympathised with the idea that we Europeans had corrupted the noble savages. They were from the start devious, aggressive, and self-important, much like the rest of humanity. Western liberalism had now made them sanctimonious as well. I drank some wine. Even in the shade I felt choked with the heat.

'Well, you've got it all now,' I said.

'All what?'

'The land. You can have it back. All yours.'

He sat up and gave me a look of withering contempt. For a moment I almost felt alarmed.

'Oh,' he said, slowly, with heavy sarcasm, 'thank *you*.'

'I can't see it makes any difference,' I said, wanting to dismiss the subject, 'if it's what you've always wanted.'

He knitted his large hands together, fingers clasped, and held them up in front of him in a manner which seemed, fleetingly, to be too dramatic and theatrical.

'*Tangata whenua*.' He pulled his hands apart. 'The people...and the land. Go together.' One hand dropped and the other withered its fingers like a dead plant. 'Without the people, it's *nothing*.'

I sat through the silence that followed, looking away, mad at myself for getting involved in a useless argument on his territory, on his terms, all uphill against his natural assumption of the moral heights; and mad at him for, in spite of all that, making me seem to be talking down to him, to be trivial and boneheaded. Then I realised that in a curious way I was merely an audience for him, that he was creating a performance of some kind, slightly overstated in its gestures and verbal mannerisms, and not completely within his control. He waved his hands towards the statue.

'All that, *duty*, and *loyalty*. To what? He gives everything away, for what?'

'The British Empire, I suppose.'

'Yes. And where's that now, eh?'

He tensed and leaned forward. I could tell that his agitation, the great tension working in the muscles of his face and body, had very little to do with any provocation I might have given him. It stemmed from some much more powerful disturbance inside his own experience. It was packed behind his eyes.

'I joined the army,' he said, 'because...' and here he paused, lost concentration, then regained it; 'anyhow, I joined. They talk a lot about your duty and what it means, and they have...an oath of loyalty and you sign all these papers, of course, you never think, I mean, what the whole...What they want is to, to just scrub you out, and put someone else there with a gun and they want to be sure that person they've made will do what they say and press the trigger when they give the word. That's it. That's what it means. They have to count on that. And it works. But it's not *you*. And you don't want all these *bastards* coming out with this bullshit about *loyalty* when it's all over, and shoving these bullshit memorials up in every fucken' town because it's all just—'

He stopped. His face was glistening with sweat. After a pause he sat back and wiped his face with the back of his left hand. I gave him what I hoped was an expression suggesting sympathy. The tension lessened.

Deliberately coarsening his voice, thickening a Maori accent, he turned and shouted across the dead roses at the statue: 'Hey, chief! You an' me, the big suckers, eh boy?'

The journey to Wellington would take two or three hours; we cleared up and prepared to leave. I threw the empty wine bottle into the rose garden. Apirana stared.

'I do everything like they're going to come back tomorrow,' he said; 'I thought, if I don't it might muck things up. It'd mean I didn't really believe that.'

I repressed the impulse to laugh. He was being faithful to a system that had cheated him, in the hope that his fidelity would somehow charm it back.

'I told a lie back there,' I said. 'I only paid out cheques on the first day. I've stolen everything else.' He gaped at me. 'I thought, when they come back, they'll understand, they'll make allowances.'

'For you, maybe,' he replied flatly. I saw his meaning. I'd misjudged him. He laughed. 'You look honest. Could've fooled me.'

'Nobody did a very good job on me, either,' I said. 'I've no sense of duty at all.'

He grinned and picked up the bottle to carry it back to the land rover.

'Hey. I might be your conscience,' he said. Although jocular, this sounded just a little odd. I felt the need to dispel the sensation.

'No, you're too big.'

'I'm not so big.'

'You're still too big.'

He hooted with laughter, which was not at all strange, because we were, after all, supposedly operating a series of jokes.

'How about dark?' he asked; 'too dark, maybe?'

I could laugh at that, since the joke was really on him.

On the long drive south past vacant fields, through towns sucked dry of life, I had time to think about what his spasm of anger might mean. It had made him elusive, as though a solid core had spilled out like mercury, glittering, cold, poisonous, running into unreachable corners. It was now urgent that the city ahead should provide survivors, more people, or at least some answers to help.

We drove by the rim of the ocean past a Kapiti Island hovering in shades of transparent blue on the edge of the world. Everywhere seemed sealed in hot glass, held behind the window of an empty oven, and I could only watch it from a distance with the coldness of this new fear running inside me. I had to confront the possibility that Apirana, weapons instructor, with his submachine guns and assorted bayonets and skinning knives; that Apirana might not be completely sane.

I looked in the rear-view mirror at my reflection to gauge the extent to which this would affect my expression. And I thought: was he only joking when he said that I could have fooled him?

The white motorway ramps curved along the seafront like stone rivers lifted into the centre of the city. Thousands of houses lay against the hills locked and shuttered with the sun fixed on them. The harbour water was flat under the mass of heat and quiet. A death scent from decaying animal carcases hung over the docks. The inner streets were cemented in shade by tower blocks, banks, offices, every rack of windows reflecting empty sky or a waste of more blind windows. The stopped moment of 6.12 was undisturbed. We were at the end of our journey. We stopped. The silence absorbed our engines.

CHAPTER TWENTY

'What's this stuff?' He prods at the dish with a fork.

'Abalone.'

'It's not bad. I don't go for that caviar.'

We dine in style in the candlelit dining room high up in one of the big new hotels towering above the Terrace.

The windows show a dead city in twilight, like an architect's model sunk in deep water. Our candles are reflected in the windows. Only the small slits of glass at the top will open. When a slight movement of air stirs through them, the candle flames shudder and the dark patches on the walls of the dining room flutter like huge moths. But of course there are no insects any more.

The silence has been suffocating, and Apirana has set a battery tape recorder playing. Soft bossa-nova music is defeating the death-feeling, pounding it away discreetly. He talks about rigging up a generator in the basement of the hotel: he says he could get one from the hire pool or an army depot. I can tell he's been thinking about his little rituals of honesty and the way I have flouted the conventions. But he doesn't want to chase all the implications too far so he has given up making payments for what we need and begun to take whatever we want, leaving me to do the rest of the thinking and arrive at reassurances. He expects me to produce some answers; he assumes I will 'work something out'. I wonder if this is how they have regarded us for the last two hundred years. And if I will know how to act my part.

His enthusiasms are all technological; he discusses the water supply, warning against drinking water without first boiling it, describing the purifying tablets they use in the army when on active service. He seems to want to keep talking.

I lift the bottle of French champagne, and pour some more.

'I'll stay off water altogether,' I say.

'Yeah. Good idea.' He accepts, and drinks. The crystal glasses sparkle in the candlelight. 'Good stuff, eh?'

'It ought to be.'

'Like you say, they'll make allowances.' He laughs and belches. 'Uh. I'm lowering the tone of the place.'

We look out at the city. A brief foraging session in one or two shops has opened up the prospect of vast resources of loot. I'm amazed at our restraint. I suppose the barriers will break down fairly quickly.

Api gets up and ambles to the window, holding his glass. He touches the fawn-coloured curtains.

'Velvet.' A pause. 'How the other half live.' He stares out. 'I once came here with a girl, a couple of years ago. To Wellington, I mean, not to this place. Couldn't afford this. Stayed in some dump, somewhere. Not much doing, Sunday evening. Just like now, except the street lights were on. It could be Sunday with a power cut, out there.' He gives a quick snort of a laugh. 'What a dump. Eh? Look at it.'

'It's not much,' I agree.

'When we got here today...I thought there'd be *something*, though. Didn't you?'

He turns to me. I can see my reflection sitting at the table, my face whitened by the light collected by the starched tablecloth, the gleams of highlights from glasses, bottles and silver cutlery glittering steadily. I look confident.

'There was nobody in Auckland,' I reply. 'I didn't expect Parliament would be in session or anything like that.'

'Well...I was just thinking...there are some bastards, I wouldn't mind if they never come back.' He becomes pensive, swirls the champagne in his glass, then drinks it all and puts the glass down. 'That's wrong, though. I know that.'

'What sort of feeling does this place give you?' I ask cautiously. 'You said at Turangi, you could sense something just out of sight. Here?'

'It's different here. I can still feel it. But it's as though there's a reason for us being here; like, an event's going to happen, and it'll be in Wellington, and we had to come here. Don't you feel that?'

'No. Perhaps you can pick up vibrations I don't get.'

'Like a Geiger counter, and radioactivity?'

'Maybe.'

He paces around on the soft carpet, hands in pockets. 'Funny, eh; I never had much idea about the future. I used to try and look forward and work out what the hell I was going to be doing, where I was heading, my life, and all that, you know. I'd think: What's going to happen to me? To become of me? You know? And...it was just a blank.'

'This event...or whatever you can sense, here; is it, I mean, can you tell if it's good, or bad, or what?'

He stops and glances at me, or rather, *not* at me, in a very Polynesian way, his eyes fixing for a moment away from mine, at a point to the left of me, and then he turns and goes back to the window. I have a feeling that the worst the world could do to these people would be met in the end by much the same expression, a pained resignation with almost no trace of surprise in it, equally appropriate for thousands of trivial annoyances, flat beer, rainy days, a missed bus, the tantrum of a child, a debt collector's letter. At school we had once been made to learn a poem which described a remote island, and the phrase used for the people on this island had stayed in my mind when all the other memories had faded or become irrelevant; 'mild-eyed melancholy'. I think the island was supposed to be enchanted, or the inhabitants drugged; their lives had no purpose, they did nothing except face the world with this expression.

Perhaps he feels the pause has taken on too much weight. He says, 'One thing I do know. I'd like a really good cup of tea, with real milk. Not that powdered stuff. Don't you miss real milk?'

I deliberately give him a silence in return. He sighs and wanders to the other end of the room, lifting the cover from the grand piano lurking in the corner.

'Twenty million cows are missing,' he shouts across the distance; 'they haven't milked for a week. What are you going to do about it?'

I begin to formulate a sarcastic answer, but he sits at the piano and starts to play, and to sing purposely off-key.

> 'Moon river, wider than a mile,
> I'm crossing you in style,
> Somedaaay...'

The moon has, in fact, edged into the sky over the harbour, embalming the powerless buildings and streets in a formaldehyde white. The shadows are utterly black. Stars are flickering morse dots a long way off.

> 'Moon river, off to see the world,
> There's such a lot of world
> To see...'

He stops playing. Then shouts: 'You ever go overseas?'

'To Sydney, once. To a conference.'

'We were in Singapore. Last year. Great place.'

He comes back and sits by the table again.

'Know anything about ships? Sailing?'

'No. Why?'

'Well we're stuck here, aren't we? I'm bloody useless with boats. We can't even get to the South Island.'

'You expect to find more people?'

'Bound to be.'

'There might be one other person in New Zealand. The survival rate must be about one in a million.'

'Survival?'

'Non-disappearance, then.'

'We could have missed people. You'd have driven past Waiouru, I might have missed you by ten minutes. There could be people out there in the bush, could be months before they even know anything's wrong. Deerstalkers. Anybody.'

'I doubt it.'

'One in a million, that'd still be a hell of a lot in Singapore.'

'What would you do if we got to Singapore and there were a dozen Chinese or Malays or whoever they are? What's the point?'

'The point is—'

'What would you do? Sing "Moon River"?'

He bangs the table, his eyes glittering, lips tight.

'Well what're you going to do? Eh? What if there's an accident? If one of us gets sick? Then what? You get appendicitis, or something. You want *me* to cut you open, eh?'

A coldness goes through me, as though my stomach and intestines are actually being exposed to the air at that moment. The tension has squeezed this psychotic idea from inside his mind. He spreads his big hands down on the white tablecloth and looks down at them. Then he says, more quietly, 'We stand a better chance if there's more people. We don't know how long it'll go on, do we? What about women? I mean, there might be...there's no reason why…' His head sags and shakes. 'Oh, hell, I don't know.' Then, silence, perhaps memories of barrack-room Malaysian prostitutes.

'If we start panicking, we've had it,' I say, as evenly as possible. 'We've got to think logically. Right?' He nods. I take a deep breath. 'Look. Today we've driven for about two hundred and fifty kilometres. What did you notice about your windscreen?'

'Notice? Why?' He looks up.

'Not a single insect. No flies. Mosquitoes. Moths.' I waved my hand at the open windows. 'After a week, not one.'

'So what?'

'We used fruit flies in our research. In genetics you need something which breeds fast. There used to be *billions* of insects. There should have been thousands of survivors. Flies have a two-day breeding cycle; they'd lay millions of eggs. They'd breed like mad, and there are no natural predators to keep them down. But we haven't seen a single one of any species.'

'They all disappeared, then.'

'There are two other possibilities. Think about it.'

He stares at me with a frown, a long, slow minute.

'No females.'

'Yes. Or?'

A pause, then he says, 'They're all sterile.'

I nod. His head sags down again. The tape has run to its end; the music has gone. Outside, the city, livid, drained of colour, is spread out beneath our reflections.

'Oh, Christ,' he whispers. Then, 'How could you find out?'

'I can check the local research centres. The chances are, that the first option is correct. The most obvious solution is usually the most likely.'

The tone of my voice makes him glance up at me; I sound much calmer than I feel. He seems only half-convinced, as if he doesn't want to believe that I can be so cool at this moment, so objective.

'You mean, that they all disappeared?' he says.

'Yes. But I can check radiation levels as well.'

'With Geiger counters?'

'And with more sophisticated equipment. There are whole bands of radiation'—and I hold up my arms, sideways—'from ultraviolet out to cosmic radiation, through gamma rays, and then at the other end, from infrared through radar out to radio waves. I know enough to be able to check if there are any abnormalities. But'—and here I lean forward and look intently at him—'I can't do it without your help. To fix electrical equipment, to make power.'

To my relief, he responds, and his face becomes animated again. He nods vigorously.

'Okay. Yes, okay.'

'And we'll have to set up a radio transmitter and a receiver, and do lots of monitoring over all the wavebands.'

'Yeah, sure.' Then his expression clouds. 'Doesn't radioactivity...doesn't it cause sterility?'

'Only in very large doses.'

'I thought—'

'It usually changes the genetic structure...in various ways. '

'Could you tell if that had happened?'

'No. Only if there are some *Drosophila*—I mean, fruit flies, around.'

I seem to have convinced him that I know what I'm talking about, and he relaxes, looking apologetic. The last few sentences have been hard for me.

'Sorry I was...you know.'

'That's alright. I should have explained a bit more.'

'I just thought...there'd be someone here, in Wellington.'

'If there's anybody else in the North Island, I should think they'll come here sooner or later.'

He nods again, and toys with some food on a plate.

'How long do you reckon somebody would last before they...cracked up?'

'Hard to say. Not much more than a week or two, I wouldn't think.'

'Be a few days, for some people.'

'It would depend on their jobs, I suppose. On how they were trained to cope.'

'Huh.' A half-laugh; he presses some pieces of uneaten asparagus to a flat paste with a fork. 'And we were trained, eh?' Then, throwing the fork down, 'Well trained.'

'It's not just that. It's what you get to know about life, as well.'

'Is it?' He yawns, rubs his face, seems to be suddenly tired. 'Not much life left to know about.' The expanse of dead city has an almost hypnotic effect. 'It can't all be just for us,' he says. 'I'm not that important.'

I smile back; but in not immediately replying with an agreement that neither am I of much importance, I realise that perhaps he has set a test for me, and I've unwittingly confirmed something for him. In fact he looks away with a wry expression as though inwardly amused and only half-concerned to conceal it.

I did not want to have to know, to understand, very much about him. It had not seemed necessary. Now I can see that I have no choice. My survival might depend on it. Because *he* is finding out about *me*, gathering information in odd ways, casually, perhaps not with any motive but because this is what he is used to; his life must have forced him to spend a lot of time trying to understand Europeans. I am at a disadvantage. I would not have said—and this comes to me with no great blaze of revelation—that I had ever begun to understand even myself. I *knew* a great deal, I knew many things; but there was some impediment which stopped me from comprehending; it made large patches of shadow. And now—

I shall ignore his ploy, if that's what it is. I pretend I'm not interested; and after a pause I see the chance to ask a question I've been feeling uneasy about since we met. So I say, 'You remember when I said dead things didn't disappear? How did you find that out?'

He stares at me with a much more distant expression, as if puzzled that I should ask.

'Dead animals on the road. Opossums, hedgehogs. Dead flies'—and he holds up his hand, spread out flat in midair—'stuck in cobwebs.'

For security against any outside threat we have locked and barred all exits and entrances. We occupy a suite of rooms on the eighth floor. The corridor door can be locked, and there is a press-button locking mechanism on the connecting door between our two bedrooms. I realise that we would both like to close and lock this door, but for either of us to do so would be such a significant action that it can't be done. I try to stay awake. The silence tightens. Then slackens. Sleep is as treacherous as ever.

She turns suddenly and looks at me as I hold the door of the black car open after the slow walk down the gravel path from the edge of the oblong pit. The earth has battered down on the wooden lid. To earth. She knows beyond my face. Everything. Ashes. The look warns against touching her. She is driven away. Cases are packed, boxes filled, papers signed, it will all go. An empty house. Dust.

In dreams different times in the same place melt into each other.

The stones by the church, in the churchyard, are upright in waves of grass, the wind rushing over the grass, and I can see their ages and names, and think how the names planned to get here. Enormous journeys, faces set hard; strange expectations at the end. The stones have grown yellow and grey with tissues of lichen like dry brains covering their letters. Everlasting Peace. Dearly beloved. Arms of the Lord. A glorious awakening.

I am dissecting tissues and cellular structures, finding the motives and impulses inside the smallest items of life, pulling apart the micro-secrets. Billions of these build into illusions of free will. Coded protein chains transmit memories and instincts. Nerve chemicals form commands inside muscles, enough to make a hand move back, a head turn, an arm go still. I shall discover the source of all this, expose it for what it is. Faces whitened by fluorescent lights inside rooms with no windows or way out will stare with the recognition of my discovery.

We may be on the verge of a breakthrough. He pushes his steel-rimmed spectacles back with the forefinger, smiling, the dentures glistening more than the real teeth. Well, he says, the last thing people want to know is that everything is decided for them by influences they can't control. Or know damn all about. Can't hope to understand. They don't want that. We find out the truth because we don't have any choice. Nothing else works, empirically. I sometimes wonder what we could do if we gave them what they really want out there. Illusion. Very powerful. The alchemists had the right idea. They dealt in both.

That was because they never knew the difference, I say; and the lips unwrap the shining teeth again.

He is walking away along the white corridor and I have not said what I have to say. The words choke back. There are questions. Terrible, overwhelming problems. My resources had proved inadequate. Why didn't I make it clear? I had reached the most adverse conclusion. He goes away as if he half-knew.

CHAPTER TWENTY-ONE

'It's Sunday.'

'Is it?' I count the days. 'Yes. I suppose it is.'

He leans against the doorjamb, his arms folded, holding a black book. We are about to go upstairs and make breakfast. No eggs, no bread, no milk. I am tying my shoelaces.

'They put these in all the rooms.' He waves the Gideon Bible. 'I was thinking about, er...you know.'

'About what?'

'Aw...I thought I might go to, you know, to a church.'

I stop and look up at him.

'Oh.'

'Couldn't do any harm, eh?'

'Or good.' My head is down again.

'What?' A pause. 'You never know.'

'What will you do?' I ask.

'Well...sort of...pray, I s'pose. Dunno really. I just thought...' He sighs, looks at the cover of the Bible, embarrassed. 'We were always bein' packed off to church when we were kids. It gets to you after a while. 'Course, it's years since I went.'

I stand up.

'What did you do last Sunday?'

'There's a church at Waiouru. I went in for a while.'

'You don't have to go to a church to pray, do you?'

'No. S'pose not. Seems right, though.'

'I don't have any religious beliefs.' I say this rather formally, uncertain about the areas we are moving into.

There is a pause; then he says, 'We were Methodists.'

'Well...if you want to, then...' and I shrug.

We go out of the room into the corridor, and begin to climb the stairs to the dining room. He brings his Sten gun, holding it pointing down. He climbs in silence.

'What will you pray for?' I ask, momentarily reckless, as we enter the dining room and see the early morning sun streaming in on the littered plates and empty bottles from the evening meal; 'that everyone will come back?'

He glances at me with a slightly puzzled expression.

'That nothing bad's going to happen. That it'll all work out. And...we'll be...you know, okay. We'll be saved.'

I stare out at the bright day, the silence rampant like a dead animal on heat, the harbour water flaring into an incendiary light pinching my eyelids almost shut. He speaks casually as he clears the table, stuffing bottles and remnants into a metal waste bin. The word 'saved' has no special inflection. Should it have? What does it mean?

When he says it, what image in his mind does it connect to?

It had not occurred to me that we might be 'saved'. I thought we already had been.

Having agreed that we should stay fairly close together, I have to accompany him in his search for a church. The idea that Sunday is a special day does exert a curious pressure, powerfully reinforced by the deserted streets and closed shops. It seems hard to avoid talking in whispers.

But the expedition becomes farcical. The first church is Roman Catholic, and Apirana tells me to drive on. We are in my car with the windows rolled down. The sun is hot. He is wearing dark trousers, black shoes and a white shirt. I presume this is part of his civilian clothing. His sleeves are rolled up to reveal a tattoo on his left forearm. He props his left arm out of the car window and keeps tapping the outside of the roof or door with his fingers, betraying irritation, probably wishing he'd never suggested this expedition, wanting to find a church and get the ludicrous business over and done with. I hide behind dark glasses and an indifferent expression, as neutral as possible, easy for me to maintain. But he misinterprets this. It adds to his irritation.

We locate an Anglican church and he decides it will do. I wait in the car. He gets out and goes up the steps. Of course the doors are locked. It is still really 6.12 am on a Saturday. He comes back, sweating, gets in the car, slams the door.

'Could break in, but it wouldn't be right,' he says.

'If you like,' I suggest tonelessly, 'I'll break in. It's all the same to me.'

He goes tight-lipped. I try to think of some way I can safely disarm any vague religious notions he might have about what has happened. They can only be dangerous. He is already very tense. I suppose Bibles have a bad effect on weak-minded people. And churches act like echo chambers on psychotics.

'Never mind,' he snaps; 'doesn't matter.'

I swing the car into a wide turn and drive aimlessly along Willis Street and down the canyon of Lambton Quay. He lapses into a sullen silence. A lolling, spastic idiocy seems to have invaded the space between us. It is hard to know how strong it might be. My hands go clammy on the rim of the wheel. We are the only people left in the world. Every other living thing has gone as if nothing more than the images of a film bleached out of existence, wiped from a screen by a burst of light in complete silence; evaporated like bits of tissue in a furnace. And here we are. Not talking to each other.

What should I do? Apologise, sympathise? That would only pander to the absurdity. He started this. Does he need to be given a way out?

I stop the car in the shade; flick the key to kill the engine.

'This is stupid,' I say. He shrugs. There is a long silence. Suddenly he asks if I believe in anything. He says it sarcastically. I reply that I haven't had the kind of life which would keep me believing in very much.

'Maybe you should think about it,' he says.

Now I can use some righteous indignation on him.

'Don't you think I *have*?'

'You're not the only one who's had a bad time.'

'I know that. But you asked *me*, so I'm telling you.'

He looks at me.

'You haven't told me anything.'

He's right. I don't want him to know too much. I remember the Maori boy years ago outside the house in Herne Bay and how he seemed to be able to make such dangerous and accurate deductions about people who were total strangers. But now, if I'm careful, in control, I can select what to tell. Otherwise he might wonder why I should want to conceal everything.

So we sit there in the car, and I look ahead at the empty street from behind my dark glasses, my hands resting on the steering wheel; and the Maori props his back against the far door and stares at me; and I tell him about Peter and Joanne, and how one evening whilst I was answering the telephone and getting towels from the airing cupboard the child had drowned in the bath. I tell him as much as I think necessary. He presents an impassive, sombre expression. Perhaps there is a morbidity in him which needs feeding, or needs the consolation of finding a lot of disorder inside what must appear to them to be our peculiarly tidy lives. Or it could be part of the Polynesian obsession with death. That must have been what hypnotised them with Christianity. Mysticism, sacrifice, cruelty; sporadic self-pity disguised as compassion: yes, it appealed to them. Worst of all, the insistence on guilt. A tumour in minds, a whining to be forgiven or made miserable. Obscene that this should persist when people had so much power over their own lives. It must make them always expect the worst. And get it.

When I stop, damp with sweat, he says nothing. I turn and face him blankly. He looks down. Then he speaks, quietly: 'You say you don't go for religion. But you believe in evil. You saw that animal on the road. Or whatever it was. You said it was evil.'

'Yes.'

'What did you mean, then?'

'It was something which would...destroy life. For no reason. Something which thrives on destroying life.'

'Having a reason makes a difference, you reckon?'

I lean on the steering wheel and sigh.

'Oh, I can't argue round all that. We'd be at it for weeks.'

'Well,' he says slowly, 'I'm a soldier. It's my job to go out and kill people, if I get the word. Just orders. They don't give *reasons*. So am I evil?'

I feel an itching like static electricity inside my spine.

'Have you killed people?' I ask, as evenly as possible, as if it's a very everyday question.

'Have you?' he replies.

There is a pause. The silence is so enormous that the ticking of the car clock and our watches expands into the emptiness like the rattling of frantic insects locked in hollow metal boxes. We hold our breath.

'Who'd ever admit it?' he says. 'Anyway, what's it mean? You blokes sit in your offices or laboratories or wherever, and you make the new weapon, you test it on animals, kill a few hundred rats and monkeys; and then you give the weapon to us, and you say, go on, use it. So who does the killing? Me or you?'

'I've told you about my job. I didn't do any weapons research.'

'I bet you killed a few animals.'

'Well, in the course of—'

'Yeh, yeh, I know.'

'I don't see what you're getting at.'

'Where you draw the line, man, that's what. Was it okay, when you did the experiments and killed them, you know, was your mind okay about it?'

The white bone of my knuckles shows through the skin and cable of veins standing out over the stretched tendons on the back of my hands. And yet I think he wants to be made to confess something himself, that this is all full of his own double meanings.

'I didn't like doing it,' I say, 'if that's what you mean. But we thought some good would come of it.' A pause. 'I can't see the point of all this now.' He has withdrawn again, is staring into his thoughts. I decide to take a risk. 'Have *you* got *your* mind right about whatever you did?'

'What?' As if he hasn't heard.

'Do you have anything special you have to pray about?'

He shakes his head, not really in denial, more like the gesture of somebody avoiding an insect that might sting.

'The way I see it,' he says, 'it's like one bloke digging a hole and another one's filling it in. I mean, if I believe, and you don't believe, we just cancel each other out, eh?'

'I don't think it works like that.'

'You don't know how it works.' He smiles wearily and waves his hand. 'Drive somewhere. It's hot.'

I start the car and drive along until we emerge near

Parliament, the spaceship of the Beehive building coiled up against the sun. The conversation, or interrogation, has slid away deviously; I feel the danger of having wrenched hidden questions into the open and let them loose without getting answers.

'Let's go in and have a look,' he says, indicating Parliament. So I drive into the grounds and stop by the front steps. Api gets out, lifting his Sten gun from the back seat. I take my shotgun and hold it in the crook of my arm as I lock the car doors.

'Be careful with that thing,' he mutters, as I turn; 'hold it down.' He shakes his head. 'Why'd you lock the doors?'

'You never know.'

'If there's anyone around, you'll get a ticket, parked there.'

I unlock the car boot and take out a hammer and a tyre lever.

'We'll have to break in,' I explain. We set off up the steps.

'I've always thought about doing this,' he says, and grins and points the Sten gun at the doors.

We are suddenly archaeologists breaking into the tombs of our own civilisation. A week, a thousand years. There are no cobwebs but the dust is already gathering. The insides of halls, corridors and rooms hold a concentrated faded smell, musty, an accumulation of hot afternoons. In the old building our noises are rustled and hollowed in stone spaces; we walk on marble, then squeaking polished lino. We cross to the Beehive. Tufted carpets muffle sounds.

The sunlight rests everywhere in large blocks as if ordered in bulk, laid down, and forgotten. Space curves round uneasily, hiding more empty space.

For some reason we start to talk louder. The corridors of the central service and power core of the building are in the dark ages. Thick fire-stop doors close slowly behind us, squeezing every atom of light out. We grope back. Apirana wants to go down to the Civil Defence emergency operations room, which is apparently in the basement; but we will need a torch.

'I'll go back to the car,' I say. 'Stay here, so I know where you are.'

'Don't worry. I'm not going *any*-where.' He puts his gun on a table and sits down. I walk away. Looking back through the glass panel of a door I see him place his elbows on the table and clasp his hands tightly together in front of his face. He leans his forehead down on his hands. I hurry through to the old building and out to the car, get the torch, and walk quickly back. He has taken a bottle of whisky from a bar and is pouring some into a glass.

'On the house. Have one.'

'I think I will.'

I get a glass and join him, leaning my shotgun against a chair.

'Cheers.'

He drinks quickly and refills. We are both nervous. We sit with our backs to the window so we can keep the corners of our eyes on each side of the cineramic warp of the room. Although we know there is nothing there, round the curve.

Apirana rubs his hand over the tattoo on his left arm, a greenish-blue mark on smooth brown. It seems to represent a cross or a sword. The words LOVE and HATE intersect, blurred.

'Neat, eh?' he says, in a mockery of a thick Maori voice, the tone suggesting an odd ambivalence, a self-parody; 'You know what a boob tat is?'

'No. I've no idea.'

'A tattoo done in jail. Or borstal. Or DC.' He glances up. 'Detention centre. Or remand home.'

I drink some more whisky. It burns inside my throat.

'It was when I was a kid,' he says; 'nothing really. I got in with these kids a bit older than me. We stole a few cars, you know, messed around. Just bored, I mean, nothing bad. The cops fell on us like a ton of bricks.' He pauses, rubbing his arm slowly, staring into the memory of what happened. 'And we got done. In court, the whole thing. Sent me to a...lock-up for kids. A place of detention for juvenile offenders.' His voice becomes formal, sarcastic. Then he looks at me. 'You know what goes on in those places? Nobody does. You'd never know.' He gives a sudden snort, like a laugh, cut off, covering his left arm with his right hand. 'The warders were ex-cops, ex-drill sergeants, South Africans, Rhodesians. Full-time bastards. You face the wall. Stand to attention. They keep you there for hours. They put a pencil between the wall and your forehead. You got to hold it there. If it drops they punch you in the kidneys. You go down, they kick you. They know how to do it so it doesn't show. That's the welcome room. They make you strip. Shave all your hair off. Spray you with delousing powder. Shove you under an ice cold shower. Back to attention with the pencil till you dry off. Or fifty press-ups.' He nods, staring into space. 'They break kids pretty easy. I've seen them make kids go face down and lick their boots. I mean, really do it. Lick the mud off. Or dog shit. I've seen them do it.'

There is a long pause. Neither of us moves. Then he says, 'But even after the welcome room...I knew they couldn't break me.' He stands up and walks away a few paces, his back to me. 'Anyhow, I was broken.' Then he walks off slowly, trailing his fingers on tabletops, wandering around the big curved room, in and out of the pieces of sunlight.

'What happened?' I say, finally. I feel sick. But I keep my hands anchored round my glass. He stands about five paces away, still rubbing his arm slowly.

'I'm a bit of a fake, really,' he says; 'a phoney, you know; all that stuff about *tangata whenua*, I can say that, but...you know what broke me? When I got through the welcome room at that place, got locked up with the other kids...well...most of them were Maori. And they had a few who kind of ran the place. At their level. They had their own welcome. The screws—I mean, the warders—they knew what went on. It went on all night.' He paces up and down, looking at the carpet. 'I knew nothing. Well, I thought I knew a bit. But nothing, really. I didn't know people could... You wouldn't believe it. My own people. What they did, and made me do. And they were *Maori*. That broke me. The screws, cops, South Africans, you expect them to be bastards. You could deal with that. But when your own people fuck you. And make you, make you—'

He closes his eyes, stops; then, heaving his chest full of air, goes on in a rush. 'And the other thing was, I mean, all the time I was in there, it wasn't more than seventy miles from home, and they let you have visitors, once a month, and letters. My old man had a car. My brother had a motorbike, and he was working ten miles away. Okay, I knew they weren't much at writing. But...all the time I was there...they never came to see me. Not once. Nobody. That, I mean, that...'

Swallowing hard, and pausing, for the first time he looks directly at me. 'You know what? I thought, if I was *dead*, it'd be okay. They'd take a week off work, they'd go a *hundred* miles to a *tangi*, to your funeral. They'd make a real thing of it. But I was just alive. Too bad. What the hell. Who am I, anyhow? And I wanted to be dead, to force them to be there. My family.' The tone of his voice changes, thickens to the recognisable parody of Maori speech. 'Great bloody people, with the *aroha*, eh? Everyone says that. Must be true. *Eh boy*, you know that, eh?'

His eyes fill up and glisten. In the fury of the last sentence he leans towards me, contorted with the expression of the parody, his voice going hoarse. He straightens up, flicking his head sideways as if the stinging in his eyes is a nuisance he can shake off. His control reasserts itself. I sit hypnotised.

'I thought maybe they never came to see me because I'd let them down. Disgraced them. I hadn't done anything very bad. And they didn't ever care much about the law, the cops, the court, that was all pakeha shit. But I thought, maybe that's it. I could have understood that. Then. Then

I got out. I went home. And life was going on. Oh, they said, you're back. You know, like that. Oh, you're back. Get the spare mattress out. We're off down to the pub. Get some chips, eh, here's five bucks, see to the kids, will you? And that was it. They said, hey, and next time, don't get caught, boy. Happy people. I hadn't got them down, at all. They'd really taken it in their stride. Hardly noticed. Was that good? You think I should've understood? Don't you reckon, after everything I'd been through, I should have known better? I was still very stupid.'

He comes back, sits down, rubs his hand over his face briefly.

'My mind was full of strange ideas, considering.'

The impulse, which seems to be outside my own power, to move my hand across the table in some gesture of understanding weakens halfway. I prevent complete surrender to it, but it's there, and he notices.

'And back at Turangi,' he mutters, 'when you said you didn't have any family, there I was, acting the Maori, "What, nobody?", like that was the weirdest thing. Jesus.'

'But you went home. Last week. You went back.'

He nods, slumped in the chair.

'Yes.'

'Why?'

'I don't know. Because...I didn't know what else to do. Or maybe I'm still a bit stupid. There must be something in me that's not, I mean, that wasn't completely'—and he appears to hover on the brink of the word 'dead', which I know is what he intended to say; instead he says, after a moment—'rubbed out.' And looks up. 'You know? Still there.'

I nod. He seems a much weaker person now, more vulnerable. His voice carries on, his own line of thought imposed on mine. 'Maybe it's in everyone,' he says; 'somewhere. No matter what happens.'

He says this vaguely, its implications not fully considered. I don't show what I think of it. If he had looked through a microscope at even the smallest bits of life he would know that the basic impulse is self-preservation. Everything else is decorative, spare-time indulgence. Or, as he should know, treachery, delusion. Yet I feel sympathy for him. It produces itself from this not wholly controllable source within my own experience, something I've set my face against. The movement of my hand across the table was almost as involuntary as the muscular reaction of the limb of a dead animal in dissection, causing the same moment of surprise. But it did have its reason. I can't help it. Is that dangerous and treacherous for me? The feelings he described were the same as those which once nearly beat me down a long time ago; I see the process repeated and extended around another person with the force of a breaking wave, a great mass of social equipment, splintered emotions, broken words, panic, pain, all pounded together indiscriminately. And against what the rational part of my mind tells me, that people losing their balance will convulsively grab at each other, even clutch at strangers by instinct, there is the realisation that something mysterious has to be taken into account since our admission of those vague feelings of recognition between us. The idea that we are not in fact strangers to each other returns unnervingly. It is still inexplicable, beyond this.

With a great effort I stand and pick up the torch.

'Well,' I say, 'come on, we have a lot to do.'

He makes a visible effort himself to concentrate on the immediate moment and push back the confusion the past has begun to loosen and unravel within him. We re-enter the compressed dark of the inner core of the building to find the stairwell, me leading the way with the small beam of light. My hand trembles and the light is unsteady. I am afraid of being trapped again. We go down, along curving corridors, through doors, round and down.

In the lower service areas the light reveals bunches of cables, pipes, wires, ducts, the dead tendrils of the building's nervous system. Without power the place is worse than useless. Control panels show that even the curtains over the windows upstairs are electrically operated. The spaceship is as dead and inert as the pyramids.

And there, in the basement, we find the Civil Defence emergency room, a hollow at the centre of the web of dead circuits, its emptiness holding back the pressure of all the layered tons of concrete. There are telephones, maps, charts; no answers, no signs of surprise. The torch beam seems to dim, as if the darkness is heavy enough to eat away its energy.

'There should be an emergency generator,' he mutters, searching along the walls with the flat of his hands, like a half-blind archaeologist looking for carvings. I hold the light, silent, as he stumbles around. Then I say, 'There's nothing here.' And again, 'Api, there's nothing here. The torch won't last much longer. If we lose this, we'll never find our way out.'

He stops. I hear him sigh.

'Yeah. Okay.'

We trace our way out of the maze, coming up from the catacombs. In the stairwell we climb up flight after flight, making for the top floor. The air pressure lessens. Finally, breathless, we emerge into a hot corridor patched with sun from skylights. A lettered panel says Cabinet Room. The door is unlocked. We go in. A circular table is set beneath a central light well, a roundel of blue sky above. The polished wood gleams. There are soft-upholstered swivel chairs arranged neatly around the table, facing clean blotters and ashtrays. The same vacancy. Traces of dust. A wall clock, gold hands stopped at 6.12; brand name, Omega.

The climb up here has made me light-headed. Absurdities present themselves with no resistance. I look at the round table and think of the court of King Arthur. An enchanted castle. Well; they're all as far gone as that, now. I draw out a chair and sit down, resting the torch and gun on a blotter. Api saunters to the other side of the table and does likewise. The sky is Camelot. Specks of dust float through the column of sun. We say nothing. We seem to be still on the spaceship, machinery silent, in planetary orbit, moving very slightly, the sun mark edging perceptibly across the circle of the table. I remember stories about space journeys which might last ten, twenty, or even hundreds of years. And here, a jumble of history below; the marble floors and Ionic columns, the fleur-de-lys carpets, Victorian ironwork, ageing photographs, bits of Maori carving, concrete air-raid shelters; it's an ark of museum pieces. The end of history; futile junk. So much human effort gone for nothing, all the odysseys, armadas, crusades, cathedrals, epics, symphonies, all heading for 6.12 am last Saturday, a huge perspective with every line focused on a hole in space. Omega. Full stop. The enormity is meaningless. I can feel nothing about it.

Api swivels in his chair, his arm extended, finger tracing an arc across the dust on the table top. His face is back in shadow.

'This is all real, isn't it?' he asks suddenly.

'As far as we know, yes.'

'I mean, what if it's a very good fake? Just like the real thing?'

'And we wouldn't be able to tell? Like the reversed polarity. Is that what you mean?'

'Yes.'

'What for? Why?'

'To watch us. See what we do.'

I shake my head, taking the chance to make the denial I missed before.

'We're not that important.'

'It may only be real to us.' He taps the table.

I sigh.

'You're saying that we're the odd ones out. That everybody else is safe in the real world and they're wondering what happened to us. Because we're missing from the real world. Is that it?'

'Yes.' The voice is soft behind the column of light. 'Well, you know; people go missing. They just vanish. What happens to them?'

I can't see it's any use wasting time on this line of thinking, so I say, off-handedly, 'If this is a replica world, then it'll have enough anomalies to be detectable by the kind of scientific tests I'm going to run.'

'You reckon?' His voice is almost toneless.

'Yes.'

'It is important.' He moves his arms from the tabletop so there is only the black submachine gun lying there with the sun fixed on it like a spotlight. 'Either we find out what happened to them,' he says, 'and find how we can get them back...or we find out what we missed last Saturday...and how we can join them. The second way might be easier.'

I sit impassive. In a way I feel sorry for him because I can understand how he has missed drawing the correct conclusion from what has happened, in particular my description of the crashed plane in Auckland. There is something pitiful about his idea, and it relates to his childhood terror of being abandoned; a pathetic survival of the wish to ransack empty space for the people who ought to be there, to conjure them into existence, combined with the other deeper need to run to the crowd and be forgiven. That is all this means. And he still doesn't know.

He makes a move to get up.

'Do you mind if I ask something?' I say, rather formally.

'No. Go on.'

'Why did you join the army?'

There is a short laugh.

'Oh. Dunno really. Maybe I thought I was a real tough guy after all that. Or...maybe, nothing could be worse.' He pauses. 'And, like I said, I'm a bit dumb.'

He deliberately undermines the reply by the last phrase, using something we both know to be untrue to let me know that he will not answer my question, it's forbidden territory. Perhaps he wants me to deduce that it's all untrue, and hence an oblique warning: his toughness is an illusion, and there were worse experiences after that. It's like the Maori warrior making a ritual scary face as you put a foot forward onto his ground and at the same time placing a stick at your feet which you may pick up if you want to go further. The snag being, that to pick it up, you have to lean over and expose your neck to danger.

We are outside, in the sun, and as I unlock the boot of the car to put back the hammer and tyre lever, I see a glint of steel. Perrin's metal box. I'd forgotten about that. I shall have to find some way of opening it. But not when Apirana is around.

CHAPTER TWENTY-TWO

We make an illusion for ourselves. We seem to be in control of the world but it means nothing. So we hurry through the emptiness like animals that have to keep moving to live. For more than a week we keep ourselves working hard.

To make sure there is nobody else, we drive round bleating the car horn through the suburbs and the Hutt Valley. They are graveyards without bodies. The wind blows over the hills and shakes the grass and trees. Bright plastic flags snap in the air above used car lots. The world is a heap of dead machinery and closed rooms.

We rob shops when we get hungry, eating cold canned food; then speed back to the city, the silence unzipped by the motor then fastening up close behind us all the way.

Apirana fixes a radio transmitter and receiver. We transmit words and morse; we receive nothing. I work at the university, wandering around the various laboratories of the science buildings, visiting the observatory on the hill, checking books in the library, always with Api hovering around to make machines work, to link diesel generators to transformers and power circuits. He insists on installing a generator in the basement car park of the hotel, and we have lights, refrigeration and hot water again. The generators replace the silence with a constant humming and vibrating beneath us, a machine noise like the engines of an ocean liner. We switch off when we want to sleep.

So there is the illusion of meaning and power, centred on us, made by us for ourselves.

With the help of books I delve into areas of physics I can remember little about. I dutifully make checks on radiation levels, the various wavebands of radiation, the positions of fixed stars and constellations, even the cellular structure of plants. All appear to be normal, except for a slightly above-average level of radioactivity around me, no doubt a result of the time I spent in the research centre. I conceal this from Apirana. It would only make him unnecessarily nervous.

In the evenings after work we read from a heap of books and magazines looted fairly randomly from shops and the library. We talk about small things from the past, avoiding what might be dangerous, or deep, by some unspoken consent, except that one evening he drinks several cans of beer and tells me, or the room in which I happen to be sitting, about his woman and how she had promised to wait for him when he was sent overseas; then, after he got back, neither of them were really the same any more, she had changed, couldn't understand him, had rejected him. As far as I can tell, most of the bitterness of this came from the admitted fact that the woman *had* been faithful and waited for him; and I think he is aware that he must have been the one who had changed, though of course he will not say this. I only half-listen; but I wonder what had happened to him that she could not understand or live with.

He wakes with a headache and says he won't drink beer anymore. It isn't good for him. He will drink other things he doesn't like too much.

These trivialities are embedded in our existence, changing focus and dimensions according to our moods or our sense of our own importance. At one level we still seem to want to behave like stranded travellers waiting for normal services to resume, exchanging small talk, thinking: This can't continue much longer; or even: If we behave in any other way, it implies a longer wait. On what would be the Friday of the second week, it occurs to me that Crusoe was alone on his island for more than twenty years. And I think: *Dear God, no*; but without any feeling of being heard or watched. The sense of absence is too powerful for that.

On a second trip to the Hutt Valley, Apirana breaks into the television centre at Avalon and removes a videotape playback unit and a large box of canisters. He sets up this unit in the dining room at the hotel and plugs it into his power supply. The programmes in the canisters seem to be capsules of the most mind-corroding Californian serials. Large cars pursue each other and explode in colour. Guns are fired, biro-red blood squirts from white shirts. Comedies erupt with pre-recorded howls of laughter every eight seconds. Api watches for a while, then switches off.

It seems to have made a mockery of all his technological expertise; worse, for both of us, it's too disturbing a reminder of the old world, it stirs up an unnerving mixture of contradictory feelings. In between looting, we are caretakers. We have enough power to feel we may be the guardians of everything, and if we could remake the world I suppose we would want it to be better. What had he said?—'There are some bastards I wouldn't want back,' or words to that effect. We don't say anything more about it. But in fact there is a hell of a lot we would not want back. We're in limbo, stuck between a gone world which presses threats and memories in on us, vividly, one moment, then falls away into a sullen gulf of ages ago; and a future which is nothing. Which we must not think about. Or speak about. We make each day out of nothing. It is like leaning into space, blindfold. We are powerless to do anything else.

The weather becomes dull, then clears to a hot sun again. One late afternoon on a bright day, Api says he is going for a swim in Oriental Bay; he wants to collect shellfish and catch fresh fish. The water is flat calm, iridescent blue. Wearing blue swimming trunks and equipped with goggles, snorkel, flippers and a spear gun obtained from a sports goods shop, he wades out from the beach and sinks beneath the surface. I sit on some rocks, the Sten gun nearby, watching him wallowing around. I doubt if there are any sharks. And he says he's a good swimmer. But I feel uneasy. He dives several times, the black flippers up-ending, sliding under the surface tension. The glass-like top of the water becomes liquid in ripples, then calms. I've forgotten my sunglasses; I can't see beneath the brightness of the water, it's all polished and sky. He seems to be under for a long time. I stand up. There are bubbles, a faint swirl. The nightmare closes in quickly. It's no use shouting. I clamber across the rocks. Nothing. The light hurts, I can hardly see. The water here must be about a metre deep. I step in, onto sand, and wade forward. He is there, by the next rock, breaking through the surface, blowing water from the snorkel, his hair matted. He wrenches off the mouthpiece, exhales and laughs, eyes crinkling behind the glass visor. The water seems to slide off his skin, over its smoothness, as it would from the skin of a child; he lies back, drifting towards me, the bright line of water making its way up his chest and throat, the ripples shaking his image until it dissolves, childlike, a convulsive movement beneath the pressure of my hand on his head forcing him below the surface with hardly any pressure at first but then a firm hold of my spread hand pressing down to meet the sudden resistance from below, the eyes wide under the water and collecting all the light; child, I know, the struggle, the movements are only instinctive and I can help you hold firm against them because I know from what you let me see in your eyes that you have no control over those movements and this is what you want, this is why you looked to me, still, now, in unbelievable bright liquid staring, the eyes will stay open even after the limbs have all gone slack and the hand has slipped back from the side of the bath. Why don't the eyes close?

A sudden wrench on my arm pulls me forward and I almost lose my balance. The head jerks away. A kick thuds onto my kneecap. In the same instant the water explodes upward, splattering my face in a shock.

The Maori is standing, the spear gun held straight at my chest, less than a metre away. He gasps for breath. The saltwater runs down my face. I blink it aside. We stare, fixed; his eyes wide behind the beads of sea on the glass panel. He spits, savagely.

'What the hell you think you're doing?'

The different images from this and the other day unravel themselves like straightening reflections pulled different ways from a distorting mirror.

How did he trick me? He fooled me into thinking he was drowning. For a moment he's about to fire the spear gun, to kill me. He sees that fear in my face, my amazement at his impulse, his overreaction. He lowers the gun, eyes still fixed on me; chest heaving, mouth open. With his other hand he pulls off the goggles and flings them onto the rocks.

'Don't—' The words stick in my throat.

'What?' he says.

'You tricked me.'

'Jesus!'

There is a tight, clenched silence. We are both trying to work out what has happened. We both want explanations. Excuses, at least. There aren't any. Are there? My mind writhes around. All I can say is, 'You shouldn't have.'

'Me?' he asks, screwing his face into exaggerated bewilderment. '*Me*?'

'I thought you were in trouble. You tricked me.'

'I bloody well *was*!' he interrupts. '*You* weren't fooling, were you? Eh?' He leans forward, very much a stranger, mad, holding his fist towards me, index finger pointing. 'Don't ever try that again. Ever. Right?'

'You were making a joke of it,' I manage to say.

'What?'

'Drowning. You know my son drowned. You shouldn't have done that.'

The anger melts away from his expression; all his facial muscles relax, and his whole body seems to sag. He obviously hadn't thought about it at all. The realisation deflates him. His eyes waver and move away.

'Oh, Christ,' he mutters. In a sudden movement he turns and hurls the spear gun out into deep water. Then, head down, hands on hips, he shakes his head.

'I'm sorry,' I say, the words directed not really to him but to the other images from the past sliding away deaf beneath liquid, under cold earth, into the folds in my mind. I never said it before. It would not have been understood. But I never said it. I'm sorry.

'So am I,' the Maori says. He wrenches the flippers off, climbs out of the water onto a rock and extends a hand down towards me. 'Come on.'

I look up. It makes some kind of sense to him. Not to me. I can't comprehend it. The words cover something which will not be looked at, which is too elusive. All I know is that I have a conscious mind which has adapted itself to a very strange existence. Inside the control that holds my expressions and gestures I suddenly feel helpless, like a thing evolved in liquid under different pressure and weaker gravity, bones gone soft inside a hard shell, carried up by a wave against my will and thrown onto land under a light far too strong.

I raise my hand and he helps me up; solemn, subdued.

That evening I move my eyes from the book I am trying to read, and find he is gazing at me over a glass of wine, thinking intently. Our eyes collide and he slowly looks away. When I try to say that I was afraid of something else, that it wasn't him I was pushing down, it was the memory, it was being reminded of what for me was a nightmare coming up from the past; he drinks carefully and then says, Well, it felt like me, to me.

It is a reply which might sound like one of his self-mocking jokes playing on the responses of an imaginary Maori, a stereotype less intelligent than himself yet part of an identity which is inside him somewhere, useful for saying awkward things. The permission to be frivolous has gone now, so the remark sounds hard. I realise that he dived beneath the water today to play a casual joke of the kind he might have tried out on one of his mates. The extent of his miscalculation went beyond what either of us had imagined; and now he has to estimate how far I am from being one of his mates, and cope with knowing it could be an immense distance. His intuition may have failed him; I may be immune to it in ways he hasn't thought about.

He has been betrayed again. Perhaps he looks back over memories which may be clearer than mine and casts this into the balance.

The evening goes on. Separated from the machinery which used to slice it up and deal it out, time has already become psychological, and although we've kept our watches going to our own guess of hours and minutes, the figures ticked off by the hands no longer have very much meaning. The days appear to have distorted and stretched in places as much as the nights. Within a few hours even a slight lessening of the tension makes the day's events seem to fall back a long way into the past. We want this to happen. So it happens.

Beneath what seems to be vulnerability he is resilient; there are concealed resources for absorbing surprises and making adjustments. My admission that I was not consciously in control of my actions has diminished me, and his manner changes in small, scarcely noticeable details; the emphasis of his gestures, an inflection in the tone of his voice, suggests that he has assumed some of the control I have lost. There is an air of reluctance about this, of someone forced to take on extra duties but he becomes more intent and watchful as well as more decisive. I wonder if I imagine most of this from my helpless feeling. I know for certain only that the expression which occupies him later and increases in the intervals between the attention given to trivialities is a more bitter sadness than before, adding years to his features. It occurs to me that he is older than he ever told me.

I do not feel able to think about the tricks of my own mind. All the cellular energies are being expended in defence, even when the future is an inconceivable blank in which the survival of the mind can serve no useful purpose. I would like to go on living to feel the sun on my face and to have the taste of good food and drink between my teeth; but not to be forced to think, and not to have any more dreams. I accept there would not be any love. As existence reduced to its essentials, this would be less than animal. The decision that it shall prepare itself as a possibility does not seem to be mine, to be made by me. It is merely there. It always has been.

We sit looking out over the city, the darkness so powerful that the dead tower blocks can only be detected by the high spaces of straight-edged black in the night where they blot out the stars.

The faces of our reflections in the window look at each other in the glass.

'What the hell.' He puts the torch on the table. 'Your turn to switch the power off.'

I descend to the generator and make it silent; the lights fade, suck the darkness in; it compresses the yellow patch of the torch. When I get back to the suite on the eighth floor I find he has closed the connecting door between our rooms. I am not surprised. I suppose it is locked from his side. I gently press the catch on the door handle. It slides in with a click.

Now it is locked both ways.

CHAPTER TWENTY-THREE

The terror comes swiftly and simply. One evening towards the end of the second week as we are eating our evening meal at the hotel Apirana says, 'What do we know, then?'

It's the question which we have been avoiding by unspoken agreement and I know instantly that I have to face the demand that it poses. He has been patient. But he has decided to confront the truth and, in effect, call my bluff. I think he realises it will not do any good. Yet he feels he has to ask. I shake my head, spread my hands out.

'I've checked almost everything...'

'And we're no wiser?'

'No.'

The next question is the one which will not be asked: What do we do with our lives, then? In a way, it is already answered. He shows that he knows this, now.

'You know that car I was telling you about?'

'Yes.'

He had seen a car called a Lotus Elite in a salesroom a few days earlier. Apparently it has always been his dream to own one. I can hardly see the point. I know little about cars; I've never understood the attraction they hold for some people.

'I think I'll get it tomorrow.' He looks away. 'Think I'll, you know, go for a drive.'

We sit silent for a long time. My appetite has gone. I drink a little wine but it seems bitter and metallic.

What he has said has enormous implications. It's more than the abandonment of the pretence we've been enacting for nearly two weeks. He is saying that might as well stop; it's useless. But he isn't just going to lie on the beach in the sun and go to sleep. The car, in the terms in which he has described it, represents his ultimate wish; the last request of the condemned man. He hasn't been so explicit. Yet I know what it means, and he intends that I should.

It occurs to me that I have not properly decided in the last two weeks how much we have been humouring each other in prolonging the charade, maintaining the illusion of purpose in what we've been doing. There's no rancour or recrimination involved now. He isn't trying to blame me, and I'm not going to accuse him of giving up too easily. I wonder if he wants to kill himself with the car. I don't think so. No, it's just one of his final options, to admit by stealing the beautiful car that the world of people with power of retribution has gone forever; and by driving nowhere and back, he will acknowledge futility. It is odd that this should appear to be understandable and frightening all at once. We confront it so easily. I had not thought it would be like this.

'You want to come?' he asks, as we drink coffee next day. The weather is still hot but the sky has gone blank, like paper. He has dressed in white corduroy jeans and a Cadbury-purple shirt. This must be how he has conceived it in his fantasies, to impress his friends and women.

'No, I've got some reading to do.'

I know I'm expected to refuse. Should I ask where he's going, or for how long? I can't. The normal structures of those sentences are so commonplace they would reduce even this to bathos. He looks defiantly happy. It's pathetic. I stare out of the window.

There's an interval of half-waking on the border between consciousness and sleep when it's hard to remember where you are; when dreams increase in power and clarity and what you know to be the real world seems to present itself as an unbelievable absurdity. Since this real world has become just that, these moments have increased, elongated, blurred the boundaries.

He goes out. I hear the sound of a car. It shrinks into the distance.

Gradually, as I sit there, the numbness which has fixed on my mind begins to fade and I start to think what I should do.

Now might be the chance to break open Perrin's box. I could use some of the tools Apirana has collected in the basement car park.

After a few minutes I get up and go downstairs to get the key to the boot of my car from my room. I walk along the corridor and go into the room. Then I realise that although we have locked the connecting door between our rooms, we still leave the outer corridor doors unlocked during the day. I stop and go back into the corridor and pause. His door handle moves under the pressure of my hand. I enter his room slowly. And pause again. The curtains are drawn back. The bed is neatly made, army-style, all wrapped tight. Clothes hang to attention in the wardrobe. I walk forward carefully. What should I look for? I want a clue, something to tell me a fraction more about him than he has told me so far.

There's a duffle bag, black with white stripes, a small suitcase, and an army kitbag, standing near the wall. If I disturb anything, he will know. I face the case and gently lower it flat to the floor. Then I press back the fastener clips. They spring aside. It's unlocked. I life the lid. There seems to be nothing inside but some old pairs of denim jeans, maroon T-shirts, and paperback novels. Beneath all that, an LP, *The Best of Feliciano*, the cover frayed and inscribed in biro: *Love to Api XXX Bubby.*

I close the case and place it back precisely by the wall. I am sweating. Moving across the room I look over the dressing table. Various odds and ends: a plastic hairbrush, the white cord for an electric razor, a bottle of aftershave lotion, a small vinyl picture holder propped against the frame of the wall mirror containing a black-and-white photograph of a serious-faced Maori girl. The Gideon Bible, scraps of paper sticking out from the red-edged pages. A clip of bullets. A silver coin, foreign, possibly Malaysian, threaded onto a necklace chain of silver links. This is below the girl's photograph. I look up and see my reflection tensed in the mirror.

The wardrobe door is half open. Inside, mainly shirts on hangers. The black trousers, neatly creased. A dark jacket. I put my hand into the wardrobe and swing the jacket carefully round a little. There is a wallet in the inside right pocket; I lift it out. Old, brown imitation leather. It opens to reveal some ten- and twenty-dollar bills, a driver's licence, a plastic identity card, the photograph he showed me earlier of his girlfriend, possibly the same face as the other photograph but hard to tell; nothing else, except a few addresses on a folding calendar card bearing the insignia of an insurance company. I slip each item back. As I hold the wallet up to replace it in the pocket my fingers trace the edge of what seems to be another piece of card. I look closer. There must be another compartment. Yes. A zip is concealed under a fold. I unfasten it and take out a cellophane wrapper. It contains six coloured photographs; Polaroid, glossy.

The dominant colours are greens and reds. They are all outdoor photos. The greens shade from the bright emerald tones of tropical plants, leaves, and grass, to the dull khaki of soldiers' uniforms. The reds are the meat and blood of pieces of human bodies. At first it is hard to see what is there. And then it is suddenly clear. The amputated parts of shattered human beings have been collected for the photographer. The victims are presumably Vietnamese; one soldier is holding up by the hair a severed head connected to part of a shoulder and an arm, and the head is Asian, slightly bloated, an eye missing, but the face of a youth of about sixteen. It is hard to guess. Another photo shows the remnants of a man whose penis has been removed. He is naked, sprawled like a shop window doll, very pale on stained dark grass and reddish-brown earth. There is a photograph of a pattern of parts of bodies set out on dark earth. All the photographs include glimpses of the soldiers standing around. A fair-haired man in a khaki singlet features in two pictures. The last photo shows a large heap of mutilated bodies; above them, two men looking at the camera, arms resting on each other's shoulders. The man on the right is grinning, his white teeth the only feature visible beneath the shade of a forage cap. Both men are dressed in combat gear, and both seem to be Maoris. The one on the left, who has tipped his helmet back rakishly so that the sun on his face is making him squint, is Apirana Maketu.

CHAPTER TWENTY-FOUR

The easiest way to kill him would be with sleeping pills in a drink. He will not suspect anything. I have left everything exactly as it was. So I have the advantage.

How dangerous is he? He seems fairly normal, but I know that can be deceptive. The retching sensation rises in the back of my throat again. I hold it in, swallowing hard. I am in the dining room, seated, holding the arms of the chair.

I must remember what he said, try to think back. He said, they wanted to make him obey orders, to pull the trigger, to kill. Then later, he said, that Sunday, nobody would admit—or was it, nobody would believe—the answer, if you asked, have you killed people? And he asked if he was evil. I remember that. And then tried to dodge, turned it all around, aimed it back at me.

He hid from me about how long he'd been in the army.

In war, yes, they'd obey orders. Shoot. There were no clear battlelines. I know that much. But what's that got to do with those...obscenities? What would make them do *that*? And pose themselves in pictures of it? Who would *keep* such things?

What if he wanted me to find them? He could have locked them away somewhere, more secure. I might have done exactly what he expected me to do. He wanted to confess all along. But he couldn't. No, that doesn't make sense. But insane people *don't* make sense.

I get up and open the top windows. The air is humid, unmoving. A white haze hides the distance. The hills look like piles of waste by a pool.

Before, the land had threatened or unsettled me by its nothingness, it had seemed to want to suck living and moving identities dry of life and absorb them into the vacuum. Now I can sense a more active vibration emanating very faintly from beyond the temporary structures of these rooms and blocks. As if it had detected after a huge spread of time spent silent and waiting, a hint, finally, of complete triumph; and now it was daring to stir itself for the kill. Softly, like a thing furred with decay, something immensely ancient becomes intent and flexes its death-energy. It has been there forever. The Maoris must have absorbed it for ages without fully knowing, like inhaling the spores of a mould or a bone-marrowing radiation. Those carvings, the masks of faces howling outwards from their shelters, must have been meant to repel it. Or to want to throw it out, like vomit. That braying sound I thought I heard by Taupo as the sun went down the night before I met the Maori, that might have been its signal. It wanted an answer, an echo from the base of our brains. It knows what is inside.

I stand there, firm against it, my mind forcing back the hostile resonance. The rancour is almost a perceptible taste. It will be cheated of me. It will not win.

A screech of noise echoes round the towers like an animal trapped in machinery. My heart stops, in shock, then pounds away at double speed.

There is a shout. I look down from an open window. The figure is standing by a bright red car, waving and sounding the klaxon horn.

'Come on down!'

I get the shotgun. At the top of the stairs I stand and pause, taking deep breaths. I must keep control.

Below, he is leaning on the car, excited, one arm extended across the roof above the windscreen, the owner embracing his new toy. Posing for a photograph. The images blur in front of me.

'Well?' he asks.

'Where did you go?' is all I can say.

'Motorway to Porirua and back, then on the Hutt motorway.' He seems impatient, and taps the top of the windscreen. 'See anything?'

'What?'

'Look.' He points. I move closer, puzzled. The windscreen slopes back, reflecting a distorted stretch of the concrete block and the white sky. A long smear extends up the centre of the glass on the outer surface. I lean over, glancing at him. He is on the other side of the car, nodding, eyes very bright.

The smear is what is left of a disintegrated fly or wasp obliterated at high speed, a blotch of pulpy yellow pus and dark red blood flecked with bits of black. I draw in breath, my teeth and lips clenched tight.

'A fly,' he says, triumphantly. I straighten up. The butcher's red of the car burns into my retina. 'It means they're still around,' he goes on. 'You know what you said.'

'It means you killed an insect,' I reply.

'What's wrong?'

'It doesn't make sense.'

'Why not?'

'Just one? After three weeks?'

'There'll be others. I mean—' He stops.

'There would have been more. The rate they breed.'

'We might not have seen them.'

'We'd have seen them all right.'

'It was when I was coming back, along the motorway, just now.' He turns, points, and turns back. Then, uncertain, the excitement gone, he stares at me. 'Well what does it mean, then?'

'I don't know.'

'You must bloody know. You said, when we—you *must* bloody well know.'

'I said if there were any left, they'd breed if they weren't sterile.' He closes his eyes, suddenly, and bangs his hand on the roof of the car. 'Maybe there was only one left. And you killed it. Or maybe—'

'Maybe what?'

'Somebody's playing a joke.'

He opens his eyes.

'Oh, for Christ's sake!' There must be something about my manner which for the first time, as his excitement subsides, strikes him as different. He detects a change. 'What's wrong with you?' he says. 'Anything happen, while I was—'

'I don't feel so good today. That's all.'

'How? How d'you feel?'

'It's nothing.'

'Oh, come on, man, if you get sick—'

'It's just a...stomach ache.'

'Bad?'

'No. It's okay.'

'We both ate the same stuff. I'm okay. You didn't drink any water?'

'No.' I move back towards the hotel. 'I'll just take it easy for a while.'

He stands by the elegant machine with the death-mark smeared down its face. Brave soldier. You expect a medal?

'I'll clean it off then,' he says. A pause. 'There'll be others. They'll start to come back.'

I turn, holding the glass door, and look at him. Not very long ago I would have taken a scientific view of the phenomenon. Now the structure of objects which compose this scene and have blended into the making of this event seem malevolently organised. I have been too naïve.

I say nothing. I nod, and go inside.

He spends the rest of the day tinkering with the car

engine. I sit upstairs pretending to read one of the books, a Koestler theory about synchronicity. I can't eat in the evening. He has a meal alone at the far end of the room. We make small talk.

The blocked panic inside me makes a pain like acid dammed against nerve endings. I start to see strange objects. There are bits of litter scattered here and there on the carpet. Scraps of paper, wrappers, corks, cellophane glinting in the light, dark marks, shadows, things half-seen under chairs and tables. From the corner of my eyes they change. The carpet is dark green. There are stains. White bits of raw bone. Human segments. A red edge on flesh. An eye knocked from its socket. I can't look directly. The book trembles. I steady it on the chair arm. The pain has narrowed my range of vision so I can only look ahead, and my spine seems fixed to prevent efforts to move.

He comes and sits opposite, still chewing, and puts his feet up on another chair. The bones and muscles work beneath the surface of his face. He drinks dark red wine. And even jokes about the insect.

'What if there was only one, eh? And I had to hit it. I mean, kill the only one left!'

He clasps his arms on his chest, holding the stem of the wine glass. His eyes glance at his wrist, then at me, then back at his wrist after a pause. The action is nothing. But it happens at the dangerous corner of my sight. It's not ordinary. Not at all. I know what he is doing. He can detect my pulse rate from the vein next to the carotid artery in my neck, he's timing it for sixty seconds by his watch. Abnormal. Extremely abnormal.

Was that really his face in the photograph? The inner muscles slide around deviously. I try to connect the images. He swallows; the face skin goes slack as though hanging from the upper bones of the skull. I remember my own face in the mirror and how something has the power to change what is familiar and remould it beyond recognition.

'You should get some sleep,' he says.

I unlock the connecting door between our rooms on my side. He is in the basement switching off the generator. I place the gun ready by the bed. I shall stay awake. And wait to see what he might do.

When the light goes the darkness is so complete there are no walls or ceilings, and the sensation with eyes open or closed is the same, a great floating and turning in space.

CHAPTER TWENTY-FIVE

The long oblong panels shine down a white fluorescent illumination even and clear over the whole room. They dehydrate colours and cast no shadows so that everybody in the place moves around with no shadow as if in a new dimension. They have begun to cease to exist.

The whispering seems to stop when I turn. I happen to glance at people who are talking and see them look away in another direction furtively. The usual secrecy of the centre has an added intensity. It thickens around me at a certain distance. When I enter rooms or move towards people there is a feeling that new conversations are suddenly begun, and certain subjects are avoided. They no longer mention their wives or children.

Perrin leaves a paper on my desk. The research committee want a report on our work. There have been doom-laden articles in scientific journals about the ethics of genetic engineering: *US Experts Warn of 'Terrible Risks'.* There is talk of a departmental investigation.

I am in the car going back to my flat in the winter dark, rain spotting the windscreen and the wipers rhythmically flicking it away, cleaning a space, flicking it away, and I remember the needles on the dials of the sonic frequency machine at the lab flicking across and back time and time again. Then there is a noise, a squeal of a dog and the tyres, and I can hear my own pulse. I come up through the darkness and the doctor says you probably have slight concussion, it wasn't very serious, just a bump, these tablets will help with the headaches but be careful with them.

Atkinson is driving me back from work until my car is mended. Probably shouldn't say this but in strictest confidence of course Perrin is a bit worried about you, the strain of, er, and then we have been working very long hours on the project, it's bound to tell, and you're due for some leave so why not take a couple of weeks off and have a bit of rest, Bay of Islands, Coromandel, Taupo, somewhere you can get away from it all.

Well, I'll tell you what I think and I don't much care if it reaches Perrin's ears. He wants me out of the way when the next quarterly research committee meeting comes round. No, it's true. The research grants will be cut next year and he knows his project will get downgraded if he hasn't produced any results. Whilst I'm away he'll persuade the D-G to have me transferred back to your section because you're short-staffed. Then he'll use my idea for high frequency sound waves and when it works his section will get all the credit.

Oh now I don't think that's it at all, I'm sure he has

your best interests at heart and there is a bit of concern about the possible effects of high frequency sound waves, well, concern about the effects on basic metabolisms and the resonating of the molecular structure, it's very much an unknown quantity. And the physicists are worried about this 'feedback amplification problem' or whatever they call it, about which we know less than zero—

You're in on this, aren't you? He's put you up to it.

No, for heaven's sake, it's not like that. All I'm saying is that now you've had this accident with the car and been shaken up a bit, you have a good reason to slip off for a couple of weeks.

I see the truth. I can tell by Atkinson's tone of voice. I might say the wrong things to the committee; they want me out of the way. Perrin is afraid.

I am in the flat at Takapuna. There is never anybody there. I work later hours and fill the time to avoid having to spend too long in the flat by myself. At weekends I lose track of time altogether. One day I am in a shop and I cannot remember why. One Sunday it is evening and I find myself sitting staring at the wall. For how long? Have I had a meal? I go into the kitchen and check the dishes in the sink to try to work out if I have had a meal because I cannot remember. The plates have piled up. It is not possible to tell. One evening I wake in front of the television and a singer comes on and I shout for Joanne to come in because he is her favourite singer. Of course Joanne is not there. I am aware of what is happening.

Then one day at work there is a mistake. The frequency setting on the sound modulator is turned from low, B1, to much higher, B10, which is easy to do because the figures look similar and the decimal points are not clear. Inside the radiation chamber I have samples of DNA molecules from a range of viruses, fungi and bacteria, and from selected insects, birds, and animals, including human samples.

It should be quite straightforward. I am alone in the radiation unit and the door is closed. I switch on. The samples have already been irradiated. The insulating headphones clamped over my ears register the tonal signal of the frequency. I know immediately the setting is wrong. But in the instant it takes to reach up and switch off, I feel something gigantic happen, something which seems to stop time and rush through the structure of the room and the cells of my blood and the inside of my skull. It waves me aside like a wing beating past. The sound is a great slam of reverberating white noise in the distance of somewhere else altogether, another universe, far beyond the frequency of what animals can hear and see; unimaginable. Even as it happens I can feel that it's still only a hint of something even more immense, a near miss in the dark from a pitch-dark force like a locomotive the size of a planet brushing past the front of my face. Because it seems to be both inside and outside me at the same moment the feeling is dream-like, of being lifted and shaken in sleep. But I manage to switch off. The whole impulse must have lasted less than a second.

The room has gone suffocatingly quiet. The floor is sliding and leaning up against me, banging my arm and side and then pressing on my back. The long oblong panels shine down from the ceiling above very even and clear.

They cast no shadows. People appear. They move strangely. Their faces look down at me.

Then Perrin is saying you have been working too hard, either you go on leave or the department will have to temporarily suspend you. The words are rehearsed. His face seems already dead, the skin a cellophane wrapping over a pack of dehydrated meat.

The electron micrograph pictures show that I must have forgotten to place at least half the taxonomically diverse organisms in the radiation chamber, because the molecules of *Bacillus megaterium*, at .60 on the ratio scale, and the fungus *Aspergillus niger* at 1.00, and all the other bacteria and viruses, are structurally normal, but the slides of the DNA samples from insects, at 1.41, animals, birds, and human beings, all in the range from 1.36 to 1.40, are completely blank. The machine cannot be faulty because it registers the lower organisms.

I know I may be unable to remember. I have to admit to myself, as well as to Perrin, that I cannot be absolutely certain. So he has what he wants at last, and I shall go on leave, after checking and rechecking the slides that show nothing. Because if I am not at fault, then the entire structure of biomolecular science falls apart and all my work falls with it. I have been feeding years and years of effort into an idiot's waste bin. It has been my whole life. And I have given up much more than any of the others; very much more. This was my only area of certainty, a clean world in a capsule where there were clear rules and no shadows, all sealed and protected against the outside, like me; it was all I could rely on. Had I uncovered a black hole at the heart of it?

I would admit the lesser of two evils with most of my mind, and say I may have been wrong for a moment.

An intense tiredness begins to drown me. The strain to resist it becomes more and more difficult. My effort trembles the faces and the shape of the room. The danger shakes me. When I hit back against the people staring down, the dream splits open. I wake to find the Maori clutching my left wrist, looming over me, indistinct in the half-light of a torch which is propped on a chair by the bed. He's got a gun in his other hand. We stare at each other for a moment until I can divide the dream images from the reality of the dimness here.

'You were shouting,' he says, letting my wrist go. 'You okay?'

My mouth is dry; I have trouble speaking.

'Yes. It's alright.'

He sees me looking at the gun.

'I didn't know what was happening.' He exhales and walks slowly to a chair and sits. I can see enough of his expression to detect an unusual nervousness.

'Nightmare,' I say. He nods.

'You remember it?'

'No.'

It is true; no deception. The events of the dreams slide past me as if I have tunnel vision and can't turn to look back. They seem to gather at the back of my head at an unseeable point.

'I remember mine,' he says. He becomes pensive.

'What did I shout?'

'Eh? Oh, don't know. Couldn't tell.' His face composes

itself into a carving of frowns. 'I think I always remember mine,' he repeats.

'What are they about?' I ask, as tonelessly as possible. His features don't move.

'Things that have happened to me.' He sighs, then nods towards the window. 'It's raining. Getting colder now. End of summer.'

I listen and there is the faint sound of rain rustling on the window.

'I reckon we ought to get out of Wellington,' he says suddenly, as though he's been giving it some thought. 'I don't like it here. I think it's...'

'It's what?'

'Aw...kind of...I think it's getting at us. Don't you?'

'Where will we go?'

'I can work an outboard motor. We could get one of those small boats and cross Cook Strait. There might be someone in the South Island.'

'You said you didn't know anything about boats.'

'I can work an outboard.'

'I'm useless with boats.'

'We could make it. Wait for a calm day.' He rubs his face wearily. 'It'll be okay. But you get better first, eh?'

'Alright, then.'

There is a pause. I can see that his concern for me is a dry piece of calculation. How much should I trust him? He's had chances to kill me. But he needs me alive.

I don't think he knows how closely I observe him, or what deductions I can make. In the movement of expressions across his face an almost childlike openness is always being betrayed or replaced by something hard and at the same time subtle, exactly like a mask carved in great secrecy a long way from the light, covered in intricate, devious designs all with concealed meanings; the result came from the gradual working away in half-light of opposing forces, one trying to wear down the other and being blindly resisted.

'I once heard this story,' he says, 'ages ago, can't remember where I got it from. It was about these people who are trapped some place. There's this door or gate, I think. It's fastened up. The point is, when they work out the right words to say, the door will open, or they'll be able to get out some way. Each one, separate. Different words for each one. Or for some of them, they have to do something, and that will open the way out. They don't all see what it is.' He glances at me. 'Because it's whether they understand what went wrong, how they got trapped there. They've got to understand, and then and then—'

He stops. The same impulse to confess; I see the reason more clearly now. It forms itself into a religious image filtered through second-hand legends from *Pilgrim's Progress* or Dante or *Grimms' Fairy Tales*, stories I can remember too, vaguely.

'Abracadabra,' I say.

'What?' He turns and looks.

'The magic formula. When you say the right words the door opens on the cave full of treasure. It's from the *Arabian Nights*.'

'Is it?' He frowns and shakes his head. 'No, don't think that was it.'

'You still think we missed something good because we survived,' I say, wearily.

'Well. Is this good?' he asks, waving his hand at the dark. 'You do all those tests, with machines and bits of paper. How would they tell you? They know down from up, and north from south, but they don't know good from bad. You said, the world's the same as far as they can tell. I mean, we know that's not bloody true.' He stands and looks down at me. 'I still reckon there's a reason why we're here.'

'There doesn't have to be.'

'There's got to be. And we could be the last people to ever know what the hell it is, because if we knew we wouldn't be here.' He picks up the torch and holds it down so that both our faces are obscured. 'Try and remember, when you wake up.' His voice shades between a plea and a threat; without seeing his features it's hard to tell.

'Remember what?'

'What makes your dreams so bad.'

He walks back into his room, the pool of light held down, vast shadows hunching and slanting over the walls and flat ceiling. The door closes and the lock clicks this time with no furtive secrecy. The sound is meant to snap against my mind.

Everything has changed. I know he is a murderer. How have I let him get so much power? What does he think I forget?

The rain increases. It rattles against the window like tapping fingernails.

The day breaks from a pack of heavy clouds. Rainwater glistens everywhere like impacted glass. He wants to drive down to the harbour near the swimming pool to select a boat. He persuades me to go with him in the Lotus Elite. I eat breakfast and am apparently recovered so there is no excuse to stay behind. I have to admit the car is rather good. It smells very new inside and everything squeaks slightly.

'I wanted one in lemon yellow with tan upholstery,' he says, as we drive down the Terrace, 'but this was all they had. Red and black. Bit crude really.' He wrinkles his nose. 'I've got good taste, you know. Where are the rich suburbs round here? That's where they'll have the best cars, eh? I wouldn't mind having a go in a Jensen. Or a Rolls.'

The banter seems to go on regardless of me or the weak attempts to respond. The displaced word 'they' has sealed itself in a special vacuum. His joking breaks this open with a subversive mockery directed outwards at the negative force, taunting it.

The car hisses over wet roads. The rain has stopped but loaded clouds are coming in to land too low, colliding with the tops of hills and being torn to mist in a slow film. The single windscreen wiper flicks away remaining bits of rain with a few arrogant movements, then squeals to be stopped.

I walk around the wharf whilst he explores the boats and breaks into several sheds looking for equipment. There is a long building on one of the jetties with sliding doors set back about three metres from the edge of the jetty. As I stroll along by this building I feel strangely reluctant to walk directly round the far corner; as if I might bump into something. So I stop, about five metres away, and then walk out diagonally to the edge of the jetty and continue to stroll along, so that I can see round the corner from a distance before I reach the end of the building. There is nothing there. When I get to the end of the jetty I turn and look back. Apirana is standing by a boat on the slipway staring at me, unmoving. I turn and walk to the other side of the end of the jetty and look down the back of the long building. There are only a few rusting cans and a couple of lifebelts there. When I walk back into Apirana's line of sight around the corner again he is still standing in the same attitude, gazing with catlike intensity at the corner of the building where I reappear. I stroll along back to the slipway, and look down at him. He has a spanner and an oil-stained rag in his hands.

'What's wrong?' he says.

'I don't know. I just felt nervous about going round the corner.'

There is a pause.

We both stare back at the jetty and the long building. Water slaps on the concrete slipway and boats heave and creak against rubber tyres looped over the edge of the jetty. The water out in the bay is a sullen green, bursting open in places with curls of foam from the tops of waves; a ripped quilt with a heaving underneath.

'You see anything?' he asks. I turn.

'No. Why?'

'I just looked up. I thought something was going to happen. I saw you stop, and walk out and go round.'

'There's nothing there.'

'Where's your gun?'

'The shotgun? Back in the car.'

He fumbles in the pockets of the waterproof windbreaker he's wearing and produces one of his handguns, a .38 calibre revolver. His Sten gun is lying by the slipway. He holds the revolver up and puts it on the jetty at my feet.

'You ought to carry one of these,' he says. When I hesitate, he insists. 'No, take it. It's safer than the shotgun.'

I pause, then pick up the gun. It weighs heavily in my hand. I put it in my pocket. I'm wearing a parka from one of the sports shops we looted two weeks ago.

'Alright. Might as well.' I glance at him. 'What did you expect to see?'

He wipes his hands on the rag, looking away.

'Dunno. But when you went behind the building there...I wasn't so sure you'd come back.'

The cold goes into my bones; I steady myself against shivering.

'You were looking straight at me when I came round the corner.'

'Yes. I knew something would come back. But I mean, I wasn't sure what.'

'Oh, come on. You didn't even pick up your gun.'

'If you'd come round the corner and found me pointing the gun at you—'

He shakes his head, leaving the possibilities, the conclusion, open. It's murderous. The fact that we're nervous about each other has been recognised and used; potentially deadly, but so easily and simply done.

'Yes. I see.' I look back at the building and then down at Apirana. 'Something almost happened, then.'

'Too right.'

'I thought, it's a kind of joke. Nothing here, though.'

'That was the bloody joke.'

He turns away and goes on with his work, checking a large outboard motor attached to a small launch. I sit down on a bench at the side of the jetty where I can see both the building and Apirana. The breeze chops at the water, wrinkling the reflections in puddles on the level concrete path. Obviously the weather won't let us escape for a few days yet. It will be too rough in Cook Strait.

The outboard kicks and roars to life, churning the water and defiantly biting aside the silence which has stuck like a glutinous mass round the wharf. Apirana's teeth grin in a white line across his face and he gestures with his thumbs raised. The boat is tied to the jetty. He tests the motor; the tone and pitch of its snarl change as the propeller blades chew at the sea. Patches of dirty froth bob on the surface. The smell of oil and carbon monoxide blows around. The noise seems to clear the air with the violence of a released animal. I sense that Apirana knows this, and he brings the roar to a crescendo before cutting it silent. A few minutes later he joins me on the jetty, wiping his hands clean on a rag scented with petrol.

'Good motor. We'll have a few practice runs here before we take her out.'

'Have to wait for the weather to clear. You won't get me out in this.'

'Should be okay in a coupla days. You get seasick?'

'Yes.'

'So do I. Don't know what canoe we came on.'

He covers the engine with a tarpaulin and closes the shed door. Then, picking up his Sten gun, he says: 'Let's go for a drive, eh? Get away from here for a while. Show you how she goes. Up to a hundred in seven seconds.'

'Alright. Take it easy though. The roads are wet.'

'Yes, officer.' He gives a mock salute.

We get in the car. The seatbelt presses the gun against my ribs. I decide not to loosen the belt. Apirana starts the car and turns it in a wide sweep, blatting the exhaust towards the wharf. Then we take off along the quayside roads and out along the Hutt motorway rising in a long curve by the bay. The mass of the city falls behind in a jumble of grey and white towers. We go faster, easily, the speed pressing us down gently in our seats. The speedometer flicks to a hundred and past. The dipping front of the car sweeps the air apart smoothly. Apirana glances at me and grins, turning the wheel to glide by the odd car and truck standing empty in the lanes. We're not expecting anything to happen, we've won for today, it's all shrinking behind us in the distance, and when the figure, the woman in a blur of white dress, darts out from a stalled car waving her arms frantically I hardly have time to shout. We jerk to the left in a vicious screech of tyres skidding on the wet road, sliding sideways, Api cursing and wrenching the wheels as he lets the brakes go then treads down again and, wham, there's a heavy thud, the hills and sky whip around, the seatbelts wrench at us, and we slam to a stop against the dividing rail facing back towards the city.

Hit by the side of the car in the wide skid, a doll-like figure sprawls on the far lane, white dress rippling around in the wind. I scrabble at the seatbelt catch, punch it free, leap out and try to run across but the skid and shock of the crash make me stumble like a drunk. Api can't get out. His door is jammed on the crash rail. He can't free his seatbelt. I turn back as he shouts, but he's clawing his way free over my seat and yelling to me to get to the woman.

She lies in a twist on the road, barefoot, one leg splayed out awkwardly, head facing up, blood starting from long grazes on her outstretched arms. She is a Polynesian, young, mid-twenties, skin a soft caramel brown, hair in long jet-black tendrils, one strand across her mouth. She's breathing. Unconscious. Her face looks merely asleep.

I kneel by her side, reach out, draw back the hair from her mouth. Suddenly blood runs from her nose, down the sides of her face. Api slumps opposite, his eyes staring frantically; he is rubbing the palms of his hands in convulsive movements on his jeans, cursing; No, oh God, no, nothing I could do, she just ran out, I couldn't—Jesus, what can we do—

He drags a handkerchief out and goes to dab at the blood on her face. I make a movement to stop him.

'Careful. Don't move her.'

He glares at me. I begin to take off my parka, to cover her. He takes off his jacket, too.

'Get rugs from the cars, coats, anything.' I tell him. He sprints off to ransack the stationary cars whilst I look after her as best I can. The blood has gone very dark and congealed. I gently tip her head back, feeling her skull. Then I draw her jaw down to open her mouth. She might choke on the blood. Her white teeth part.

Api comes back with rugs. He makes a pillow for her head but I motion him away. We cover her.

'Drive back and get an ambulance from the hospital,' I say. He looks at the car vacantly.

'I just—I never saw her, she just came out—'

'Her leg might be broken. I think she's got concussion. We can't take her in the car—'

He stands, starts to run, comes back.

'You go. I'll stay with her.'

'No. You drive. Get an ambulance. There'll be first-aid kits and stretchers in it.'

He runs to the car, climbs in, crashes the gears and drives off towards the city, a grind of metal as he pulls away from the dividing rail. The tyres screech. The blue haze of burned rubber blows away. The car noise fades.

I look down. She's still breathing regularly but her face has gone the white of candle wax and the bloodstains look very dark. I'm shivering, going into shock myself. I walk to the dividing rail with its dented impact scar and smear of red paint; leaning over it I retch and vomit, barking out acid remnants of the tinned fruit I ate for breakfast. Then I stumble across to the woman and kneel by her, helpless.

He's right. What can we do?

Where did she come from? The car is an old white Cortina, heavily rusted. It seemed as if she was hiding behind it; as if she ran out at the last moment.

She moves slightly, making a small whimpering sound; her head lolls sideways. There are too many rugs and coats on her. I carefully lift my parka from her feet and replace it with a tartan rug Api brought from the old car. She is barefoot. About eight metres away there is a sandal on the wet road. I put my parka on again, the gun heavy in the pocket.

Come on, Api. Hurry. Come on, man.

I rub my hands on my arms. It does seem cold now. The sky has gone darker. It might rain again.

Where has she been the last three weeks? I stare at her wax face. She looks more like an Islander than a Maori. Samoan, perhaps. Not that I could really tell. From Auckland? Not from here, any of these suburbs. We checked them all, thoroughly. We drove for miles, and ages. *We checked everywhere.*

She moves again. I think she will die. I sit on the wet concrete and hold her hand. The knuckles are grazed. The hand is not very warm; but soft, and limp.

I look round. The emptiness seems to expand into an even vaster nothing, grey-blank, taking some part of my mind to a distance and letting me see the scene separately. The sky and hills are stuck together. The horizon has vanished. We are two figures on a great concrete arena, a stage without edges. How could we have done this? How?

Don't die. I massage the hand gently. I lean closer to her face and whisper, you mustn't die. You'll be alright now.

There are no witnesses.

Nobody sees.

Or hears.

CHAPTER TWENTY-SIX

She lies in the bed at the hotel where we have so carefully placed her; unconscious, all night, so not in pain, not knowing how much she should be in pain. In the evening we light candles, but Apirana goes down then and starts the generator for the electric lights. The candles seem wrong. Neither of us speaks much. We watch her intently. If our will to make her live counted for anything she would be awake. But it doesn't, and she is not. She becomes the centre of everything; broken, silent. Again, the mystery has wrenched itself into a new shape. It has contracted and become more urgent, and at the same time expanded, seizing new areas.

We have brought her to the hotel because we have food and power here; these rooms are on the first floor. But we argue at the far end of the room, away from her, in low voices, urgently. He wants to take her to the hospital for an X-ray. I convince him we couldn't operate the machine, even with power; we don't know how. He insists I drive there to get drugs. I do so, leaving him sitting by her, shocked and pale. She's got to be alright, he says.

At the hospital I collect penicillin, an oxygen cylinder and mask, morphine, sleeping tablets, hypodermics, valium and librium, a nitrous oxide cylinder and some chloroform and antiseptics. Back at the hotel I again try to detect if she has broken her legs; the left leg below the knee looks swollen, but there is no apparent fracture. She may have internal injuries, or broken ribs. There is bad bruising. Perhaps we only hit her a glancing blow. But when she was thrown onto the concrete, she may have fractured her skull. Even if we knew that, what could we do?

We clean the blood from her closed face, bathe her arms and knee with warm water and antiseptic, and apply bandages.

Neither of us can sleep. We take it in turns to try. I leave Apirana watching over her, the light dimmed to a small glowing patch. He smoothes the hair back from her forehead with his big hand, resting his hand lightly on her forehead, and when I lie down in the next room I can hear him whispering to her.

An hour later he comes through the connecting door into the room where I am staring at the ceiling and says we should have tried to find out her name by searching the car. If we know her name it may help.

I say there is no point going out there now, in the dark, it will be light in five or six hours.

He says he will go when it's light. He thinks she is Samoan. There is a long silence after he returns to her bedside. Then I hear his voice again but in a different tone; still low, yet more decisive and speaking as if somebody is listening to him. I get up and walk to the door and look in. He is kneeling by the bed with his head buried in the Bible. I watch for a moment and then go and lie down again. At some point I fall half-asleep to the pulse in my skull of a windscreen wiper beating away bits of blood on glass.

At dawn he goes out to search the car on the motorway. I sit by the woman. Her breathing is shallow and regular. A new colour has gradually come to the surface of her skin, a translucent light gold. She looks peaceful and beautiful with the composed expression of someone who is settled down ready for an immense journey. At the same time I know this to be a deception, a collection of mere surface effects. Her metabolism is deceiving itself. As I watch her I see the change begin to take place within half an hour. It is as if the message passed from one level to another, and the survival mechanisms of the inner chains of command realised what was happening and began to resist. The same old sequence; involuntary, uninterested in whether the main process might be good, bad, peaceful, beautiful, or anything else; just the spasmodic struggle for survival at any cost. A restlessness and a disturbance in the steady rhythm of the breathing, barely noticeable at first, is the start of the change. I wonder why I have to watch this. Like any war, because in every sense that is what it is, it will be useless and frightening; it will make nothing but pain. I have to sit now and see it beginning. The map of her face is gradually altered; new lines are drawn. The peace is at first only faintly disturbed. Then it disappears, seeming so unnatural and fragile, not at all a normal condition but an irrelevance.

I can not whisper any consolations. It is never any use and the waste of words made in the past to people who never heard has drained a hollow inside me, of words sent into mute spaces and abandoned spirals. Hard to remember the time when I tried, and wished people to listen.

She begins to move her arms feverishly in small movements over the bedclothes. I put my hand down to hold her wrist but it pulls away. Her face frowns and tightens and I lean over and gently hold her arm.

I sense that I am being made to play a part. He has put that idea in my head, said it, in various ways, shown it, over and again. It was there, on the motorway, the feeling of being posed in a scene, the hills ranged around, the concrete ramp an immense stage or set and the silence waiting. The day before, he was alone, and given a warning. He came back with blood on the car. Then he made me drive with him. I had to be made accomplice to this.

The daylight seeps between the curtains. I reach up, pause for a moment, incomprehensibly stopped in the most normal of movements; then I pull the cord to split the curtains open. The light falls into the room in a soft rush like something which has been dammed.

I hear him returning. He will not have found any evidence to let us know who she is or how she came to be there. I can tell that we will not be able to find out. I am facing facts which seem to be part of a pattern of necessities. It demands that she remain as inexplicable as ourselves and the world we are in.

He is angry that the car has refused to provide clues. I think he must have almost torn it to pieces. Nothing.

'Is she waking up?'

'I think so.'

'Is that good?'

'She'll be in pain.'

'Get the morphine.'

I shake my head. 'Not yet.'

An hour later when I come down from the dining room with food and coffee, she is moaning and threshing about, trying to say words. The fragments of syllables could be Samoan. Her dark hair spreads over the pillow and tangles across her forehead as she turns from side to side. Apirana tries to hold her down.

'You know how to give injections?' he asks.

'Yes. But I'm not sure if we should.'

He looks impatient. 'Give me the hypodermic.'

I hesitate. His lips compress.

'Give me it.'

'Do you know how?'

''Course I do.'

He says it flatly, cutting argument, holding his other hand out, snapping his fingers impatiently. I hand the filled hypodermic to him. He lifts it, tests for air bubbles. Yes, he knows how.

'Hold her.'

I lean over and steady the arms. Very cool, he swabs a

vein on her left inner forearm with antiseptic, throws the cotton wool aside and sinks the needle in. I look away.

I suppose his photographs don't show all he did in Asia.

He is by her, smoothing the hair aside from her forehead as her movements slacken and the pain seems to disappear. And he is dabbing her face with a clean towel moistened with cold water. I watch him from the corner of my eye as I make the coffee at the far end of the room. His image is still the face in the photograph, smiling over human wreckage, the meat of dead people. What does he think he can do? Make this one come alive?

I have pocketed powerful tablets from the hospital. I stir his coffee, turning my back to him.

No.

The day over the harbour looks white and rainy and hard like a ceramic basin in the light of a bathroom, flecked with water. I take a bottle of whisky from the bar and go down the stairs to the room again. He wants whisky, not coffee. The room smells medical. Antiseptic and soap. The drug has stunned the woman to a new kind of rest. As before, it is deceptive; this time, a chemical parody.

He shoves some food into his mouth with his fingers and sits heavily in one of the armchairs. I sit opposite and sip the hot black coffee; he swills the whisky from the bottle, coughing, wiping his mouth on his sleeve and staring up at the ceiling. We say nothing. When he speaks, half the bottle is empty and he is speaking to himself.

'There was no way I could have missed her,' he says.

Then, 'Like she was hiding, and she just ran out.'

After a while, he says more quietly, in a slightly different tone of voice, 'You know, they look just like us.'

This is so strange and disconnected that I stare across at him. He seems to be asleep. And then, in a few minutes, an agitation comes over him as though he had absorbed the convulsive movements of the woman. What is happening to him appears trance-like, cataleptic; he is involved in unseen events. I wonder how safe it is to be near him. My gun is in the next room. Should I—

He begins to speak to whatever he sees, evenly at first, but increasing in intensity. 'There was nothing I could do. Shouldn't be there. No. Request information. Vee Cee, sector one; repeat. No, it's not them. Get out for God's sake, *get out*. Oh Jesus. Jesus, no. *No*.'

He breathes faster and writhes in the chair, his hands and arms flexing in spasms, left hand clutching the bottle to his chest. Slowly the movements stop and his head comes forward, chin down. He draws his arms around himself and shakes his head, his voice so soft it becomes almost indecipherable.

'Don't want report. It never happened. No need you see, no need for that. Doesn't make any difference, now. All of them? Look at this. Go on. What's wrong? Can't hurt you when they're dead. Too late now. What they want to hide for, eh? Hiding, there. Ran out. Close range, rapid, seven point six two.'

There is a pause, then the tone changes again.

'They look like us...Like the Maori...Look at them... look...' Then, suddenly: '*Kill the bastards! Fire! Kill them!*'

There are still words, receding, repeated; finally they go away.

He stays asleep for more than an hour. I get up and move to the window to sit by the woman. The buildings outside seem to be crowding closer because we are on a lower floor, great blocks of wet stone compressing the space and silence. The threat I had felt from the piles of land out there has forced itself into the room. There is a scent of death, an unmistakeable compound of blood and rancid adrenalin, and something else beyond that, more bitter and frightening. I am aware of it. I shall be ready.

I move, and he wakes and looks around. He rubs his face in his hands, tensing his fingers against his forehead.

'What did I say?' he asks.

'Just...there was nothing you could do.'

He puts the bottle on the carpet and leans forward with his head in his hands, wearily. There is another long silence. Then, 'They say you should remember.'

'Who does?'

'The psychos. Head-medics. Shouldn't hide what's in your mind. Bad for you. Bullshit. It just plays over and over and you can't change it. So what's the fucken' use?' He looks up. 'If you forget...you're lucky. God, I know that.'

I walk across to the table by his chair to make some more coffee. And when he lifts his face up from the intentness of staring down at his clasped hands with the fingers tightly clenched round one another, I'm confronted by an expression almost like pleading. It struggles to keep its hold on his features as though other impulses are straining against betrayal. An attempt to pronounce what could be the word 'please', directed towards me, half succeeds.

I stand quite still, my features not reacting. At the heart of this disaster he wants me to rescue him, to make a gesture of redemption and unravel everything by reaching out with whatever words are needed to absolve and forgive him. Of course I cannot do that. I make no sign, give nothing away of understanding or even knowing.

The emotion goes from his expression, replaced by a twitch of self-contempt; then he turns and he gets up and blunders away to the darker end of the room. The bathroom door slams, as though kicked.

CHAPTER TWENTY-SEVEN

'People might start to come back just a few at a time. Not everyone all at once.'

He says this unconvincingly. We are standing by the bed. I am about to reply when the woman opens her eyes and gazes up at us. We both start. It's like a corpse come to life. Her eyes widen, she focuses on us, her face reacts in terror. A moan becomes a whimpering attempt to scream, a dreadful noise. She tries to push back with her hands. Then the noise chokes, the eyelids fall, and she is unconscious again. It all happens in an instant, like a convulsion, as though a swimmer floating in deep water had turned over in a sudden cramp and found she was facing down into death liquid, eyes pressed open by the depth looking down, air gone.

We stare at each other. Apirana puts his knuckles against his teeth.

'What's happening?' he says, through his teeth.

'The morphine might be wearing off.'

'No. Can't be. Any more would kill her.'

We watch. She is becoming agitated again, taking deep breaths. He paces by the bedside.

'Why did she scream? When she saw us?'

'She must have been alone for three weeks,' I say. 'It must have affected her. We had less than a week.'

He stops.

'Yes. Jesus! What she must have been through.' He turns and points at me. '*You* checked Auckland. You were there for *days*. You said there was nobody.'

'I couldn't go down every street. Don't start *that*. She could have been anywhere. Don't start on at me about bloody Auckland.'

The moans are getting louder. Her lips try to form words again, and then the face contorts with hurt. She begins to make a series of gasping noises which rise one after the other into cries of pain, wrenched out, agonising, unstoppable.

The Maori clenches his hands over his ears, closes his eyes tight.

'Oh, God. What can we do? Oh, Christ—'

He comes at me, his face glittering with sweat.

'Give her anaesthetic. For Christ's sake.'

I draw back. He gets the bottle and some cotton wool and pushes it at me, trembling. He is going to pieces very badly. I feel afraid. The rising moans and cries go on and on, unbearable.

'You see, I told you,' he shouts. 'What do we do? Stop it, we've got to.'

I pour some chloroform onto a wad of cotton wool; the smell fills the room. As I hold the wad near the woman's face, Apirana slumps at the edge of the bed and reaches out towards her, plucking at the bedclothes, whispering, I'm sorry, please, *please*, tears thickening his eyes.

The cries subside. His head goes face down onto the bedspread, hands outstretched. He mutters in Maori.

The chloroform forces a sick dizziness into my face and throat. I get up and wander along the room and drop into a chair.

Time slides sideways. Where am I going?

'Where are you going, then?'

Atkinson smiles, head round the door of my room.

'Oh. Coromandel. Couple of weeks.'

'Very nice. Hope the weather holds.'

I gaze at the door after he goes. We take no notice of the weather in the research centre. I have noticed that the sun has been hot and the sky clear on my way to work. I look at the door. Where *am* I going. My chair swivels gently to one side. I open the desk drawer, take out the sleeping pills prescribed after the accident; still nearly a full bottle. The brown glass is cold in my hand. I shall go to a motel.

Another knock at the door. Perrin, now. I pretend to be busy with papers.

'Just clearing up,' I say.

'Yes. Er...' he pauses, pushing his glasses back, deciding not to say whatever he came to say. 'Well, I'm going over to Eric Thompson's for a few drinks. Usual

Friday conference. Did you give Hibbert the computer programmes?'

'Yes.'

'Good. Right. Well, ah, have a good time.'

The door closes. I speak after he has gone; just, 'Goodbye.'

By seven o'clock the centre is deserted. I walk down the corridor and knock on one or two doors. Nobody. Then I descend to the radiation unit. The levels are normal. My identity card slots into the decoder and the steel door opens. I wait to make sure I'm alone. Then I go in behind the sound modulator. The panel at the back lifts out. Inside are the wires leading from the frequency controls to the dials on the front of the generator. Very carefully I reach in and tug the red wire loose from the B12 circuit. Then I replace the rear panel and clip it back into place. As I go out and close the door I can feel a vestigial smile pulling at the corners of my mouth over my tightly set teeth and neutral expression. I could tell by Perrin's shifty manner that he intends to return later or perhaps early tomorrow, Saturday, when nobody's here, and give the B12 programme a short trial run. I know he's insatiably curious. Well, when he tries it, the machine will overload and blow its circuits. The frequency will go higher without registering on the dials. There won't be any danger because the circuit breakers should cut power at a certain point. At the very least the resonance might give him a headache for an hour or two. But the modulator will be out of action for at least a fortnight, and by then I shall be back.

The door closes and the word I have already spoken seems to still hang in the air with the staying power of formaldehyde.

Goodbye.

Have I done everything? Shredded my papers. Yes. I walk through the main laboratory dehydrated by the fluorescent light. A white rat stands against the wire of a cage twitching its pink nose, finding me in the sky of its albino eyes. The rats always struggled worst. Goodbye, *Drosophila.* The light goes out on the double helix, the billion-year helter-skelter, the tangle of threads on the genetic chart.

I think how strangely the water untangled and floated the hair apart as the surface combed it upward into every separate filament. Goodbye is forever. Peter; Joanne.

The light is clear, dry, an empire of another element. Perrin will open the doors, and do what he has always wanted, tap on the barrier, push his way into the next billion years. All by himself.

We may even go at about the same time. Not a good thought for such a long journey. An adverse conclusion.

I am driving with my back to the west and behind in the mirror the earth is tilting its mass of hills up to bury the last of the sun. The gold on the land ahead goes quick. I am moving towards the darkest part of the sky. The car seems to lift and rush on through the warm air. To Coromandel. And the stars—

The echo of a great rending in the air, a vibration which elongates into a sound like a scream, tears from one memory to another, dragging images from different times together, then apart, into pieces.

The Maori is shaking me awake. The room reconstructs itself. Once more the screaming and moaning from the figure on the bed, and the chloroform to daze the sounds.

He lifts the edge of the sheets. 'Look.'

Her leg is bluish-black, grotesquely swollen. I stare.

He drops the sheet, turns away and looks out of the window, arms folded in a tense clasp.

'It may be broken,' I say.

'The blood's not circulating.'

'It could just be very bad bruising.'

He sighs. 'The car hit her. It's broken inside, somewhere.'

'Should we put a splint on it, then?'

'No point, unless it's reset.' He leans his forehead against the window. It seems to be afternoon. It is hard to tell. 'Gangrene,' he says. I lift the sheets cautiously and look again. 'If only we could work the X-ray.'

'Can you reset bones? Even if you can see on an X-ray where it's broken?'

He doesn't answer.

'Well, I can't,' I say.

'Don't suppose you can,' he replies, facing out. 'I mean, what the hell can you do? Eh? Go on. Tell me. What the fucken' hell can you do?'

I replace the sheet. Then I say, 'If it's gangrene, there

would only be one thing to do.' My throat has gone very dry. 'You're right. I couldn't do that.'

'You don't know.'

'Yes, I do.'

I walk away, across the room towards the door to the next room. He suddenly hurries after me and grabs my arm, stopping me, pulling me round to face him.

'You know what I think? Eh?'

'Look, for God's sake—'

'I think you don't feel a bloody thing. That's how you get by. Go on. Look in the mirror. That's how you look. You're a piece of stone. You look at me like that. Listen. I'm not some piece of shit you trod in. What *are* you anyhow? You don't feel anything, you don't believe anything, don't know this, won't do that; don't fucken' tell me what you won't do, you—'

I wrench myself free and shove him away. We stand glaring at each other. I smother the impulse to hit back with what I know about him.

'Go on,' I say. He shakes his head.

'What's the bloody use.'

'Yes, what is the bloody use?'

'Bastard.'

'What good does it do?'

'You're dead, aren't you?' He thumps his heart. 'Stone dead, boy.'

'Because I'm not yelling and howling?'

He clenches his fists. 'You don't even *know*.'

'I know you're doing enough for both of us.'

'Oh, I'm just a dumb *hori*. So's she. I mean, what

the hell. A couple of *horis*.'

'There's no audience. Go on if you want. Nobody can hear you.'

'Is that why I'm yelling and howling? Because I thought someone was listening? Ahh! I really must be dumb, *eh boy*?'

'You know why you're doing it.'

I am in deep, now. Is that going too far? He tenses and comes closer again.

'Why? Come on. Tell me. Why?'

'You're doing it for yourself.'

Only the fact that I hold steady against the reflex to flinch as he jerks his fist back stops him from hitting me, from completing the action. He freezes. Then, 'You bastard.'

His arm drops. Again, he shakes his head, reasserting his defences and his control. 'You just don't know, do you? You're just dead.' And he turns and walks back to the bedside and sits down again. 'Doesn't matter,' he says; 'too right, it's no good, you wouldn't know. It's a waste of time.'

There is a long pause. He stares vacantly at the bed. I move towards the door and look back.

'You ought to take a valium,' I say.

He doesn't even bother to glance up.

'Go screw yourself,' he says.

The shotgun is fully loaded. I check the .38 revolver and make sure the safety catch is off. I lock the door.

In the evening he bangs on the door and calls my name. I open the door. My jacket is hanging over a chair nearby, the revolver easy to hand in the top inside pocket.

'I have to go and see to the generator,' he says. 'Stay with her.' His face is set hard. He goes out.

The woman is in pain again, on the borderline of separate nightmares; the moments of apparent waking seem to mark the transition from one horror to another.

What I detected beginning, in the space of ages ago, is still going on. Her resistance is fierce and blind and immensely strong, as though the pain had found it could feed on itself. Her face seems to have shrunk.

I hear him returning. You were wrong, I think, about how I felt towards her. But it is too late for that to make any difference now, and I will say nothing.

He takes a chair, turns it round, and sits astride it, elbows resting on the back. After a long silence he says, 'She's dying, isn't she?'

'Yes.'

What else can I say? What does he expect?

'I suppose we keep giving her the morphine.'

I nod. When I look at him I want to judge how much he is willing to rescind so that we can continue to have some kind of existence. After this admission, it is now only a matter of our survival. I must force myself to make allowances for him. I have to try.

But his hand is resting on his mouth and his eyes show nothing but a hard glittering. Suddenly he says, 'You know what mercy killing means?'

My lungs seem to be compressed momentarily, and I have to swallow a deep breath to keep back the pain from my ribs. It is like being struck.

'What?'

'Mercy killing. You know, don't you?'

I stand up and move away, stumbling over something.

'You don't walk out on this,' he says.

But I find my way to the next room, slam the door, lock it and lean against it. My brain holds me back from an immense sloping surface down which I would slide until my weight has taken into space and dropped.

The door shudders. His fists pound on the other side. I won't hear what he's shouting. I get the revolver and hold it up in both hands, pointing it at the door only centimetres away. The gun sways wildly. The banging on the door has vibrated my spine. I think of the bullet pulling apart his face if I fire the gun. My hands go down. He stops. I can hear him breathing and coughing. Then he moves away, and minutes later there is the sound of his voice murmuring; I strain to listen. Verses from the Bible. At first the voice is urgent. After a while it falls and becomes a monotonous droning. Useless, wretched gibberish.

I pace to the window and down to the other end of the room and back, again and again. The terror has begun to run faster, to go beyond control. There is no escape.

'Listen to me. Listen. I know about the clocks. I have to tell you. You hear me?'

It is much later, in the middle of the night, and he is thumping on the door again. I don't know if I should answer. But he persists. Finally I stand by the closed door.

'What do you mean?'

'I know why the clocks stopped. Six-twelve. At that time.'

I pause. His voice becomes calmer.

'Look, for God's sake, man. Open the bloody door. We have to talk.'

I take my jacket off the chair and drape it over my arm, hiding the revolver which I hold in my right hand, finger on the trigger. Then I carefully unlock the door and open it. He stands there, dishevelled, clutching the Bible, an odd bright look on his face. Because the generator is still humming away in the basement the electric lights are on, although he has dimmed them all except a wall light and the small lamp by the bed. The woman is lying there, drugged, her head on one side on the pillow.

'Well?' I say. He holds up the Bible tightly in his left hand.

'It's in here,' he says. My heart pushes down, as if deflating, like my lungs as I let my breath out. I pretend to fold my arms within the draped jacket so that the concealed gun is aimed at him. He turns towards the wall light and opens the book, flicking through the pages.

'The number of the beast. Six and six plus six. That's when the clocks stopped. Six-twelve. The number of the beast, in Revelations.' He glances up. 'You saw the beast on the road, that night. Listen: 'the kings of the earth, and the great men, and the rich men, and the chief captains, and the mighty men, and every bondsman, and every free man, hid themselves...and said hide us from the face of him that sitteth on the throne...for the great day of his wrath is come; and who shall be able to stand?'

I begin to say something but he shakes his head and stares away into a vacant part of the room to deliberately avoid my eyes. Then, quickly, he says, 'You tell me the truth, if you think this is wrong. You can't. You don't know. I believe this. Every man is hidden. Everyone. It's a prophecy. The end of the Bible, the very last thing. There's nothing else.'

For a moment, unlocking the door, I had let myself believe from the tone of his voice that there might have been an answer. Now I look down at the carpet and feel the old weariness, the anger flattened by disappointment.

'Don't you see?' he says.

A new voice suddenly pronounces a sentence, what sounds like a whole coherent sentence in Samoan, a question. The woman's eyes have opened. They stare vividly black against white; large, shining in the electric light. She speaks the sentence again, not looking at us. Apirana moves across to her, still clutching the Bible. I follow and stand behind him as he sits on the edge of the bed. Of course we don't understand what she is demanding. Her lips seem dry.

'I'll get some water,' I say, turning.

'In the jug. Glass over there.'

Awkward, with the gun still clasped beneath the jacket, I fumble to pour a glass of water. The two Polynesians, he with his back to me, she whispering the important sentence again, are together in the pool of light by the bed; and for the first time I realise what must be at the centre of his own solitary horror: of not being able to understand a single word, not able to help her even by speaking. Everything is a total, closed, secret. It seems like a cruelty meant precisely for him. And I think: he must be insane by now.

I return to the bed. Just as I move to the edge of the light, the woman dies. Her head goes slack and lolls sideways, her eyes half close in a still look at nothing. The movement of the head spills a trace of liquid from the corners of the eyes and this runs slowly down the face. In the final instant, when her eyes lose the room, her features seem to collect in a softening of skin the memory of the settled expression which had once been possible. The effect is beautiful even though I know it means nothing more than the death of nerves and tendons moving through the structure of her face and the golden colour is only the shade of the light.

The Maori reaches out towards her left hand, clutching at her and staring. When I go to take her pulse, to make sure, he shoves me away fiercely. No words are spoken.

I wait, then leave him sitting there, staring, numb.

CHAPTER TWENTY-EIGHT

From the next room I hear him begin to howl in Maori, a dirge, the kind of wounded cries that they sing at death. It breaks across a range of piercing tones marking weakness and pain, then moves to a different level, more powerful and defiant. I have never heard anything as unnerving. It violates the boundaries between human and inhuman, like the echo of a voice returning from darkness amplified and changed in tone by the enormities which have repelled it. The sound that goes furthest into my head suggests the scraping of insolence against a hard edge of terror. There are others, less recognisable, so clenched in intensity that in the end there is no way of separating the worship of death from the struggle against it.

In spite of this, in an uncontrollable rush from consciousness I drift into a sleep. I am lifted a long way above the abandoned city and all its houses and blocks of towers are laid out dead below, miles of dark stone and glass and ribbed iron. And in the centre, a tower with one speck of light, a solitary dot. The only sounds on earth come from this; a diesel feeding energy into the concrete space, and the wail of a prehistoric death chant. When this fades I hear the whispering in the distance of the old dream I've had many times, indecipherable; the voices I will not hear.

At light I wake, rise, and listen. The place is very quiet. Again I fold the jacket over my arm and go into the room slowly, holding the gun hidden. He is still in the same place, sitting upright, head lowered, chin on his chest. I stand opposite. His face comes up. Has he been asleep? His eyes point in my direction. There is no response when I speak his name. I say it several times. Then he says, 'Get out.'

The corpse is pale, like a shell; an arm is extended and the empty eyes are half open. A smell of antiseptic and dead sweat presses into my throat. I walk round the bed and pause as I go by him. Without looking at me he reaches his left arm up and makes a pushing gesture to get rid of me. The jacket slips and my sudden grab at it makes him turn and stare. He sees the gun. I step back.

He does not seem surprised, he just looks slowly up from the gun to my face and back down to the gun again.

'Go on,' he says. He turns so that he is facing me, very passive and without any expression. His left hand moves gradually through the air towards his face and the forefinger extends until it almost touches the centre of his forehead. Then he says, 'Here.' And there is a silence. 'Go on. Do it.'

I am back in the next room, leaning again on the door, knowing that within minutes I must understand my life, I must force my memory to the very centre, the holding power of every defence. I must remember. *He* told me that, days ago, when he heard me shouting in the dream. Then, in there, he said the opposite. *Forget*, don't remember, blot it out, it does no good. I still have no choice. I can't—

Cells tense inside my head. I feel the pain, of what he pointed for me to do, through my own skull.

When I look again into the room only moments later he has vanished. I stand in a stupor. I heard nothing. But the door to the corridor is half open. I stride to it and glance along the passage into the grey light. The door to the stairs is squeezing shut furtively with a faint hiss of its automatic lever.

Quick. Will he have gone up to the rooms where the guns are, or down to the car park, to his jeep? I run along, haul the door open and look up and down the stairwell. No sign of him. So he must have gone down, out on the top floor of the car park building. Still clutching the revolver, I jump down the stairs three at a time, kick open the exit door and run out into the great cavern of the car park. The generator is humming in the lower level, the basement. I flick on the fluorescent lights and run behind the nearest row of cars, crouching. The jeep is parked next to my car against the far wall. I stop and look. The noise of the generator makes it hard to hear. *Damn*. I was wrong. He isn't here. He tricked me. He must have gone up one floor, then left the stairwell and run along the corridor to the other set of stairs. Now he'll be up on the eighth floor with his weapons.

I dash to the jeep and pull the tarpaulin back. What did he leave here? Boxes of ammunition. The practice grenades. Some real ones. I take two out and slip one into each pocket, making sure the rings connected to the release catches don't snag.

He will come down after me. I won't be able to hear because of the generator. I run along to the ramp which leads down to the next level. The machine noise gets louder as I descend. Along, and down again. There it is. I pause, then crouch behind the generator, glancing all around. When I switch it off, the sound falls into a long drone and the lights shrink. The machine dies with an animal-like convulsion, then the lights seem to be blotted out by silence. Enough grey light is coming in through the open side of the parking building to show the exit doors from the hotel staircase about ten metres away. I dodge across and get on the far side of a concrete pillar. By looking at the reflection on the side of a black car standing to the right, I can still see the exit door I think he will come through on the left.

The silence solidifies. I can hear nothing but my own breathing and my heart thudding like mad. I still can't think what's happening.

There's a very faint sound, somewhere above. A clicking, and a rustle. Silence, then more rustling, and silence again. He must be on the upper floor, with the jeep. What will he expect me to do next? Or *least* expect me to do? Is it any use trying to reason with him? I don't even know if this is the real thing. Are we trying to kill each other?

'Hobson!' He shouts, from above, the echoes making the voice seem everywhere. 'Hobson! Throw the gun out where I can see it.'

I look up, trying to see where he is. There are more movements, then a pause.

'I know you're down there. Come on out.'

'Maketu!' My voice is hoarse. 'For God's sake, this is stupid.'

'Too right. You want to kill me, eh?'

'No no—' Is he moving closer? 'Listen—'

'You don't get a second chance, boy. Throw the gun out.'

'Apirana!'

'Shit to that!'

'I don't want to kill you.'

'Like hell. Throw the fucken' gun out.'

He's trying to work out where I am. He's moved closer, now he's somewhere on the next floor, above and to my right, near the sloping ramp about fifteen metres away. I move behind the black car. There is a silence. Then: 'Going to count to three. Throw the gun out where I can see it. You better do what I say, Hobson. I'm not fucken' around. I mean it.'

A pause. I transfer the revolver to my left hand and take a grenade out of my right pocket.

'One.'

How can I pull the pin out without putting the gun down? Sweat itches down my face.

'Two.'

I reach up and hook the metal ring at the top of the grenade onto the projecting handle of the car door and keeping my fingers firmly round the grenade to hold the striker against the side, I tug the ring loose. The percussion cap will only set the fuse burning when I let go. He showed me that the day we drove down from Turangi.

'Three.'

There's a rustling movement above, a metallic click, and something bounces down the ramp and rolls across the concrete floor a few metres away. Grenade! I swing my arm back and lob my grenade over the tops of the cars towards the ramp. As I duck down behind the car I see he's thrown a *practice* grenade, a thunder flash, not the real thing, just to scare me with the noise. Too late. In the next second I hear the real grenade I've hurled at the ramp hit a concrete column and clatter onto the slope and I hear him yell, *Shit!* Then the thunder flash explodes with a loud firework bang and the grenade straight away detonates in a shattering explosion, huge bursts of noise echoing in the confined space, shrapnel from the grenade whacking hard concrete, whining in all directions, something punching the side car window to green crystal, a spray of broken bits of glass bouncing over me and across the floor as the main echo of the explosion blasts back from the far wall, compressing the air.

An acrid cordite smell and a haze of blue smoke hangs beneath the ceiling and drifts down. Beyond the ringing inside my ears I can hear nothing. No sign of movement. I slide up and peer through the back window of the car towards the ramp. Nothing. If he was hurt, he'd be making a noise.

Now it's for real.

I turn and run, still crouching, to the door which leads to the inner hotel staircase; pause in the doorway and gently pull the door open. I listen, then slide inside into the darkness, closing the door very quietly. I feel around in the pitch dark for the stair rail and move my feet forward till I tap the first step. Then, gun in my right hand again, I carefully work my way up the steps to the next floor. By the next door I stop and crouch, pushing it outwards with my left knee and operating the handle with my left hand.

The door opens soundlessly. I point the gun out and push harder, coming up from the crouch. Through the ten-centimetre space I see a figure moving slowly behind the nearest row of cars, back to me, facing away, then glancing round. The moment he sees me he whips round and brings the automatic rifle up. I get only a fraction of a second to leap back and slam the metal door before the first wild bullet hits the concrete lintel. The gun bangs away like a pneumatic drill on metal. I throw myself frantically up the stairs away from the door. The firing stops. I go on running up, bounding up in the dark. The handrail knocks against me.

I just have time to gain the next floor before the door below is kicked open and I hear the clink of the metal grenade hitting the concrete wall. I panic, first pushing on the door handle instead of pulling. Then it's opening and I'm diving inside. The explosion roars up the concrete shaft of the staircase like a cannon firing. The pressure slams the door behind me and jolts the hotel so hard that white powder comes showering down from the corridor ceiling.

I'm back on the first floor. Without thinking, I run along the corridor and into the room where the woman's body is lying. The daylight is stronger. The open doors from this room and the next show the corridor clearly from here to the staircase door. I prop myself in the doorway and hold the gun steady, looking back towards the staircase. The white dust settles on the carpet. I wipe the sweat from my face onto my sleeve. There is no way out now. This is it.

The minutes tick by. Where is he? Behind that staircase door? He can't rush into the corridor because the door opens the wrong way. If he pulls it open far enough to throw a grenade down the corridor I'll have time to close this door and step behind the concrete wall of the bathroom.

The angle of the door handle begins to change, so slowly I can hardly be sure at first. Yes, he's there. Then, a long wait before a dark line starts to widen along the side of the door. It opens no more than a few centimetres. I'm blinking back the sweat from my eyes and straining to see.

'Hobson!' His voice barks down the corridor, booming from the concrete shaft of the staircase with a string of curses. 'You come away from there, you bastard.'

I suddenly realise he won't throw any grenades because of the woman. Even though she's dead. He won't do it. The shouting goes on.

'You're fucken' mad, you know what you are, you fucken' *porangi* bastard? You better not touch her. You hear that, pakeha? Stay away from her. You hear?'

I let him work himself almost hoarse with rage; then I yell back, '*You* killed her, Apirana!'

I use his first name deliberately, drawing it out mockingly. 'Apirana. You killed her.'

A choking noise, an incoherent word, bursts from the gap in the door. I tense my finger on the trigger of the gun and hold the weapon as firm as I can with both hands before I shout, 'Like you killed them in Vietnam. Is that right? Killed the women and kids, chopped them up? Apirana! You're the one who's mad, *boy*!'

The air seems to split sideways. I fall back into the room the moment the submachine gun jolts from behind the far door. The firing, like perforated steel being ripped apart, whacks dozens of bullets into the corridor, splintering wood, bursting glass, in a great roar. Lights explode. Sparks crack from concrete hit by steel. The doorjamb is chainsawed to bits, chopped apart, pieces flying everywhere. The banging and splintering seems to roar on for ages, and all I can do is crouch inside the doorway, press myself down and pray for the bullets to end.

When it stops I can't move. I hear the staircase door thud open and then a clattering sound, like a gun being dropped. I have to force my body to get up.

Smoke and dust, tasting of cement and cordite. I nerve myself to glance out, quick. He is standing at the far end of the corridor, arms slack by his sides, his gun thrown down on the floor. I level the revolver at him but stay well inside the shelter of the edge of the door. And there we are, for a long minute, the blue haze clearing from the air.

Then he begins to walk forward in a vague way, stumbling over the gun, his hand going out to the wall to steady himself. He kicks the gun aside without looking down. And comes towards me another two steps, keeping his right hand on the wall. His face is quite blank, as though he's finding his way along in total darkness. I move out to stand in the corridor, still holding the gun at him with both hands, my finger on the trigger.

'Stay there! Keep back!' I shout. 'I'll fire.'

He doesn't seem to hear. Slowly he advances down the corridor directly at me.

'Apirana! For God's sake!' My hands wobble. 'Stop!' At the last moment he knows, I can see in his face he knows I'm going to shoot, maybe a fraction of a second before I know, myself, I will do it.

The gun jerks back as I pull the trigger. The explosion seems to hit him in the chest with the force of a hammer, sending him sprawling away against the wall. He turns, one hand on his chest, the other flat on the wall; then he goes down suddenly onto his knees and forward on his face.

I lower the gun. A shuddering comes over me, making my arms flick around uncontrollably. The gun drops, unfixing itself from the tightness of my fingers. As I walk towards him, he pushes himself up with his left hand, half sideways, lifting his face, his legs making useless crawling movements on the carpet. His eyes fix on my shoes. The dazed expression pulls back to a sudden hatred, his lips gather, and with a huge effort he spits viciously at my shoes.

It is all blood, gleaming down his chin and out of the sides of his mouth as he spits, then rolls over onto his back in one movement. His hands hold deep red liquid on his chest.

I crouch by him. He looks directly up towards me. For a moment his eyes widen, as if amazed, the black shining surrounded by yellowish white. Then he says, 'Hemi. You're dead, Hemi.'

The eyes slip sideways. A rush of darkness comes from his mouth.

CHAPTER TWENTY-NINE

There is a finely furnished modern hotel room lined with soft carpet and velvet curtains. The corpse of a young Samoan woman is lying on the bed. The door leading to the room has been smashed by machine-gun bullets and the corridor beyond is gouged with bullet scars and littered with dozens of cartridge cases, bits of wood and metal, broken glass, and the body of a young Maori. Each object is a part of an enormous mystery.

I lean against the wall. So strange, that I should kill him. I don't understand it. Here I am, staring down at him, shaking my head and speaking his name over and over: *Apirana.*

We were the survivors of millions. How could it happen?

I look down, dazed, at my shoes. There are glistening flecks of spittle and blood on them. When I try to unfasten the laces my hands can't do it, but I have to take the shoes off, so I rip the laces out and hurl the shoes away. Why do people die with their eyes open? What do they see?

Now he knows. Don't you? He tricked me. Gave me that gun. Knew I would do it. Finally, he decided, he saw the way out, he knew how it had to be ended. I thought I could break him down by flinging a few words out of the dark at him. But he used me to cancel all that. To pay it back, and escape.

When I drove to Coromandel, to Thames, I remember thinking, What if they are counting on this? As I checked in at the motel at Thames and paused at the bottom of the stairs holding the iron rail that vibrated, I was wondering if I had been even more skilfully manoeuvred than I would have believed, into going up this staircase with the bottle of sleeping pills clinking in my pocket. The alternative, of course, was that it would never have occurred to them that I would have the guts to do anything remotely like this.

The spiral of the iron handrail curving round reminded me of the ribonucleic chains, the resonance of proteins that could be vibrated apart, and the genetic sleep in every one in a million that could be shaken awake; the survival mechanism. Near the top of the stairs I had lifted my head to look at the great scatter of starlight over the Coromandel Peninsula, thinking of spiral nebulae and how immensely important our research was, in the pattern of the universe, how worthwhile, at a distance; and I'd stumbled and nearly fallen. When I clutched the handrail I thought: If the universe wanted to stop me, it had its chance there.

Then the absurdity made me laugh as I entered the motel room and locked the door. The self-destroyer doesn't want to die by accident.

I am very methodical. My work has made me believe that almost nothing can happen by accident.

I remember: what? Holding the bottle of sleeping pills and wondering if this was a mistake. To make myself know why I had decided to do this I would have to force my mind to betray itself, to break down the last remnants of the instinct for survival at any cost. I had no idea how hard that would be, how much terror it could make. It would be terminal.

Now I arrive at it again. I have to cheat a far worse, more imbecile, senseless, existence. But it will still not be easy, unless I comprehend, at least a part, a fragment.

It does not take long to break open Perrin's metal box. I carry it to the dining room on the top floor and tip all the papers out onto a table. There are thin card folders, memos stamped with security numbers, minutes of secret meetings. And a small diary, entries written in a biro scrawl like the secretions of an insect. It is all about bureaucratic scheming, mostly financial. Perhaps written to justify himself in case he fell dead some day. I flick from page to page. Then I see what might be my name. Smoothing the book open, I take it closer to the window. The sun is dissolving the clouds over the harbour, the shadows of the clouds sliding quickly across the water. I look down at the diary.

...difficult decision but have advised D-G it would be best to withhold such information from Hobson as it might jeopardise the entire project. In the early days not much was known about the effects of radioactive isotopes on chromosomes, and precautions were somewhat haphazard.

The tests show no abnormalities in the children of any other staff members and the consensus would seem to be that infantile autistic symptoms of the kind manifest in the Hobson child cannot be linked with any certainty to radioactive genetic damage to the male parent. Dr Franklin is the only dissenting opinion; from his research into immunology he believes that genetic alteration rather than damage has taken place. This seems academic to me and in any case incapable of proof. The consequences are equally unfortunate.

I move away from the window. Chairs and tables push against me. I sit down and fix the book flat on a table under my hands. After a while I move my hands aside and stare down at the pages again.

We are a relatively small unit and the departure or defection of any staff member would be a serious setback. I would regard Hobson's psychological and neurological condition as demanding particular scrutiny in view of this. Have given assurances to D-G on basis of Report 7A/42.

The pages seem to turn themselves as though the light is splitting them apart and fastening them down. Later I see only this reference, jotted amongst notes about research grants:

> Re. Hobson child, it now seems that syndrome includes self-destructive behaviour characteristic of lethal factors in genetic mutants even at basic cellular level.

I look out of the window. It may be afternoon by now, a bright day with a blue sky and violently glittering water. I close Perrin's book. If anyone was here, I could hand it to them and could say, very clearly: Yes, I killed him.

A carbon copy of Report 7A/42 is in one of the folders, a thin piece of almost transparent paper. It is packed with the usual psychological jargon. I am peculiarly calm, but the process of decoding the jargon and seeing what it means has a shocking effect. The sentences spill out like maggots from the paper, coming alive, unfolding themselves as I read, spilling over the edges. I think I even hear a rustling noise, and I stop, and it goes and then returns, like the whispering which once surrounded me in the empty spaces of the great room full of light. And I go on reading.

What always seemed so ordinary to me is transformed, turned inside out. The words make me see myself very close, from a distance. I become 'the subject', and secret observations of my behaviour produce words like 'paranoia', which means a fear in the subject that he is being secretly observed. There is mention of suspicion and withdrawal, of self-destructive impulses. The subject may compensate by a series of sleeping or waking dreams which assume for him the force of reality itself. The most central aspect of all this is the control of the memory. The ability to change or obliterate the past in specific areas may become automatic, no longer a conscious act. It may be a means of holding back bad memories or a compensation for not being able to affect the course of everyday events in the present. Something which is a conscious weakness becomes an unconscious strength. At that level it can produce psychopathic results. Actions can be destructive whilst the mind remains creative and inventive. Dreams retain the truth and replay it, a super-reality.

The subject sits at the table and lets the almost weightless piece of paper float from his hand.

At the motel I had spread out the sleeping pills on my palm and known what would make death beyond all doubt. What had I admitted to myself that would account for such an action? I had realised that Perrin would die, I even imagined him entering the research centre at that moment and switching on the machines; but that was a matter of betrayal for us both, not demanding a death from remorse or guilt in return. It would seem accidental. What else? Peter was dead and Joanne had gone. How many tablets was that worth?

I put my head back now and gaze up at the white ceiling. From a long way off, the faint glitter of reflections on water sends wavering ribbons of soft light very slowly across the surface above me. The real light on the water, I know, is hard and metallic, it hurts the eyes. I remember the Maori hiding beneath it, and the downward pressure of my hand. Then the struggle, against a force of my own making, a will inside me to blot him out. Gradually the image of his head sinking, and the face that just died in the corridor below with its eyes that refused to see me and mouth that spoke to nothing even as it drowned on itself, both blur into the image of the child I helped to death. Now I know I am going beneath that surface myself, here, in the room with the liquid reflections rising across the walls to the ceiling, the memory pressing on my face and submerging the resistance in my mind. I know that I killed Peter. A darker flood rises even above that, like the death pouring from the mouth of the body below. *I hated him*, the child was an embodiment of what I hated, a parody of myself; sealed off from all feeling of life. My gift to the world was a mutation of my own nothingness. The shock when his eyes had finally looked at me was recognition. We saw ourselves in each other.

The self-deceptions break down like a shell of bone collapsing under pressure. The realisation bursts inside me with enormous force: the lethal factor is within myself; *it is me*. My reflection is all that stares back from glass and water and unclosed eyes. *I was the cause*. Worse still, immune to the Effect. The mechanisms meant for my removal had gone massively wrong, events had turned inside out like the twist in the Moebius loop or the endless protective repetition of the double helix.

Disconnected images revolve in front of me and begin

to overlap in loose focus. There is a world somewhere which continues without me; and yet my consciousness can perceive it. There is another, full of clear sequences trapped in a mind of broken matter, a circle of limbo where beasts squat and run and a figure I seem to recognise appears from mists over and again, and I must kill it and escape. There is a world in which doctors discuss the continued brain activity and rapid eye movements of a patient deep in a barbiturate coma and wonder what kind of world he inhabits. And a future in which a scientist's hand moves to switch off a machine an instant before it pulses back into the electromagnetic grid of an entire planet a resonance which will be the decoding and unravelling note of all basic protoplasm, so that only those with the strangest immunity would be isolated from the transformation. Or the instant is missed, and there is a world vibrating as if struck by a massive hammer. In another world, evolution enters a new dimension.

I am standing on the flat roof in bright sunshine. The images twist round, inseparable, tightening together like the strands of a rope. I look down. I have the power to break them. It is a sheer drop to the flat concrete of the path next to the street ten stories below.

I look round. It is a fine afternoon. I remember so much. I think of being alone in the motel room at Thames in the nearness of ages ago as I selected some tablets and swallowed them. But it was uncertain, not like this. Now I climb over the safety rail and stand on the edge of the drop. No remorse. This will be complete, and finished. I believe in nothing else. Because nothing could be worse.

All I have is the power to end.

I lean outwards and let go.

The pull of the earth takes hold of my spine, my limbs spread over space. There is the breath-beat of falling, spiralling, the air pushing hard for a moment and then letting go. The light splits open my eyelids. It is brilliant, drained of colours, painful. An immense silence rushes around me. My throat is trying to make a noise, to beat it back. The light pulses red. Then the silence explodes.

I was sitting bold upright in bed breathing fast and staring at the wall. The daylight was streaming into the motel room through the slats of the blinds. I seemed to have been awake, and asleep, for ages. I lay back and remembered where I was. The silence persisted. My watch at the bedside had stopped at 6.12. Reaching out, I shook it and the second hand began flicking round again. How long had it been stopped? I got up and went to the window which looked out onto the main road; my arm moved up towards the cord of the blind. What?

I paused. What was happening? The casual movement, everyday, ordinary, towards opening the blind had been interrupted by something, by an impulse to stop, which had no sensible origin at all. It was so curious and *extra*ordinary that I was pausing not because of the impulse itself but in a conscious effort to find a reason for it. But I had forgotten. My mind seemed to resist. The silence pressed in thickly. It was exactly like forgetting the name of a place you've visited dozens of times; it's just on the tip of your mind but you can't find it. You stop and think, and when there's no answer you go on. Perhaps, later, you will know.

Then I reached up and opened the blind to the enormous light.

Text Classics

Dancing on Coral
Glenda Adams
Introduced by Susan Wyndham

The Commandant
Jessica Anderson
Introduced by Carmen Callil

Homesickness
Murray Bail
Introduced by Peter Conrad

Sydney Bridge Upside Down
David Ballantyne
Introduced by Kate De Goldi

Bush Studies
Barbara Baynton
Introduced by Helen Garner

The Cardboard Crown
Martin Boyd
Introduced by Brenda Niall

A Difficult Young Man
Martin Boyd
Introduced by Sonya Hartnett

Outbreak of Love
Martin Boyd
Introduced by Chris Womersley

The Australian Ugliness
Robin Boyd
Introduced by Christos Tsiolkas

All the Green Year
Don Charlwood
Introduced by Michael McGirr

They Found a Cave
Nan Chauncy
Introduced by John Marsden

The Even More Complete Book of Australian Verse
John Clarke

Diary of a Bad Year
J. M. Coetzee
Introduced by Peter Goldsworthy

Wake in Fright
Kenneth Cook
Introduced by Peter Temple

The Dying Trade
Peter Corris
Introduced by Charles Waterstreet

They're a Weird Mob
Nino Culotta
Introduced by Jacinta Tynan

The Songs of a Sentimental Bloke
C. J. Dennis
Introduced by Jack Thompson

Careful, He Might Hear You
Sumner Locke Elliott
Introduced by Robyn Nevin

Fairyland
Sumner Locke Elliott
Introduced by Dennis Altman

Terra Australis
Matthew Flinders
Introduced by Tim Flannery

My Brilliant Career
Miles Franklin
Introduced by Jennifer Byrne

The Fringe Dwellers
Nene Gare
Introduced by Melissa Lucashenko

Cosmo Cosmolino
Helen Garner
Introduced by Ramona Koval

Wish
Peter Goldsworthy
Introduced by James Bradley

Dark Places
Kate Grenville
Introduced by Louise Adler

The Quiet Earth
Craig Harrison
Introduced by Bernard Beckett

The Long Prospect
Elizabeth Harrower
Introduced by Fiona McGregor

The Watch Tower
Elizabeth Harrower
Introduced by Joan London

The Mystery of a Hansom Cab
Fergus Hume
Introduced by Simon Caterson

The Unknown Industrial Prisoner
David Ireland
Introduced by Peter Pierce

The Glass Canoe
David Ireland
Introduced by Nicolas Rothwell

A Woman of the Future
David Ireland
Introduced by Kate Jennings

Eat Me
Linda Jaivin
Introduced by Krissy Kneen

Julia Paradise
Rod Jones
Introduced by Emily Maguire

The Jerilderie Letter
Ned Kelly
Introduced by Alex McDermott

Bring Larks and Heroes
Thomas Keneally
Introduced by Geordie Williamson

Strine
Afferbeck Lauder
Introduced by John Clarke

The Young Desire It
Kenneth Mackenzie
Introduced by David Malouf

Stiff
Shane Maloney
Introduced by Lindsay Tanner

The Middle Parts of Fortune
Frederic Manning
Introduced by Simon Caterson

Selected Stories
Katherine Mansfield
Introduced by Emily Perkins

The Home Girls
Olga Masters
Introduced by Geordie Williamson

Amy's Children
Olga Masters
Introduced by Eva Hornung

The Scarecrow
Ronald Hugh Morrieson
Introduced by Craig Sherborne

The Dig Tree
Sarah Murgatroyd
Introduced by Geoffrey Blainey

The Plains
Gerald Murnane
Introduced by Wayne Macauley

The Odd Angry Shot
William Nagle
Introduced by Paul Ham

Life and Adventures 1776–1801
John Nicol
Introduced by Tim Flannery

Death in Brunswick
Boyd Oxlade
Introduced by Shane Maloney

Swords and Crowns and Rings
Ruth Park
Introduced by Alice Pung

The Watcher in the Garden
Joan Phipson
Introduced by Margo Lanagan

Maurice Guest
Henry Handel Richardson
Introduced by Carmen Callil

The Getting of Wisdom
Henry Handel Richardson
Introduced by Germaine Greer

The Fortunes of Richard Mahony
Henry Handel Richardson
Introduced by Peter Craven

Rose Boys
Peter Rose
Introduced by Brian Matthews

Hills End
Ivan Southall
Introduced by James Moloney

The Women in Black
Madeleine St John
Introduced by Bruce Beresford

The Essence of the Thing
Madeleine St John
Introduced by Helen Trinca

Jonah
Louis Stone
Introduced by Frank Moorhouse

An Iron Rose
Peter Temple
Introduced by Les Carlyon

1788
Watkin Tench
Introduced by Tim Flannery

Happy Valley
Patrick White
Introduced by Peter Craven

I Own the Racecourse!
Patricia Wrightson
Introduced by Kate Constable